Eva and Henry

A Cape Cod Marriage

Irene M. Paine

authorHOUSE®

AuthorHouse™
1663 Liberty Drive
Bloomington, IN 47403
www.authorhouse.com
Phone: 1-800-839-8640

The novel Eva and Henry, A Cape Cod Marriage *is based on the life experiences of the author's great grandaunt, Eva Paine Smith. All characters of the Paine, Smith and Cole families are based on real people. As much as possible, the major experiences of the main characters are based upon actual occurrences, as ascertained from family historical data. However, many facts have been embellished and literary license has been taken in developing the thoughts, conversations, and daily actions of the characters. Many characters are totally fictitious, and have been used to illustrate the societal issues of the day. Visit* www.EvaandHenry.com *for more information.*

First published by AuthorHouse 9/9/2010
First revision 3/22/2011
ISBN: 978-1-4520-4643-3 (sc)
ISBN: 978-1-4520-4644-0 (hc)
ISBN: 978-1-4520-4645-7 (e)

Library of Congress Control Number: 2010909442

Printed in the United States of America

Dedication

This book is dedicated to my husband, James G. Wolf.
Thank you for your constant encouragement
and unconditional love.

Acknowledgments

I must heartily thank many people who read *Eva and Henry* in its various stages and helped me with form, purpose and direction. The novel began as a short story written at the Provincetown Art Association Museum during a winter writing course led by Pamela Mandell in 2003 and 2004. All writers attending the workshop read my first attempts and offered encouragement, including: Martha Hyams, Annie Hall, Wendy Willard, Jane Rowe, Sharon Teichman, Mary Ann Bragg, Laurel Guadanzo, Mary Alice Wells and Harriet Miller. Also supportive—JC Garner, thank you for lending me the little volume, *Tokology*, which provided a view to women's health issues in the nineteenth century.

I thank Pamela Mandell for her exquisite professional service in reading the novel as a finished first draft and offering me the strength to go through many revisions. Pam's questions and comments helped me to correct inconsistencies, empower characters, develop plot, and break the book into chapters.

Continuing the process, I thank my draft readers: Pat Selmer, Laurie Higgins, Arlene Kirsch, Annie Garton, Gayle Adams, Maryln Zupicich, Juliane Soprano, Deborah Wolf-Saxon, Becky Roshon, Martha Wolf, Stevie Wolf, Sarah Paine Curley, Evelyn Paine, Heidi Schuetz, and Dan Wolf. Dianna Morton and Shelley Sloboder, thank you for taking drafts to bed with you at night and falling in love with Eva and asking for more. You both helped so much in so many ways. And my two readers from Dune Hollow Writers in Orleans—Joan

Flynn and Ginia Patia—your encouragement was motivational for me through a tough winter. Helen Purcell of Wellfleet, I am deeply indebted to you for your proofreading, and also for your support. Thank you to my professional coach, Dru Jackman, for keeping me inspired.

I thank David Wright of the Wellfleet Historical Society for letting me dig around in ship's logs, and thank you to the Cole family of South Wellfleet for sharing the writings of Charles F. Cole. Thank you to Captain Reuben R. Baker, Jr. of Wellfleet for sharing a volume of family history with me. Thank you, Merritt Frazier, for sharing your historical documents on Wellfleet with me. And a big thank you to David Kew for locating an archived newspaper account that was crucial to the story, and also for your keen interest in Wellfleet history.

I thank Annie Dillard for her suggestions to me twenty years ago regarding the craft of writing a novel. I thank Anne LeClaire for her thoughts and advice she recently offered me on revision and publishing.

I thank my father, Robert S. Paine, and my uncle, Abbott O. "Jay" Paine, for telling me stories about their grandfather's sister, Eva Paine Smith. By keeping her memory alive, they ignited my desire to reconstruct her marriage.

I thank my husband, Jim Wolf. He encouraged me for hundreds and hundreds of days as I wrote about Eva Paine and Henry Smith. He read each draft of the novel and pushed me to become a better writer. I love you for giving me the gift of your attention. And to the rest of my immediate family—I thank you for taking me seriously whenever I said I was writing a book. Thank you for giving me the space to go shut myself in with my computer and get it done.

~

Eva and Henry

A Cape Cod Marriage

Irene M. Paine

Preface

April 6, 1938

No bride knows what her marriage will bring; she must move forward in faith. Or perhaps the compelling force is not faith. Perhaps it is pure desire—the human desire to be with the beloved in the fullest sense of the phrase "to be with." Whatever the impetus for the union, until she has gained experience, a bride can only entertain expectations.

At twenty-one years of age I understood this. But I was eager to marry and therefore allowed my anxious excitement to trump any doubts. I soon learned that marriage is so much more than the prescribed path to consummated passion—it is a journey of continuous challenge, and I am indebted to that journey for enriching my life.

I am seventy-three years old now. When I look back, which I do frequently, I'm certain that although I was romantically naive as a young woman, I was also fully aware that I could only hope and pray my marriage to Captain Henry Smith would be long, fruitful and happy.

I cannot protest that I did not understand the hardships endured by the wives of mariners. Being born in the Cape Cod village of South Wellfleet, my life was attuned to the rhythm of sober departures and joyous home-comings. My grandfather, my father, and my brother all came of age sailing the New England coastline. I was acutely aware of the demands of coastal life, as was everyone who lived in South Wellfleet in the 1880's. I married Henry with my eyes wide open.

We were fortunate to live in the neighborhood of Paine Hollow, which was proudly self-sufficient, if not prosperous. Tidy white-washed farmhouses and their companion barnyards spread like a quilt across the valley and down to the shore of the bay. As a little girl, I believed that everyone had as many cousins, aunties, and uncles living close by. The feeling between neighbors was such that we would call a man "uncle" out of respect, even if he wasn't, and I was in my twenties before I unraveled the family tree enough to understand who my true aunts were and who had been bestowed the title through close friendship with the Paine family. It was in this peaceful setting that I spent my years with Henry.

My memories of our marriage are sharp and colorful—even more so than the events of recent times—because I've read and reread the faded handwriting in my journals. The charcoal portrait of Henry, which hangs at the foot of my bed, is the last thing I see at the end of the day as I admire his smooth brow, his intelligent eyes, and his youthful cheeks. When I close my eyes and fall to sleep, I am young once again, walking arm in arm with Captain Henry Smith.

～

CHAPTER ONE
After a Long Winter

April 28, 1886
South Wellfleet

The cold nights still produce a thick frost that crunches underfoot in the morning, but blooming yellow flowers proclaim the arrival of spring. Daffodils and forsythia brighten our grayish brown landscape with exclamations of color and promise us that green leaves will soon appear on the naked trees. The energy of renewal rises in our human population as it rises in all things natural.

Today a momentous occasion was marked in South Wellfleet, although it may have appeared a modest event to some. After a long winter hiatus, the fishing fleet raised sail and departed from Blackfish Harbor—and for the very first time, I accompanied Captain Henry Smith to the wharf to see him off.

The courting season of the idle winter months has claimed me as a woman in love, and I've emerged from my twenty-first winter with the intention to be wed. I am delighted that Henry is to be my husband, and I am to be his wife. But to our observing neighbors, the premier appearance of Eva and Henry together on the wharf was no doubt comical.

I felt like a wing-flapping hen chasing after her rooster as I ran to keep up with Henry—for every stride he took, I was compelled to take two. Both of my hands were occupied holding my skirts up off the rough planks while I prayed I wouldn't trip. Always a step ahead of me, Henry moved firmly down the wharf, carving a path through the crowd. Despite the fact that I was forced to abandon all attempts at a sedate, ladylike composure, I must admit it was a thrill to be with Henry in his element.

He wore his derby with nonchalant casualness, setting it back on his head at a jaunty angle. Of course Henry wears the hat as all the captains do—to signify that he is a master and not a crew member—but his hat is a bother to him, and he refuses to wear it with any seriousness.

There is no stuffiness to my Henry—no false airs about him at all. At twenty-seven years of age, he is tall and strong. His piercing blue eyes constantly survey his surroundings. A decisive stance and alert expression convey the message that he is confidently at ease. He sports a full mustache that completely covers his upper lip and droops down past the corners of his mouth. I recently teased Henry about his mustache, suggesting that it is a compensation for his receding hairline.

"It keeps my mouth warm in a cold gale," he replied to me. "Be careful now, Eva, or I'll grow myself a full beard like the old timers do. I'd rather have ice freeze on my beard than on my face during a winter storm."

I have not mentioned it since; the mustache is quite enough.

As we approached the gangplank of the *Dora Freeman*, Henry slowed his gait and took my elbow to help me cross over onto the schooner's deck. He was immediately solicitous when he noticed I was out of breath. He gently stroked my cheek and smiled down at me.

"Wait here, Eva," he said. "I'm going forward to check the rigging, but I'll be right back." Henry called two of his crew to the bow, and I was quite suddenly standing alone, my cheek burning where he had touched it.

I acclimated myself to the slight rocking of the vessel and turned to watch the people of South Wellfleet streaming down the wharf, dressed in their best Sunday winter woolens. An expectant hum of laughter and conversation filled the chilly air. Old friends eagerly greeted one another after a long winter of spending too much time sitting around coal stoves. The customary send-off meal provided added incentive to leave cozy parlors; on every schooner the galley cooks worked below deck, perfecting their specialty dishes.

The good Lord had indeed been most considerate in answering our community prayer by providing a fine day for the fleet to leave the harbor. The sun weakly warmed us, as it does in April, and a strong breeze ruffled the sheltered waters of Blackfish Creek. Out on the deeper waters—past the protection of Lieutenant's Island— dancing white caps indicated excellent sailing conditions.

The freshly caulked and painted schooners were tied to one another, side by side, five vessels out from the wharf. In consideration of Henry's prestige, the *Dora Freeman* was one of those tied directly to the wharf and easily boarded. But no one present, not even the oldest aunties and grandmothers, minded the exercise of climbing over the gunwales from one schooner to the next, as it provided an opportunity for the men to gallantly offer their arms to the ladies and for the ladies to take those strong arms and lean upon them.

The decks were soon crowded with happy people. Plates and casseroles and cakes appeared from inside picnic baskets. Uncle William Paine, who is too old to go fishing this year, brought out his fiddle to console himself with a lively tune and quickly had folks smiling and tapping their feet. I allowed the excitement to distract me from the knowledge that good-byes would soon be exchanged and loved ones would disappear out over the horizon.

I walked back to the stern and stood at the wheel, imagining Henry's strong hands upon it and considering the significance of the hour. We all look forward to renewed prosperity after the frozen winter. Long overdue accounts call out to be paid, and it would be a great treat to buy a fresh leg of lamb from the butcher rather than eating yet another meal of codfish chowder or salted beef.

It is true that the fleet anchored here in Blackfish Creek is much smaller than in years past—in fact, the old timers would not call it a fleet at all compared to the dozens of vessels that once sailed out together—but the remaining schooners are no less important. The bittersweet emotions involved in sending a family member out to sea will always be the same, no matter what the size of the fleet. The catch is still substantial enough so that together we accept the risk that is taken. A man could lose his life, and therefore, a mother loses a son, and a sister loses a brother, and a woman loses a husband, and children lose their father. We all know because we all have been touched by such loss.

The aroma of corned beef and cabbage came wafting to me from the *Dora Freeman's* galley stove, enticing me from my thoughts. Neighbors and crew members swirled around me and seated themselves on wooden folding chairs as friendships that had been temporarily interrupted by winter weather were boisterously resumed. New babies were presented and the loss of departed relatives lamented. Laughter and shouts rang out across the floating party. I looked through the crowd for Henry, but I could not see him.

I waved to my nineteen year-old brother as he stood on the deck of the *Mary Cole,* which was tied alongside the *Dora Freeman.* Freshly barbered and clean-shaven, Lewis looked boyishly younger than his years. His red wool shirt was spotless and pressed, thanks to Mama.

Lewis knew my secret. Watching him laugh with his crew mates, I wondered if the *Mary Cole* would clear the harbor before every man on board heard that Henry and I were planning to wed. Lewis grinned at me and then bit into a steaming cornmeal muffin.

"Come over here," I called to him. "I want to hug you good-bye one more time." We met at the railings and embraced over the sides, his feet on the *Mary Cole,* mine on the *Dora Freeman.* "Please don't say anything today before I have a chance to tell Mama," I whispered. "I can't have her hear by way of gossip that Henry and I are to be married."

"I promise not to tell a soul until we're out to sea," Lewis winked at me with false gravity.

"Don't play with me now."

"I'm not playing. You can trust me, Eva. I'm not going to spoil anything."

"I know you wouldn't do so purposely, but perhaps you might accidentally say something," I argued.

"I'm not so far removed from my own tongue that I don't know what it's going to say. Your secret is safe with me. Now go enjoy yourself." He gave me a playful push.

"Thank you, Lewis." I reached up to him and straightened his collar. "And do have a good trip. Mama and I will be praying for you."

"I know you will. Go on, now." He gave me a brotherly peck on the cheek and turned to his mates.

Mama would ordinarily have been present to bid Lewis farewell, but an irritating cough kept her home next to the kitchen stove. She was disappointed, but she didn't want to bring her cough out in public where the older ladies might catch it. Mama visits the elders when they are sick, and she told me, "I know full well what a bad cough can do to them. I'd better stay home, dear, where I am not a threat."

I did miss her presence, especially since Henry and I had hoped to surprise her, along with the assembled friends and neighbors, with our announcement. Now I would have to tell Mama without the benefit of Henry by my side.

I searched out the faces of excited men and younger boys soon to be departing. The send-off meal is considered to be good luck, and I reassured myself that all of the men present have eaten many such meals. Henry and his crew of six souls will, of course, come home along with the rest of the fleet with a jingle in their pockets. And Lewis will also return, safe and sound.

And then, there will be a wedding! The whole community will be ever so pleased to attend the wedding of Eva Paine and Captain Henry Smith. After Mama is properly informed, my task will be to write out the invitations while Henry is away.

"Have a seat, my dear," Henry spoke from behind me, at last. "I'll get you a plate."

"Oh, but I should be getting the plate for you!" I tilted my head to look up at him.

"There will be plenty of time for that later, Eva. Today, I serve you." He guided me to a chair, and held it while I seated myself. Then he bent down to speak softly into my ear. "I want to be sure you receive the best of the pot. If I let you get it from the cook, that may not happen. Now, sit right here."

The closeness of Henry's breath gave me goose bumps. He affectionately squeezed my shoulder and then went below to the galley. Whatever Henry wants, Henry gets. I see that whenever we are together. Perhaps it is the direct gaze of Henry's blue eyes; perhaps it is his height—he stands a head taller than almost any man out on the wharf—but his very presence commands attention. And then, there is the respect given for his reputation.

I know as well as anyone that Captain Henry Smith has many times over earned his vessel the title of the fleet's "High Liner," the first schooner back to market with a full load of fish, therefore fetching the best price per pound for the catch. Henry locates fish with uncanny certainty and is a calculating taskmaster to his crewmembers, knowing and asking the limits of them. Henry is never at a loss for crew; the incentive of earning a higher share at market overcomes any resistance to hard work and long hours.

I sat on the edge of my cold chair and looked about in a bit of a daze. I wore my gray wool pinstriped dress and matching jacket, topped off with a warm red cape. At dawn, I'd spent an hour on my hair, intricately braiding and arranging it on top of my head, leaving my forehead bare—a style that Henry says accentuates my hazel eyes.

I was unusually uncomfortable sitting alone. I didn't want to seek out a conversation with anyone as I waited, but I was not impolite and I returned every greeting. It was certainly being noted that Henry had brought me, his second cousin and life-long neighbor, to the wharf as a female companion. The Methodists in attendance had become accustomed to seeing us arrive for church together by sleigh through the winter, but that could easily have been interpreted as a ride of convenience, as we lived so close to each other.

Our public appearance today elevated our friendship to another level. Along with the usual jovial greetings, deep bows were offered to me by the gentlemen. Knowing smiles or cold shoulders came my way from the ladies. Henry is perhaps the most eligible bachelor in the community, and he has been the subject of intense speculation between the mothers and daughters of Paine Hollow for several years. He is, after all, in the prime of his life and should be thinking of starting a family.

I know that with our complimentary talents and intelligence, Henry and I will make the perfect pair. I enjoy the reputation of being quite proper and quick of mind. Until my graduation four years ago from the Wellfleet High School, I embraced the marvelous challenge of mastering the curriculum, from Latin to geometry. Since then, my study of music and playing the organ have kept me amused, along with recently becoming a member of the Wellfleet Methodist Church choir. And I do participate enthusiastically at the monthly meetings of our neighborhood Ladies Social Union. I consider myself to be a fairly accomplished young woman, able to interact skillfully in mixed company.

But I was definitely not myself as I sat on the *Dora Freeman*, and I was puzzled by my own reticence to laugh and talk with my friends as I usually do. I was a stranger to myself, waiting for Henry to bring me my meal. It surprised me that I was so affected; every year since I was a small girl I have attended the send-off meal in honor of one or another of my relatives, and it would never have occurred to me that I would be so reserved in such familiar surroundings.

The biting chill in the air was more obvious on the exposed deck of the *Dora Freeman* than it had been in my mother's front yard. The temperature of the sea water was still frigid; just a month ago the harbor was soundly iced in. I clapped my hands together to keep my gloved fingers from going numb. My dear friend Nettie called out to me from the deck of a nearby schooner. I smiled and waved, but didn't shout back. The people seated around me ate politely, not too quickly, greatly appreciating the food. The good-natured joking between the women and men quieted to a subdued murmur of conversation as the inevitable parting time drew near. The tide had turned and was on its way out. The fleet would sail within the hour.

Henry's absence became uncomfortable for me. I was not accustomed to sitting and waiting, and I grew impatient, but I kept my seat. I looked up at the gently swaying masts. I studied the deck of the *Dora Freeman* and imagined the toil and adventure the scrubbed planks would soon witness.

Happily, Henry appeared from below, and I watched the ease with which he bounded up the companionway towards me. He gracefully carried a plate of food in each hand, and two shiny forks peeped out from his breast pocket. Our eyes met and he smiled at me. We didn't stop looking at each other as he approached and handed me a plate of food. The blue of his eyes was the color of the sky on a perfect summer day. He sat down next to me to eat.

"You look so concerned, Eva," he said. "Where's your pretty smile?"

I had sternly lectured myself that even though this was my first time seeing Henry off, I was not going to show a faint heart. Henry is a captain, and I must be dignified in his presence. I was alarmed at the tears rushing to my eyes, and I blushed red with embarrassment.

"I'm sorry, Henry," I said. I took out a handkerchief and quickly wiped my eyes. "I'm sure the time will pass quickly, and soon you'll be back here with me. I'm just being silly." I took a bite of the tender corned beef, but it was a lump in my mouth. I attempted a smile for him.

"That's my girl. There's the pretty face I will think of," he said. "Don't wait on the wedding invitations. Send them out. I'll be home in two weeks, and then we'll be married. Soon you will be Mrs. Henry Smith."

I was quiet, my mind rushing ahead.

He looked at me with concern. "Eva, is our plan still acceptable to you?"

"Yes, Henry, of course. The fourteenth of May," I nodded. "I'll send the invitations out immediately. The first appearance of our wedding banns is due to be printed in the newspaper this week, and the second will come out next week. Then we will have advertised properly. Mama expects that Papa will be back from his voyage very soon, and Lewis will also be home for the wedding—if the *Mary Cole* can keep up with you."

"You flatter me, my dear," Henry smiled broadly at me. "Of course Lewis will be there, we can't be married without him. I have to start out on the right foot with the only brother I'll ever have, don't I?"

"I'm glad you think of him so fondly," I said. I love my brother and wouldn't want Lewis to feel that I was abandoning him.

Henry had cleaned his plate while I'd eaten just a few bites. His attention left me as he looked toward the dories stacked on deck, and then up at the two masts. He called a crew member over and asked him to go aloft and check a fastening.

"Yes, sir!" The responsive youth was off and up the main mast instantly. Watching Henry become absorbed with his responsibility, I was both proud and envious of his position as master of the vessel.

If only I had a similar station in life, one that required intelligence, a striving for excellence, a competition!

Henry's attention returned to me.

"You have no appetite, my dear," he said. "Before we get underway, I must talk with my first mate about the watch tonight, so it's time for you to go ashore. Leave your plate here on the chair and I'll see you off."

I surmised I was in the way—a female guest in a man's world, a fancy accessory in this hour of departure—and gingerly crossed over the plank, again with Henry's hand on my elbow. I was aware of people watching us as we walked across the wharf. We were the subject of many conversations, I was sure, but I didn't want to forfeit my opportunity at a heartfelt farewell. I turned to face Henry and took both of his hands with my own, causing him to look down at me. I required one last look into his beautiful eyes; it would have to sustain me for two weeks.

"Dear Henry, I know you'll have a successful trip," I said. "Please come home safely. I care for you so much." I was unable to express anything but the simplest of sugary phrases.

"Of course, my beautiful girl," he chuckled. "Don't you fret, I have sailed this route many times, in all kinds of weather. Go home now, and I will see you soon enough." He leaned down and gave me a quick hug, the wool of his coat scratching my face, his strength squeezing the breath out of me. "On my next trip out, you will be seeing me off as my wife." He smiled as he released me.

Then he crossed back over onto the *Dora Freeman*. Again I had to blink back tears, but I don't know if they were tears of frustration or tears of sorrow. I could have waited for company; many women would return to their homes without their husbands. But I decided to go alone. Henry's embrace had been hard and physical, and I wanted to keep the memory of it with me for as long as possible.

I retreated to the beach and waved at the opportunists in their rowboats who were ready at their oars, as the fording place was submerged under the high tide. "Miss Paine, over here! Miss Paine, over here!" they called out to me. I chose the closest skiff and was quickly rowed across to the opposite shore.

After paying the boy a nickel for the passage, I walked along the beach to the end of Paine Hollow Road. I climbed half way up the dune and sat down on the damp sand, looking out across the harbor toward the wharf. My hands ached inside my gloves, and I shivered even though the afternoon sun shone directly upon me, but I ignored the discomfort. I had to see the fleet go out before I went home.

The harbor echoed with shouted orders. Quickly, the guests came off the vessels, and chairs were stowed back in the warehouse. Decks were cleared, sails hoisted and lines cast off. One-by-one, and a few pairs sailing side-by-side, the schooners caught the wind and sailed across dark glittering water of Blackfish Creek, passed the northern point of Lieutenant's Island, and then tacked out across the wide mouth of Wellfleet Harbor. They will round Provincetown tonight, and tomorrow the fleet will be down on the Nantucket Shoals, with the men out rowing their dories, pulling in codfish and flounder.

"I wish you all a safe journey, I wish you all a good catch of fish, and I wish the time to fly as swiftly as you are sailing now," I murmured.

The schooners were soon reduced to miniature sails out on the horizon, and I could no longer single out the *Dora Freeman*, but I watched them all as they sailed out of sight. Then I walked home to my mother's warm kitchen.

∼

May 1, 1886

I awoke to a steamy, salty morning. The strong sunlight lifts the moisture of last evening's rain from our sandy road in waves of humidity, scented by the dank aroma that only wet warm sand can produce. It is low tide down at the shore, and the pungent smell of the exposed sand flats reaches our house on the southwest breeze. The apple tree I planted when I was a little girl is shedding its cheerful blossoms in the breeze, and there is a luxurious pink drift in the new grass below the branches.

As always, this morning I relished my dawn duty of releasing the chickens from their coop. It is a comforting and happy sight to see them come clucking down the plank into the yard, eager for their morning grain. They squabbled a bit, hopping about and pushing one another in anticipation. I shooed the lone rooster away from my skirts; he was impertinent, and I can't trust him not to peck me when my back is turned to him. I poured their feed into the cedar trough and immediately they were heads down and bottoms up—a fine flock of Rhode Island reds that Papa brought home two years ago as baby chicks. They are laying well now, thanks to the rooster, and the eggs bring me a pretty little profit down at the general store.

I am constantly accompanied by thoughts of Henry; he comes into my mind unbidden no matter what chore I am performing. I was obsessed with him even as I drank my morning tea and wrote in my journal, while just across the table Mama read her Bible. Thinking of his beautiful eyes, I breathed the air deeply through my nostrils and filled my lungs, straining against the corset stays that clench my diaphragm. I pushed my breasts against the cloth of my undergarments, and imagined myself pushing against Henry. How daring of me to behave in such a manner, but Mama is quite used to me scribbling away in my journals. If she only knew how my entries have changed, of late.

Of course, these sentiments about Henry are totally private and I cannot mention them to anyone, not even my dearest friend, Nettie. I have always been doubtful of the experiences of heroines in romance novels, yet I now could be the main character in one of them. The thought of Henry overtakes my senses, and this condition has been constant.

This is an unforeseen circumstance I don't quite know how to address. Who should have or could have warned me that the mere smell of Henry's wool jacket as he hugged me good-bye would send me into such a juvenile state, no longer in control of my intellect or my sense of sociability? I am at a tortured loss—the loss of myself as I knew me.

Today is the beginning of Henry's third day out with the fleet. It seems as though he's been gone for so much longer. Mama is also waiting for a man. Papa is away on the *Nautilus* completing a three port merchant run. Has Mama's longing for her husband always been as sharp and insistent as what I now feel? How has she lived with this for twenty-five years? I have not yet suffered for a week, and already I cannot remember the way I once was: happy and aspiring and precocious and striving. I am full of impatience. I have always been able to make something happen, but now I see that I have no control over this tender obsession. I must pay attention and go help Mama beat the rugs.

～

It is finally dark, and the peep frogs hidden at the pond's edge have begun their loud chorus. I find that I run to my room whenever possible to write out my thoughts, as I am having a strangely difficult time keeping track of them. I've been moving too quickly through the house. Today I misplaced things, not remembering where I put them down. In clumsy haste, I accidentally knocked a glass off the shelf in the kitchen.

Mama is aware of the fact that I am distracted. But until I tell her that Henry and I are to be married, it is entirely inappropriate for me to explain that I am missing Henry. I must tell her soon, as Henry expects the marriage arrangements to be in place upon his return, and if I do not tell her, she will read the banns in the newspaper and discover the fact on her own, or worse yet, hear from a neighbor. Luckily, her cough has kept her close to home these past few days. Why such procrastination, why such confusion?

I think it may help in my communication with Mama if I write down my thoughts in an intelligent manner and try to answer some of the questions I know Mama will have for me:

Henry and I have known each other all of our lives. He is the son of Papa's cousin, Arozana Paine Smith—one of our many cousins who populate the lovely valley of Paine Hollow. The seven-year difference in age between Henry and myself does not seem at all significant to me now, especially in light of the fact that our bachelor President Cleveland, who is almost fifty years old, will marry his twenty-one year old sweetheart next month in the White House. When I was a young child, I idolized Henry as a handsome older boy. He was always friendly and kind to me at family events. Mama remarked that Henry's fondness for his cousins was because he was an only child—a lonely child, she guessed.

He took the time on several occasions to extricate me from the clutches of the neighborhood bullies who delighted in tormenting me on my walk home from school. Henry was never oblivious to a little girl's troubles. He once dropped Harold Lombard into a snow drift for throwing snowballs at me, and he chased Willie Paine through the woods for taking me as a Rebel captive and tying me to a tree during one of his silly games. Willie Paine never again imagined me as a Rebel captive.

I was ten years old then and still at the lower school; Henry was seventeen and had conquered his courses in the classics, English, history, and geometry at the high school. He studied navigation at the winter fisherman's school when the ice pack kept the boats ashore. I saw him as an older brother, and wished he was, as my younger one was preoccupied with frogs and hunting rabbits and was not about to come to my rescue when I needed it.

As the years went by, I saw Henry at every family occasion from weddings to christenings to funerals—and if he was out to sea, I noticed his absence with disappointment. When he talked and laughed with other females, I found myself instantly envious. Time proved envy to be an unreasonable reaction, as Henry has never asked any lady for her hand.

Quite unexpectedly, romance came upon us like a thunderbolt. This past winter we were magnetically attracted to each other; at social occasions we barely noticed anyone else in attendance. It was as though I finally lost my patience with wishing and praying, and was no longer willing to leave our meetings to chance. I placed myself in Henry's path whenever I could. Perhaps the cold days when Henry drove me to church in his sleigh are to blame. We never would have had the time to get to know each other in such luxurious privacy had our parents been along, but the cold weather kept them at home.

On several occasions surely provided by the Lord, we glided into town through a magical winter wonderland, singing songs along the way to keep ourselves warm. While I snuggled under the lap robes, my hands as warm as the rest of me, I looked up at Henry's strong shoulders and arms and at his bare hands that held the lines to his beloved team of horses. I became all the more aware of Henry's strength when he once let me take the lines so he could warm his hands under the robe—a minute of guiding the spirited Silkie and Sinbad was all I could manage.

"Here, let me take them back, Eva," he insisted. "There's no need for you to strain your wrists like that." His gallant manners made him quite a pleasant companion.

In my mind, no other possible suitor has lived up to the likes of Henry. This should all be understandable to Mama. She appreciates kindness and consideration. And I am sure that Papa would like the same for me, especially since he has been so opposed to me leaving home for the university. He is convinced that I would not be safe living in Boston.

But here is the problem! How can I tell Mama that Henry wants to marry me, when Henry has not yet asked Papa for my hand? And, the truth is, Papa should not be asked permission, because he may not give it. He does not approve of marriage between cousins, even though Henry and I are the children of cousins, which makes us second cousins.

And further, it is I who asked Henry to marry me, not the other way around! Of course, I would never have asked him had I not known his answer would be in the affirmative. I giggle whenever I recall the flow of our conversation. I remember it line for line, which is not at all difficult, as I've run it through my mind dozens of times. Ten days ago, Henry and I were on our way home from church, rolling along in his buggy. We were discussing the Widow Matilda Chase and the way she had humiliated one of the parishioners on the church steps just after the service. I had been upset to see such cruelty.

"Widow Chase had no call at all to be so insulting to Annie Smith about the condition of her children's shoes," I said to Henry. "It is no fault of Annie's that her husband is unable to earn money now that his back is so weak."

"I've heard tell that the weak back is just the half of it, the other half is the remedy of rum," Henry said.

"Where did you hear that? That is just the sort of rumor that can ruin a family. There may be some truth to it, but it is not the whole truth. Annie has told me about the great pain Walter is in, with no relief. Who are we to pass judgment?" I was preparing myself for a good debate.

Henry did not answer my question as to the source of his information, and changed the subject entirely. "You are such a good woman, Eva," he said. "So kind hearted and fair minded. It's my loss that you are not partial to the idea of marriage."

I was alarmed. "And who gave you that impression? My goodness, Henry, why do you say that?"

"Oh, don't look at me like that." He peered down at me from the side of his eye as he drove the horses. "You've been headed for college all of your life. Your mother counts on it."

"My mother, bless her, has no right to count on me for anything." I was indignant. "I must determine my own path. Don't you agree?"

"Of course I agree." He drove along the county stage road, keeping a fair distance back from the buggy ahead of us. The horses pulled impatiently into their harnesses, knowing they were headed home to their own barn, but Henry held them back with a tight grip on the lines. "No one should chart out their life to satisfy someone else's hopes," he said. "Not even for a loving mother."

"Well said, Henry. And after careful consideration, I've decided not to attend the university." I paused for a breath. "I'm not going anywhere. Therefore, won't you consider marrying me?" I said it before I could stop myself.

"I don't have to consider it, Eva." Henry's answer was immediate and emphatic. "The answer is yes, I would be honored to have you as my wife." He pulled the horses to a halt and leaned over to kiss me.

My first kiss! I found myself laughing and marveling at how quickly the conversation had arrived at an intention of marriage. The stubble from his early morning shave had grown enough to roughly sand my cheek, the hot burn serving only to enhance my excitement.

"What a lucky man I am," he crowed. "Eva Paine has asked me to marry her!"

"Don't tease me, Henry, please! You could have asked—you should have asked."

"But Eva, I thought you had other plans. I didn't want to create the dilemma of an unwanted marriage proposal. I thought perhaps you would rather have another life than the waiting life of a sea captain's bride."

"You still should have asked me, Henry."

"Yes, I should have; I've been terribly remiss." He climbed out onto the side of the road and picked some daffodils from beside the fence. "Forgive me, Eva. Take these posies as an apology, and let's not waste any more time, please!" He presented the flowers with a flourish. Then he climbed back into the buggy, and we continued our drive smiling with contentment.

I have pressed those daffodils between my heaviest books. I will keep them always.

And so, Henry never asked, not wanting to bring undue pressure to bear against my presumed plans to attend the university. Ultimately, I had to be the one to ask him.

But this all leaves me with the original problem: How can I expect Henry to ask Papa for my hand when it was I who asked Henry for his? It is, after all, time for me to be married if I am not going to pursue my education—and Papa, of all people, knows that I am not going to go to Boston against his wishes. It is time for action. I will ask Mama to help me with the invitations and preparations. I must tell her tomorrow.

~

May 2, 1886

A tin bowl leapt out of my hands and landed upside down on the kitchen floor, where it rotated loudly on its rim before it settled down. My startled mother looked over her spectacles at me. She continued to rinse a piece of salted cod that she had been soaking in fresh water in preparation for our evening meal.

"Eva, dear, you are as jumpy as a cat today! What's gotten into you?" she asked.

I feigned misunderstanding as she reached down to pick up the elusive bowl.

"Nothing, Mama. Perhaps it's the weather. It's so warm and agreeable today. I'm restless and don't know what to do with myself."

My mother nodded knowingly. "You have spring fever. We've got to find something for you to do. When will you consider applying to Boston Wesleyan University? Cousin Isaac made sure that women can attend. He didn't forget the ladies, and would have been so very pleased to know a relative from his own home town was to go up to Boston to study."

Mama is ever vigilant; whenever I voice being even the slightest bit bored, she encourages me to go to Boston. It doesn't matter that Papa is against it. I could be gone before he knew it, she says, and the matter would be settled. I would be perfectly safe in Boston if I roomed with trusted friends. No person in Wellfleet is prouder than Mama of her illustrious cousin, Isaac Rich.

We all know his story—Isaac was born at a farm just down the road at Pleasant Point, and left for Boston as a young lad because his parents had too many mouths to feed with so many children in the family. Isaac got his start selling Wellfleet oysters from a pushcart at Faneuil Hall and went on to make a fortune in the seafood business. When he died in 1872 and bequeathed more than a million dollars to help establish the Boston Wesleyan University, he left instructions that women be encouraged to attend. I always find it amusing that Mama is such a champion of her cousin, even though he was obviously a devout Methodist, and she is an unwavering member of the Congregational Church.

"Eva, remember how you loved high school in spite of all those months of studying so late into the night? You did very well, dear. I am so proud that you graduated with honors from high school. You are a marvel. You could study to be a teacher or a doctor, or anything you want to be!" Mama launched into her familiar persuasive argument.

I smiled at her and thought of my books, neatly put away upstairs on a shelf with the examination booklets tucked into paper pockets for safe keeping.

"It's true, I did love high school," I said. "But it's been several years since I graduated—four to be exact. And I don't want to live in Boston. When is Papa coming in? It seems as though he has been gone for so long!"

I surprised myself by collapsing down into my father's chair. Mama stared at me straight-faced and then bit her lip, blinking rapidly. Immediately, her nose was red.

"He's only been gone for ten days," she said. "But it does seem to be longer, doesn't it?" Mama opened the oven door and tested the temperature with her hand, and I jumped up to get a few more sticks of firewood for her.

"I'm sorry, Mama," I said. "I didn't mean to upset you. Papa will be back soon. How thoughtless of me to worry you like this. It's just that I don't want to go to the university in Boston, even though your heart is set on it."

Mother nodded and did not say anything, but continued to prepare the fish for baking.

"I have something to tell you, Mama." I stood with my hands pressed into the kitchen table. "I want to get married."

Mama put down the glass of bread crumbs she had been sprinkling on the fish and looked up at me.

"You're not happy, Eva? You are so gifted and talented! You're not disappointed with yourself because you are not yet married, are you? Oh, are you saying that you're not happy here in the house with your brother and father and me?" Her face crumpled.

"No, Mama. Not at all," I tried to correct her misassumptions. "I said it all wrong. I love you and I love Papa. You are wonderful to live with—you have been the most loving parents to me, and Lewis is a wonderful brother. But I am in love with someone." Mama looked at me so doubtfully that I had to laugh.

"Yes, Mama, I have found a bachelor who has resisted convention for a long time, but now I have asked him to marry me, and he has accepted." I couldn't resist giving her the news in this playful way.

"Eva, you didn't." Mama had to sit down. She wiped her hands on a dishtowel and walked out of the kitchen and into the dining room to sit in her rocking chair. I followed and stood with my hands clasped behind my back.

"How does a woman ask a man to marry her?" Mama asked in exasperation.

"Mama, I had to!" I defended myself. "Cyrus Young—you remember him from my class—he was about to propose to me. He sent me the most beautifully written valentine in February."

I took a small blue envelope from the bookshelf. "Look, here it is, see what Cyrus wrote—'A maid so fair, an angel from air, my helpmate be, I'd live with thee. Always and forever yours, Cyrus Young.' I do like him as a friend, Mama, but I wouldn't want to marry him. I have been avoiding him ever since."

Mama took the card and looked at the entry, written in beautiful penmanship and signed with many flourishes. "Yes, that sounds more than friendly. Poor, shy, young man, getting up the courage to send you that." Mama had regained her composure and she gently rocked in the chair.

"I am flattered, but I can't say yes to a man just because he got the courage up to pursue me. I can't imagine being a wife to Cyrus. Thank God he didn't have the nerve to approach me in high school— I don't know if I would have had the sense then to realize I should say 'No, thank you.'"

"I agree with you, Eva." Mama patted the chair next to her. "Please sit down, dear, and tell me about your chosen one. If it is not to be Cyrus, then who is this mysterious suitor?"

I sat down and regarded my mother, memorizing the scene in front of me—a method I've acquired to take a moment when a moment should be taken. My mother sat patiently.

Sarah Rich Paine is a beautiful mother, I must say, extraordinarily so when compared to the other ladies in the Hollow. Her waist is trim due to diligent corset lacing every day, and her teeth are still present and strong due to her refusal to eat white sugar. Honey from her own beehives will suffice perfectly well for Sarah Paine. She wears her prematurely silver hair twisted up in a bun, with not a hair out of place.

Mama was elegant there in her rocking chair, in the spotless and highly decorated dining room of our home. A china tea pot on the table, a thick Persian carpet underfoot, leather bound books in the lacquered bookcase, and gilded framed pictures on the walls—all spoke eloquently of Papa's success as a merchant captain. Prominently displayed just behind Mama was the oil painting of the *Nautilus*, the schooner my father owns and sails with so much pride. From my vantage point, the *Nautilus* appeared to be sailing across Mama's shoulder. I shut my eyes and then opened them again. I could distract myself no longer. I took a deep breath, and then exhaled.

"It's Henry," I said. "I want to marry Captain Henry Smith." Mama looked down at her folded hands. I could hear the clock in the front hall ticking out the seconds.

"The sleigh rides into town this winter have had an effect," she said softly.

"Yes, Mama."

"And you went to see Henry off the other day at the wharf, not just your brother."

"Yes, Mama."

"Widow Chase brought my mail from the post office yesterday, and she mentioned that she saw you on the *Dora Freeman* with Henry and asked if you two were sweethearts, but I dismissed her question, considering the source."

"I'm sorry, Mama. Henry and I wanted to tell you at the send-off, but you couldn't come. We wanted to tell you together that we are to be married when he returns."

"But he has a temper, Eva. Remember the winter at the fisherman's school when School Master Cole had to. . ."

I didn't let her finish. "Oh, Mama," I said. "He was sixteen years old when that happened. Henry is a man now. He is not a boy anymore, and does not have to answer to any man. Headmaster Cole didn't like it that Henry disobeyed, but Henry took his thrashing and learned his lesson, and then went on to graduate. We cannot hold that old story against him now."

"But Henry broke a desk in the school room, he was so angry at being caned. He was destructive."

"Yes, Mama, but that was long ago! He's different now. Don't we have a duty to forgive him his boyhood temper if we are Christians? He has protected me. He has been kind to me. I feel safe with him. I want to be his wife."

"Hush, Eva," Mama held up her hand. She rocked back and forth in her chair. "So be it," she finally said. She was quiet again, which caused me to be anxious. And then she asked, "Where will you keep house?"

"I was hoping we could live here, Mama," I said. "Just until we have a home of our own. I know it will be some time before Henry and I have put enough by to build our own home, but if he has a good summer of fishing, then we will be able to think about it in the fall. We will have to start out very modestly. My bedroom upstairs is large enough for two, so I thought we could live here." As I said this to my mother, I realized that I had assumed a great deal concerning my future living arrangements.

"Yes, of course. I would want you to." Mama's voice was stronger. "I'm not sure what your brother, or your father for that matter, will think of you and Henry living here together as man and wife, but they are both out to sea much of the time, and you say it will be temporary. And why should we women be alone this summer when the men are away?"

"We shouldn't be. Don't worry, Mama. I will be here with you. This is a big house with plenty of room. And Papa might like having Henry to lend an extra hand around the place."

"But, Eva, you are an intelligent and educated young lady. Are you certain you want to marry a cousin and stay right here in South Wellfleet? You could do so much out in the world! Perhaps you are just at loose ends, and you need another challenge to engage your mind."

"Mama, you have to let go of that hope. I am *not* going away to Boston. I've already spoken with Reverend Moss."

"You haven't!"

"Yes, I have. And he said he would perform the marriage ceremony. He knows that Henry and I are second cousins, and he said it doesn't matter. He said that the Lord does not frown upon cousins marrying, so neither will he."

"Oh, Eva, you are far too bold a girl for me to understand! Speaking to a minister about your own marriage, rather than letting your father do that, or even your intended husband!"

"I had to know if the marriage would be allowed, Mama. The minister said yes. Won't you please help me write out the invitations? Henry wants us to be married on the fourteenth of May."

"My goodness, that is barely two weeks from today. What will people think?"

"Well, as always, some busybodies will think the worst of us. But I promise you, Mama, they will be disappointed, as a full nine months will pass by before any child is brought into the world.

"Henry and I simply can't see any reason for a long engagement. We've decided, and Henry says that at his age, he sees no reason to stand on formalities. He is ready, and I am ready. There is nothing inappropriate about it. We see it as a practical thing."

"Yes, of course, Eva, *I* do not doubt your character, but, oh, how some tongues will wag. But I must insist—you will not be married until your father is home. We will send out the invitations, but the ceremony must be postponed if your father has not returned and been properly informed. He will want to be present to give away his only daughter.

"And your brother Lewis—you must wait for Lewis. Eva, please have some patience. Why are you in such a rush?" Mama wore a plaintive look upon her face as she begged me for some explanation. I searched for the most truthful answer.

"Love, Mama. I am in love. I have never been in love. I am missing Henry all the time, thinking of him all the time. I want to be married to him. I want to belong to him. I wanted at least to choose the man I would belong to, rather than having one choose me as his belonging. Is that so wrong?" My voice had risen to a high octave. Mama sighed, and reached over to take my hand.

"No, Eva. It is not wrong at all," she said. "I think it will be all right. You are different, Eva, but I think it will be all right."

~

CHAPTER TWO
Henry's Wife

May 9, 1886

Papa has returned from his voyage, at last. Mr. Townsend ran up from his house to tell Mama. Just before the noon hour there was a sharp rap on the kitchen door, and then Clive Townsend appeared, hat in hand, his face blackened with soot. Mama ignored his disheveled appearance.

"Clive, do have a cup of tea with us," she invited him.

"I would be honored, Sarah, but I'm in the middle of brush burning. I've got to get back and tend to my fires. I just wanted to let you know that Captain Otis is in. The *Nautilus* just sailed past the point."

"Thank you very much for your effort," Mama exclaimed. "I do so appreciate it. I am beholden to you, Clive. You have gone and left your work to come tell me." My mother was effusive, presenting the broadest smile she had exhibited since Papa put out to sea seventeen days ago.

"It's no bother, Sarah. It's my pleasure." Mr. Townsend turned and left as quickly as he had come. Mama went immediately to the parlor mirror. She took down her silver hair and carefully brushed it and then re-pinned it up into a proper bun, humming as she worked. I watched her, admiring her desire to be attractive for my father after so many years together. I am determined that as Henry and I age together, I will be as attentive to my appearance. I held out her green woolen cape, and wrapped it snuggly over her narrow shoulders. She hugged me, and then went to her linen closet to fetch a canvas laundry bag.

Together we hitched Tessa, our sorrel mare, to the buggy. Mama drove the twenty-minute route up and around the head of Blackfish Creek and then out to the wharf. She kept Tessa at a trot for the entire three miles. "You'll rest when you get us there," she told Tessa as we jounced along. Mama sat on the edge of the leather cushion holding the lines, alert and attentive, her eyes straight ahead. A little smile played around the corners of her mouth.

Tessa was skittish as we approached the South Wellfleet railroad station, as she had no affection for the puffing iron monstrosity she usually encountered there. But we were between the two arrivals of the day; the morning train bound for Provincetown had already passed through and wouldn't return for another two hours, heading back for Plymouth. "Tessa, walk on!" Mama demanded of the horse, and Tessa obeyed.

We passed by our tiny railroad station, which consists of a shed with a ticket window on a raised wooden platform next to the railroad tracks. Our post office occupies half of the shed, since the mail is dropped on the platform twice a day. The next stop out is Wellfleet, and there is a proper station building there; we are lucky to have a platform in South Wellfleet. Ike Paine's general store stands next to the platform. The fresh white paint on the storefront gleamed so brightly in the sun that I couldn't look at the building. All was quiet as we trotted through.

The sandy road then took us by the Second Congregational Church, which is centered in the graveyard that provides the final resting place for many friends and family members. The church was built back in the 1830's for the convenience of our families in South Wellfleet, but now it is shuttered and silent.

Inside, the dusty pews are marked with little brass plates inscribed with the names of the charter members, Mama and Papa included. They were married in the church, and I attended Sunday school and sermons there when I was a girl. But once again, the South Wellfleet Congregationalists must travel to Wellfleet to the First Congregational Church.

"It's a pity that our church is empty—it looks so forlorn," Mama said as we passed by. I looked over through the cemetery gates and singled out the headstone of John Taylor, who as a young man had been a "lifeguard to George Washington," according to the inscription. I would rather contemplate the grave of a Revolutionary War hero unknown to me than think about the aunts and uncles and cousins and grandparents who lie buried in their coffins, dressed in their best clothing.

Many are buried with their feet towards the rising sun. When Christ comes again from the east, as the scriptures predict, those who were worthy in life will sit up in their graves to face him with newly restored bodies. I shuddered, and Mama flipped the reins to quicken Tessa's trot. She knows I am unnerved by the thought of death.

I've learned to carry smelling salts to get me through the hours of a funeral ceremony with the expected level of decorum. For months following a burial, I am bothered by the image of the beloved's coffin being lowered into the cold ground. Yes, the spirit has left the body for the deserved just reward, as I am constantly reminded by scripture, clergy and friends. There is no doubt that the deceased are no longer with us; they are not in their coffins at all. But in spite of my faith in the good Lord's infinite plan, I cannot erase from my mind that image of the carefully dressed body lying in a box and buried in the earth.

"Why couldn't this church survive?" My mother attempted to distract me with conversation. "Your Grandfather Nathan helped to build it when he was a young man, sailing the lumber down from Maine. It is so sad to me that the doors are locked now."

"Well, we don't have a large enough congregation now to pay a minister, and that is because so many of us have become Methodists, Mama."

Without realizing it, my mother had given me an opening into one of my favorite topics. She sighed. "Yes, Eva, I suppose that is one reason. If all the families who were founding members of our church were still Congregationalists, then perhaps there would be enough people to sustain it. To see our church building abandoned—I never thought I'd live to see the day. But more a trial for me that you have joined the Methodist Church. We have *always* been Congregationalists."

"I'm sorry you are still so upset about it, Mama, but at least we can ride to Wellfleet center and back again in the same carriage. Some people can't even do that. Think of the lively discussions we have comparing the two sermons on our way home," I teased.

"My dear, you know I would much prefer to sit in the same pew as you do, in the same building. Your father and I will never join you in your decision to become a Methodist, although we did not move to prevent it—you were so determined. I feel that in some way, you have chosen to leave your family by leaving the church of your ancestors.

"But I didn't want to get into this discussion about one church versus another, I just wanted to say that it is such a shame that a beautiful church like ours no longer has enough parishioners to stay open, and we now have to travel the five miles into Wellfleet to worship."

I couldn't let Mama have the last word. She had put me on the defensive. "I didn't convert to Methodism to insult my ancestors. But I much prefer the liveliness of a good Methodist service to the Congregational formality. Our music is uplifting and everyone joins in to sing willingly. I no longer dread going to sit in the pew—I enjoy it, and the Lord did mean for worship to be joyous!

"It is all the same God, and yet the interpretation of worship is so different. Really, Mama, you know that the music just drags so at the Congregational Church. The hymns all sound like dirges, and that organist!"

"Eva!" Mama acted shocked, but I knew she agreed with me. She "visits" the Wellfleet Methodist Church with me when Papa is away, and now that so many Wellfleet sea captains are Methodist, even Papa has come into the Methodist Church to attend several funerals.

"Well, it's true," I said. "I am excited to get up and go to church on Sunday, and I never was before converting. You should hear Henry sing, Mama. A wonderful thing happens—his face beams with happiness. The hymn may be ten verses long, and Henry never runs out of stamina! Oh, I just love to stand next to him and sing, it is such a feeling!" I couldn't tell what Mama was thinking—she was quiet. Perhaps she needed more discussion about the service and less about the jubilant singing.

"Further, Mama, there is more passion in our sermons! I am invigorated after listening to Reverend Moss, as he truly preaches the good news of the New Testament, rather than dragging on with the Old Testament. With all due respect to the people dear to me who attend the Congregational Church, I feel nothing but dreary when I leave a service there. I shall never be good enough to enter Heaven as a Congregationalist. It is truly by faith rather than works that I will arrive in Heaven, and this is the message that I hear from our Reverend Moss."

"Eva, dear, your enthusiasm is quite persuasive, although I forgive you at your young age for failing to realize some of us older folks *enjoy* a quiet, contemplative church service. And there are other concerns. Lewis has told me of times he has been out fishing on the *Mary Cole*, and on Sundays the Methodist captain has purposefully drifted through the nets of working boats and torn them, all the while conducting his crew to sing Christian hymns on deck.

"Now tell me, is that any way to convert a Congregationalist, or even a Catholic, by destroying their fishnets? It's embarrassing that these captains are now called 'Bible-backs,' and it is known up and down the coast that they hail principally from the town of Wellfleet."

"That only happens on Sundays, Mama. You know the scriptures say not to work on Sunday."

"Jesus himself said the cows have to be fed and watered, no matter if it is Sunday or not," she shot back.

"Of course, you're right, Mama." I said. "I can assure you, Henry is not a Methodist who would ruin the nets of fellow captains. Henry has been known to fish on a Sunday or two. He says the notion of work is open to interpretation, as you've just pointed out." I had to acknowledge that Mama knows how to make a good point when she wants to.

"You're certainly able to debate the subject, Eva. Was religion a topic that was taken up on the high school debate team?" Mama asked.

"Never! You remember our principal, Mr. Ingalls. He forbade the teachers and students to compare the merits or faults of the denominations. He encouraged us all to remember that we are Christians and to obey the Golden Rule. Beyond that and the Lord's prayer, which we recited every morning, he was against any talk of religion outside the literary discussions of the classics.

"I do miss analyzing Shakespeare's plays and sonnets, Mama. There was nothing that man didn't write about! He approached love and death and religion and treachery with equal energy."

I stopped talking, realizing that Mama was preoccupied, but she had achieved her objective of taking my mind off morbid thoughts. We rounded the head of the creek and traveled through the salt meadows down to the Southern Wharf Company. Tessa sensed some change ahead; she snorted and leaned harder into her harness. We were rewarded by the sight of the dark hull of the *Nautilus* alongside the wharf.

The crew members were at the booms rolling and tying the sails. A great flurry of people advanced upon the wharf to help offload the cargo—tons of hay that had been pressed into bales and stored in the barns of Maine all winter, and hundreds of board feet of pine lumber, cut from the Maine forests. Our livestock have eaten their way to the end of last fall's crop of salt hay, harvested from the marshes that border Blackfish Creek. Papa's cargo of Maine hay will feed the livestock through the first summer harvest. As I tied Tessa to a hitching post, I promised her I'd soon return with a treat. The sweet scent of dried clover permeated the air as Mama and I stepped up onto the wharf.

My father supervised the off-loading procedure with a booming voice and spare hand movements instantly understood by his entire crew.

"No crew members will be paid until this hold is empty! William, get down there and help Mr. Atwood with his wagon! Come on now! Ten dollars a wagon load now. Pay the clerk, pay the clerk!" Although Papa was safely home, his duties as captain would not be finished until the *Nautilus* was unloaded. After the hay, the lumber would come off and be taken to the lumberyard. Wagons lined up along the wharf, waiting for the lumber, and the horses were stomping and whinnying in their harnesses, hoping for a handful of the sweet hay.

The office of the Southern Wharf Company nestles humbly in the sand beside the wharf. The clerk inside, Mr. Avery, is as clever as any city bookkeeper and keeps detailed cargo accounts of the vessels that come and go. This hay and lumber cargo is the last load the *Nautilus* carried on a merchant voyage that departed South Wellfleet seventeen days ago.

The first leg of the trip was south to Norfolk, Virginia, where a load of ice blocks, packed in sawdust and still frozen months after being cut from the Wellfleet ponds this past winter, was exchanged for a hold full of oysters. The second leg was north again to Boston, where the oysters were offloaded, and after a thorough cleaning of the hold, a cargo of mixed household goods was stowed for the third destination of Portland, Maine.

And now the *Nautilus* is home again, with the much-desired hay and lumber and a few sweet delights, as we were to discover.

I love Mama's homecoming ritual. Some wives wait at home for their husbands to come to them after a voyage, but my mother always leaves her kitchen as soon as a neighbor brings her the news that her husband is in. It is for this very reason that people make the effort to report to her when the *Nautilus* rounds the point. It isn't every wife that gets the news delivered to her doorstep.

The fondness between my mother and father is well known, to the point where many think my mother is suffering while father is away. Since she is revered as a kind soul, quick to come to the aid of the sick or impoverished, it is the community consensus that the best way to return her kindness is to deliver the news that her beloved Otis is safely home. The eager messenger is always rewarded with the most appreciative exclamations of thanks, as if that person has single-handedly brought Papa home.

My mother made her way across the wharf, and the working men parted for her as butter to a hot knife. I snatched a handful of hay from a wagon and ran back to Tessa with it, recognizing in myself the reluctant trepidation inherent in telling Papa what I must on this first greeting after his voyage.

For the second time in my life, I would be informing Papa of my intentions, rather than simply presenting him with news of my activities or accomplishments. Two years ago I told him I had attended an evangelistic service at the Wellfleet Methodist Church and had knelt down at the altar to convert that very day. Papa met the news with a stony silence and never discussed my conversion, although, to his great credit, he gradually accepted the fact that I am now a Methodist.

My father stopped bellowing to his crew and cried out, "My dear

Sarah! You look as lovely as the first day I saw you! Give your husband a hug." He embraced my mother and looked over her shoulder at me as I came up behind her.

"Come on, my dear Eva! Oh, the two loveliest ladies in the world, and I *have* been around the world. You are a sight to come home to." My father hugged me with enthusiasm.

"I have something for you, my two ladies. Sweets for the sweet." He pulled a paper package out of his coat pocket and took a sniff. "No, it's not this one, that's tobacco." He pulled a second package out of his pocket and handed it to my mother. "Open that now and see what you think of it." Papa beamed at Mama, watching her.

"How kind, Otis. You are so thoughtful," Mama said. She untied the string and opened the paper carefully, as if it were a fine silk wrapper. Inside was a large molded leaf of sugar.

"That's maple sugar candy, just made this season," Papa said. "Take a taste, Sarah.

She did, and declared it delicious, rewarding him with a kiss on the cheek. I thought the same when I took a nibble.

"Papa, thank-you. It's so nice that you are always thinking of us." I squeezed his rough hand.

My mother turned and walked across the gangplank and onto the deck with her canvas bag. It is her custom to go directly to the captain's quarters on the *Nautilus*. There are various activities she carries on there; she dusts, she strips Papa's bedding from his bunk, she collects his soiled clothing from his sea chest. The one thing she has never done is to accompany him on an extended voyage. Many a captain's wife has sailed for months or years with their husbands, but Mama is too easily chilled. She prefers to wait for her husband to come home, and she serves the community while he is gone. I've always suspected that she bargains with the Lord: *I will serve you while Otis is away, and you will bring my Otis home to me.*

I remained on the wharf, standing next to my father. He continued to oversee the activity around us, but his men carried on perfectly well without any direction. I had to speak.

"Papa, I have something to tell you," I began. I have never had anything more important to tell him. It would have been easier for me to tell Papa that I was already married. My father is a man who accepts things that are already done, but if something is looming, he wants to throw in his opinion.

"Yes, my dear girl, what is it?" he asked heartily. As always, he expected the best from me. I plunged into the thick of it.

"I am going to be married to Henry Smith." There. It was out. Strangely, I was almost ashamed in telling him, and it was difficult to continue to look at my father's face. I had not imagined that this simple statement would be so personal when spoken to my father. I might just as well have opened my mouth and told him that I wanted to sleep in Henry Smith's bed.

Papa stared at me. Then he squinted at the horizon where the bay met sky. He pulled a corncob pipe out of his pocket and began to fill it with tobacco from his pouch—the pipe that he never smoked once he reached shore, the pipe that he and my mother pretended did not exist. At first I thought he would say nothing. I stood next to him, not daring to leave him until he replied. A minute went by, and I dreaded the thought that he might treat this announcement with complete silence, as he had my conversion to Methodism. He finally spoke.

"So, we'll be losing you, my girl," he said. He sucked fiercely on his pipe and exhaled a huge cloud of smoke. "Why Cousin Henry?"

"Because I know who he is, Papa." I couldn't talk frankly to my father about why. About how my heart went wild when I was near Henry. About the way Henry made me feel safe and desired at the same time. I tried to say something that Papa would understand. He would be the first to be upset if I met and fell in love with someone who was unknown, perhaps a visitor who had arrived by railroad and knew nothing of our ways, as the Bostonians demonstrate when they come for the summer to cool themselves by the shore.

"Yes, we know Henry. He's out fishing with the fleet right now?"

"He's due in shortly. We are to be married when he comes home. Our invitations are for the fourteenth of May."

"That soon. Well, my girl," he turned and looked down at me. "I wish you all the happiness that a long life with the proper mate can bring. This is good news. Sometimes I come home to bad news, and this is not bad news. This is good news."

Papa was quiet for a moment. Then he lifted his head and smiled. "I shall have a son-in-law," he said. "I always wondered who the lucky fellow would be. And Henry Smith is very lucky indeed to have waited for you, Eva. I wish you all the happiness."

"Thank you, Papa." I had a lump in my throat. It was as if he was saying good-bye to me before a long voyage—one that I would be taking, not him. I reached up to hug him, and then I ran back to Tessa and stood beside her, stroking her and talking to her. I needed some time to calm myself. Mama came towards me with the full laundry bag. I took it from her and threw it up over the buggy seat.

"You told your father, didn't you," she said.

"Yes, Mama."

"I thought as much," she said knowingly. "He seems a bit blue. He told me he'd be home for supper, and he wants to eat rice pudding with raisins for dessert—your favorite when you were a little girl."

"I'll make it for him," I said.

I had not expected that my father would have such tender feelings towards me as I prepare for marriage. I am, after all, twenty-one years old, and it's high time that I have a mate. But I am blessed to have such a caring father.

"Let me drive, Mama," I insisted. "I need something to do." I took the reins and we drove home in near silence except for Tessa's soft hoof beats on the sandy road—my mother grateful that Papa was safely in from the sea and me anxious for Henry's return.

~

May 11, 1886

Preparations have begun in earnest for my wedding day. As to the location of the ceremony, conversations among my parents and aunts and uncles made it clear that there is no better solution than the one offered on our wedding invitation. Henry and I are to be married in Mama's front yard. This is a decision that I made myself, since half of our relatives and friends are Methodists and the other half, Congregationalists. In order to avoid the unpleasantness of endless discussions as to the reasons why we should be married in one church or the other, and in order to avoid insulting or displeasuring anyone, the front yard will do just fine. In case of rain, the parlor will suffice. Of course, the attending minister will be our Methodist minister, Reverend Moss.

Mama has been busy expertly fashioning my new dress from five yards of sea blue silk. I decided on blue silk so I could wear the dress again. A white wedding dress is pretty and yet so impractically extravagant. Pieces of the dress have been laid out across the dining room table, and my mother sits patiently sewing for hours. A muslin sample was created first to be certain of fit and style, and now the real dress is coming together.

This morning I stepped into the house after feeding the chickens to find seven women in the parlor helping to finish my wedding dress. The sleeves were gathered and puckered by Mama and then fitted to the armholes of the darted bodice. Nettie's mother, Aunt Mary, had the voluminous skirt on her knees, and she engaged her needle most industriously in the task of gathering in the waist. Soon the bodice and the skirt will be sewn together, and then I will try on the dress and stand on the dining room table while the hem is pinned up. I was delighted to see the group of them here, working together so happily on my account.

"Eva, there are only days left until the fourteenth. Has Henry wired you?" Aunt Elizabeth asked. Her husband, Captain Wiley, is under the employ of our Wellfleet millionaire, Lorenzo Dow Baker and his Boston Fruit Company. Captain Wiley frequently takes advantage of the telegraph wires—when he comes into a port, he always wires Aunt Elizabeth as to his whereabouts and fond thoughts of home.

"No, Auntie, I don't suppose Henry has come in to a harbor to find a telegraph operator. You know they fish until the holds are full." I didn't bother to remind her of the fact that was obvious to the rest of us: Captain Wiley has a company expense account for such luxuries, and Henry certainly does not.

"Yes, but to leave a bride-to-be in such anticipation! It is only civilized to make the effort to keep in touch, I should think. Are you worried, dear?" Aunt Elizabeth looked up at me with an expression of true concern.

Henry's mother had to speak up. "Aunt Arozana" to me, she is Papa's first cousin by way of his father's brother, and therefore, Arozana is my first cousin once removed. But out of respect or fondness—and in Arozana's case, both—all female cousins of the older generation are called "Aunt".

"Henry will most certainly be in on time," she declared. "Don't fill the girl's head with worry, Elizabeth. He has never been overdue. In fact, my Henry is usually the first to return. They don't call him the "High Liner" for nothing. We can expect him momentarily!"

I glanced at Aunt Arozana thankfully, and then worried about how I should address her in just a few days time when she becomes my mother-in-law. She smiled broadly at me, the back corner of her smile revealing the fact that she has lost a tooth. Her plump face was creased only by her smile. Aunt Arozana has no frown expression that I know of, and she also has no need to squint at her needle; her eyesight is still perfect, she claims. She continued to address me.

"Eva, I've prepared the room over the parlor for you and Henry. I am sure that you two will be quite comfortable there, my dear. You'll have the best feather mattress in the house, topped with the velvet crazy quilt that I made years ago for Henry's bride. I am grateful that he has chosen *you*, my dear. I am so very happy that my Henry is to be married at last and will provide me with grandchildren to enjoy in my old age." Aunt Arozana was quite blissful in this last pronouncement as I sank into a chair and stared at Mama, and she at me. It was apparent that Henry and I would not be living with Mama and Papa. Aunt Arozana was not done.

"Of course the homestead will be Henry's when we pass on, as he *is* our only child, but even if Winslow and I had more children, Henry would be entitled as the oldest son. I am only thankful to the Lord that I am alive to see the new mistress come into the home, and I will do all that I can to instruct you on the ways of housekeeping, my dear Eva. It will be to my benefit, after all, as you will be living with me for the rest of my life! What a gift you are. I have always longed for a daughter." Aunt Arozana looked me over from head to toe, took a breath, and continued.

"Now, I know that you consider yourself to be well educated, which I allow is true, but the care of a man is not taught in our educational institutions, as of yet. No one can darn a sock like I can, it is well known—and you, my dear, will have the benefit of all my expertise. My prayers have been answered and I will have feminine companionship and comfort in my home at last. Lord knows that it has been a trial living with two men all this time with no feminine conversation or sensibility."

Aunt Arozana leaned back in her chair and breathed heavily. I waited a few seconds to be sure she had finished speaking and then attempted a reply.

"Yes, Aunt Arozana, I am very grateful, as well, to be gaining you as a mother-in-law," was all I could manage.

Mama got up from her chair and asked how many ladies would like a cup of tea and a hot muffin fresh from the oven. She counted four and left the room.

Mama has been quite happy in her kitchen for as long as I can remember, and I do not know how to do half as much as Mama does in the way of baking, stocking, setting food by, or preparing anything, for that matter. I help her when she asks for it, and I'm sure that I am of assistance, but I wouldn't know where to begin if I tried to run a kitchen by myself. As Mama left us to fetch tea and muffins, I realized how her position and Aunt Arozana's were to be reversed. By my marriage, this house would lose a daughter and Arozana's would gain one. I excused myself and followed Mama to the kitchen. She was weeping over the wash basin, looking out the window at Tess in her paddock.

"Mama, don't cry," I tried to comfort her. "The Smith's house is just a half a mile away. I'll be right down the road, and I can see you every day. It's much closer than the university in Boston, Mama. Now stop or you'll make me cry, too."

"Yes, I know, Eva," she said, not looking at me. "I'm just being sentimental. You have never left home before and taken all your things. I can't bear to think of all your things gone from this house—your clothes, your books, yourself! It was just a matter of time, though. I want you to be happy, and you shall be. Arozana is a good lady and her husband Captain Winslow could not be a more faithful servant of God." Mama respectfully referred to Winslow Smith's position as a deacon of the Wellfleet Congregational Church.

"I will miss your voice, dear, at night when we have our discussions over supper, and I will miss your laugh and your singing. But I am so very fortunate that, as you say, you will be just down the road. So pay no mind to these sniffles. It's all happening a bit quickly for me, but I am happy for you, truly I am."

Mama hugged me and then gathered the china teapot and tea cups onto a tray and told me to bring along the muffins. I grabbed at the hot tin and jumped back.

"Use the potholders, Eva. The potholders." I obeyed and followed her out into the parlor to rejoin the ladies.

~

May 15, 1886
Our Wedding Day and Night

I am a married lady now. Time accelerated as our wedding day approached. Henry sailed into Blackfish Harbor two days early, but I chose not to see him before our ceremony. We exchanged several notes up and down the road via our mutual neighbors who were more than happy to oblige Henry and me in our wedding preparations. Henry's news to me was that his voyage had been financially successful and that he waited in "great anticipation of our union." My news to Henry was, "All is ready! Papa is home, and Lewis sailed in right behind you. The invitations have been acknowledged, my dress is ready, and the day is upon us."

Yesterday morning I sat in my new blue silk, submitting to Nettie's hands as she dressed my hair for the wedding. She had walked across the road from her house to help me get dressed while her mother and mine finished the cooking together. I looked fetching indeed in the dress, and Mama exclaimed that the sea blue color made my eyes darker and my complexion lovely and pale. I decided that my long hair could be tamed by drawing it all to the top of my head and then creating a bun. Nettie declared this too "every day" of a look. She heated the curling iron on the stove, and intended to curl the locks over my eyes into the latest style, according to the Brides section of the *Boston Daily Globe.*

"Don't burn my forehead, Nettie," I admonished her as she came towards me with the hot instrument. "I can't be married with burns on my face."

"Oh, don't worry. I'm not going to burn you, silly goose," she laughed. "But Henry would marry you even if you did have burns on your face, I have no doubt."

"What do you mean, Nettie? Don't even think about burning me."

"I mean that Henry is getting himself a very intelligent wife. Looks aren't everything, you know! I know, because I wasn't blessed with half the good looks God decided to give you." Nettie spoke matter-of-factly on this old subject.

"Really, Nettie. You're a wonderful person, with so many good qualities! And I think that you are beautiful."

"Thank you, you are a loyal cousin," Nettie said. "But the gentlemen don't see me through your eyes. I've never been proposed to, and I'm almost a year older than you are with no prospects—as the old aunties constantly point out." Nettie smirked at me.

"Nettie, you say that as if you are proud of it," I said. "Here's a secret for you—Henry did not propose to me. I proposed to him."

Nettie stared at me for so long that my hair, tightly wrapped around the hot curling iron, began to stink.

"Oh, you're burning my hair now, Nettie," I protested. "You've got to pay attention, *please.*" I held up my hand mirror to watch as she unwound my hair. A springy coil drooped over my forehead. Nettie picked up another lock to wind around the iron.

"You asked him—that's innovative, Eva. So what would you have done if he refused you? We all thought that Henry never wanted to get married and would be the perpetual bachelor of the neighborhood." Nettie made a point. I didn't want to discourage her.

"I would have pretended that I was only teasing and hadn't been serious. But I had to ask the question if I wanted to know the answer. I never wanted anyone else. So, if you have your heart set on someone, Nettie, go and ask him. It can't hurt."

Nettie's face darkened with a scowl. "It can too hurt," she said softly.

"What is the trouble? Do you have someone in mind? You do, don't you, Nettie?"

"No," she said emphatically. "I have no one in mind, and I never will. I don't want to get married. I think marriage is something I would not do well with. I like my life the way it is. I like living at home, and I certainly don't want to submit myself to a man as his "helpmate.""

"Nettie!" I was astonished.

"I'm not specifically thinking of you right now. I trust and pray that all will be prosperous and happy with the marriage that you and Henry are about to make. I'm thinking of several of our acquaintances who are overwhelmed with their children, their housework, and the demands put upon them by their husbands to produce *more* children." Nettie's eyes widened as she tried to explain.

"Eva, your father is the youngest of eight children, and my father is from a family of twelve. I don't know how our grandmothers managed it all— the cooking, the laundry, the illnesses. I just cannot imagine having so many children. And you never know how many God will give you."

"You poor thing," I said. "The Lord won't give you more than you can bear. My mother only had two children, and yours had three. Now watch that iron, Nettie, you are burning my hair again." I was more concerned with my hair than humoring Nettie's mood about child-rearing.

"You know, I am just being married today, Nettie, and haven't thought of myself as a mother—although I certainly want to be one, of course. You will be a good auntie. You will see what a joy a little child can be. And then your fears of raising children will wash away."

Nettie finished with my last curl and laid the curling iron aside.

I held the hand mirror and admired the ringlets on each side of my forehead. Nettie leaned down to my face and spoke softly.

"Today is the day of your wedding. This evening will be the first evening of your marriage. You could give birth to a child as soon as next February. Your life as a mother could begin this evening! You must think about that." Nettie was very agitated.

"What is it, Nettie, what *is* bothering you?" This was not my Nettie. Nettie is always solid and competent and strong. I watched her face crinkle as tears ran down her cheeks. I reached out and squeezed her hand. "What is it?"

"It's Livey," she sobbed to me quietly, so our mothers would not hear. "I'm thinking of Olivia. She died in childbirth the very same year she was married to John Howland. And now we've lost her, never to see her or hear her voice again in this lifetime. I am still so much missing her, Eva. I don't want to lose you in the same way." Nettie looked away from me.

I couldn't think about Olivia on my wedding day. I didn't want to remember reading her name on the white marble headstone or the great mound of flowers we former school chums heaped on her grave as she was laid to rest in the Howland family plot beside John's grand-parents. The little white headstone next to Olivia's that read simply "Baby" explained everything. I began to feel dizzy, and with effort pushed the remembrance of Livey's sad funeral out of my head.

"Nettie, I must trust in the good Lord that all will be well. Everything happens for one reason—it is all part of his plan. Yes, we are sad about Olivia, but we cannot stop living and loving. Now, don't trouble yourself so much. I highly doubt that the Lord would have the same plan for me as he had for Olivia.

"We must enjoy the goodness of each day that we have here. Now tell me you're going to help me celebrate this sunny wedding day I've been blessed with. You won't lose me, Nettie—I'll still be your neigh-bor, just a further walk away." I squeezed her hand again, and made her look at me. "My hair looks lovely, thanks to you. Now smile for me Nettie. I want to see you smile."

She smiled at me, but the wet tears on her cheeks told me her true emotions.

~

Many a bride has stood with her new husband in front of a minister and friends, blushing the brightest shade of red. From this moment forward, not only would it be permissible to engage in intimate relations, it was expected. I experienced the unanticipated reaction of coming perilously close to fainting with anxiety as Reverend Moss led Henry and me through our vows. Looking out at the faces watching us, I saw couples long married, as in the cases of Henry's parents and my parents and many of our neighbors. My spinning mind was greatly affected by the realization that they had become different people because of the permission granted to them upon the pronouncement of their union—they became people who engaged in marital relations.

The circle of faces around Henry and me included the pleasant countenance of my brother Lewis, so recently matured from a boy to a man. He has no trouble attracting the attention of young ladies and will have no problem finding a mate. But my dear friend Nettie, with her warm hugs and confiding nature, insists she is never to enjoy the embrace of a husband.

I grew up with another dear playmate from Paine Hollow—Lily Wiley, Aunt Elizabeth and Captain Wiley's daughter. Three years ago she married school master Charles Cole on Christmas Day and then immediately moved to Sandwich where Charles had secured a new teaching position, to Nettie's and my great disappointment. Lily's departure broke up a lifelong threesome of friends. Nettie and I are still upset at Charles for taking our Lily away from us. But to my great astonishment, Charles and Lily arrived on the morning train to attend our wedding. I was delighted that spunky Lily brought her tiny daughter Alice along.

"She's learning to walk, and your mother's lawn is the perfect place for her to practice her steps. She'll be a year old next month," Lily told me. I had but a moment with the precious Alice until Aunt Elizabeth whisked her away to play with her, claiming grandmother privileges.

That is the ideal, to have a sweet child. That is now my purpose. And I had no idea as I stood there with Henry in front of Reverend Moss—drenched from shoulders to knees in nervous sweat—had no idea at all of how to proceed. Even though I had excelled in the study of human biology in high school, memorizing body parts on a diagram had not given me the knowledge of how my own feminine anatomy would work when called upon.

I wished Lily lived closer so I might confer with her in private. But she would be returning to Sandwich, and I have no other young married female confidant in the neighborhood. Bringing up this subject with Lily before the wedding would have been out of the question; writing about it through the mail would be most inappropriate. And I could never ask my mother questions of this nature. I wouldn't even know how to put the questions into words. I was left to explore these uncharted waters with Henry as my guide.

That thought made me blush again as we completed our vows, and I promised to obey Henry forever. Then Reverend Moss, who was dapper with a newly groomed beard and mustache, pronounced us man and wife, "till death do you part."

Uncle William lifted his fiddle and played a waltz, and Henry and I embraced one another and danced across the lawn. We were given the first tune to ourselves, but then Uncle William began a familiar sea shanty, and all those who were able, young and old, came jigging out across the grass to join us. We danced several lively scores, and then Mama rang the dinner bell loudly to call attention to the meal.

Our wedding feast was indeed abundant and delicious. This

I know through the reports and remarks of our guests, because I was not able to eat. The banquet tables placed around the yard were heavy with food: beef roasts, stews, casseroles, sausages, pickles, several roasted chickens, steaming mashed potatoes, crepes and sauce, roasted carrots, onions and beets. The women brought the dishes they are known for, as the men would eat every bite that was placed upon the tables whether or not the foods were considered to be complementary to one another. My mother outdid herself with a three layered chocolate wedding cake frosted with whipped cream. For her, I made sure to have a piece, and I fed Henry a slice, a simple action which drew great applause.

Otherwise, a few sips of water were the most I could swallow. Fortunately, I was not required to make intelligent conversation, because I could not. I observed my family and friends walking through the yard or sitting on the lawn furniture—groups of people forming and reforming as news was exchanged between all on the latest comings and goings.

Henry held my elbow and stood next to me. The spicy scent of his shaving tonic enveloped me, and I was ecstatic in the knowledge that I would not be obliged to leave his side—I could stand beside him for hours if I so chose. As he conversed with our well-wishers, I allowed him to convey the obligatory words of thanks on our behalf. For once, I found myself tongue-tied.

Henry's mother was also unusually quiet. Aunt Arozana sat in a wicker chair on the lawn, and did not move about socializing, as was her normal habit.

Holding a white handkerchief in her hand, she repeatedly wiped beads of sweat from her brow. I was comforted that I was not the only one who was anxious. However, I did not want our marriage to be a source of vexation to my new mother-in-law. Reluctantly, I left Henry and walked over to Aunt Arozana; my silk dress that she had a part in producing rustled as I crossed the lawn. She smiled up at me.

"Are you happy, Eva?"

"Oh, yes, very happy, Aunt Arozana."

"My dear, now that you are Mrs. Henry Smith, you must call me Mother Smith," she said. "It won't do to have you calling me 'Aunt' anymore."

"That will take a bit of getting used to, but I will begin immediately. Mother Smith. Are you feeling well, Mother Smith?" I leaned down to kiss her cheek.

My mother-in-law again mopped her brow. "Yes, I am very well. I have waited a long time for this moment to see my son happily married. You have always been dear little Eva to me, and I am so very content that *you* are Henry's wife."

As she said these words to me, my mind attached itself to the word "wife." The minister had pronounced us "man and wife," and my new mother-in-law was the first to use the word in conversation. Wife. Henry's wife.

I smiled at Mother Smith. The paleness of her face distracted me. I touched her brow, and it was colder than I expected.

"Are you chilled?" I asked her. The May sunlight was not yet very strong—we were still more than a month away from the heat of summer.

"Yes, I do feel a little cold," she said.

Henry walked over to us and frowned as he looked at his mother's face. "Are you having one of your spells, Mother?" He turned quickly on his heel and bellowed back at Lewis who was standing on the doorstep. "Lewis, bring a blanket out to my mother."

Immediately Lewis disappeared into the house.

"What is it, Henry?" I asked him, alarmed.

"Her heart," he murmured to me. "She sometimes has episodes."

"Good Lord," I said.

Henry quickly opened his mother's handbag and removed a glass vial of pills. He took one out and gave it to her. "Here it is,

Mother. Take your nitro. Eva, get some water." I ran to the water pitcher, poured a glass, and brought it to him. Henry held the glass to his mother's lips and she swallowed.

"There," she said. "That's enough now. I'll be fine. Please, Henry, don't make such a fuss."

"Father should take you home, Mother."

"No, I am not going, Henry, so don't even mention it to your father. Do you hear me?" She was extremely firm, using steely tones that I had never heard her employ. "I'm staying right here," she said.

"As you wish, Mother," Henry nodded. "You shall have it your way today." He turned to me. "She shouldn't push herself, but she can be stubborn."

"Henry, you shush," Mother Smith said. "Go on, you two. Shoo." She waved us away. "Go enjoy your guests."

Uncle Winslow had not noticed his wife's distress. He was down near Tessa's stable with Papa. The men were smoking their pipes, an activity of which Tessa snorted her disapproval. She trotted around her pasture tossing her head. Every time she passed by my father, he blew a ring of smoke out at her and she was off again.

Aunt Elizabeth held Alice in her arms at Tessa's fence, and the little girls of the neighborhood had joined them. They made a pretty picture, all dressed in their best petticoats and pinafores, laughing every time Tessa pranced by, her long red tail streaming behind her. A strong surge of maternal yearning passed through me as I imagined a little girl of my own laughing with such happiness.

Mother Smith rose from her chair as if to prove to me that she was fine, and she walked over and linked elbows with my mother. Together they strolled down towards the little girls. Henry left me and went to join Papa and Winslow, along with Lewis and my other male relatives. Immediately, the mariners were swapping sea stories, attempting to out tell one another, as was their habit at every opportunity.

The sound of laughter filled my ears. I stood alone, rooted in the yard where I had been raised. Looking down at my polished shoes, which reflected the sun's dull glare back up at me, I contemplated the ground upon which I stood. This was home to me and had been for my whole life.

I took a moment to appreciate the familiar landscape: the contour of the green lawn, the curve of the sandy driveway as it came in from the road, the sweet white blooms of the beach plum bushes, the view of Tessa in her pasture, and the split rail fences lining the road down to the bay. I listened to the giggling of young cousins, the murmur of female voices at Tessa's fence, and the bursts of discussion coming from the men. They began to debate the prospects of the mackerel season, which wouldn't begin until the day after Independence Day.

"I tell you, the mackerel catch will be down again this year. The fish have gone clear across the Atlantic to the coast of Africa," I heard Uncle William insist.

"I disagree, William, I think we've just fished the school out," Papa said. "It will be a sad day when the boys can't go out for mackerel anymore. Just five years ago we had twice as many boats leaving the harbor and coming home full to the scuppers after each trip."

"The reason we have fewer vessels now is because of the shoaling," Henry expressed his opinion. He was agitated—I could hear it in his tone of voice. "The bay here is filling in, and the deep water boats can't anchor here anymore. You know that!"

"True, Henry," acknowledged my father. "But I haven't fished for years, and it's not because of my age—not at all. It's because I realized it was time to try something different. But now, that blasted railroad is cutting into my cargo operation. I have to go beyond the reaches of the tracks to make any real profit! And I'm not keen on running back and forth to Jamaica for bananas like Lorenzo Dow Baker does; I *am* too old for that, I'll admit."

Captain Wiley spoke up here, as of course he would, being employed by Baker's lucrative Boston Fruit Company. "You know that the steamboat is the way to accomplish such a run, Otis. I'd never try it by sail, now that there's no need to. The winds and tides just can't be counted upon to be as reliable as a steam engine."

"So there you have it," Papa exclaimed. "We are living at the end of an era. The death of the sailing life is upon us, I tell you." My father was extremely loud. I have heard this all before—it is a constant discussion between the men, and has been since I was in high school. Henry spoke again.

"Well, I'll be six feet under before I take command of one of those belching steam monsters. They are not seaworthy—they are not safe. You lose your engine, and where are you? You're dead, that's where you are."

"Henry, show some respect!" Winslow reprimanded his son. "Captain Wiley here has been running a steamboat quite successfully for the past few years, and we don't want to wish ill will upon him."

"Yes, Captain Wiley has been very lucky so far, but I dare say that if you are not cautious, sir," Henry turned his gaze fully onto Captain Wiley's face, "You will learn the hard way that I am right. The steam engine is not to be trusted on the open ocean.

"And as for our harbor here in South Wellfleet shoaling up, any fool can see it's only getting worse. But I will sail out of here until I have to scrape out at high tide. You won't find me mooring up in Wellfleet Harbor. This is home, after all!"

Henry's father went to make a reply, and I let my mind drift away. There was no news in their conversation, and there would be no resolution today. I searched out the women and noticed that my two dearest friends, Nettie and Lily, were clearing the dishes from the banquet tables. I went and took them each by the hand, and together we walked to the fence and joined the other ladies watching Tessa. All truly did seem right with the universe.

"Lily, do you have any words of advice for me on my wedding night?" I asked quietly. "You know Mama is far too proper to say anything at all to me about this."

Lily laughed. "I have no doubt that you will be fine, Eva. You have been in love with Henry for years, whether you knew it or not. I fully expect you to be giving birth before this time next year."

"Don't rush me so, Lily! I want some time with the man." I really hadn't wanted to hear this kind of pronouncement on Lily's part; I wanted some hint as to what was in store for me in the coming evening.

"Time with Henry Smith will be hard to get—he loves the sea so much. I am fortunate that Charles is a high school teacher and comes home every night." Lily took pity upon me as she looked at my face. "All right Eva. Let me whisper something."

Nettie grimaced. "I don't need to hear it, and I don't want to hear it," she said and turned away from us.

Lily whispered in my ear, "Plan on a full body washing every morning for awhile. There is nothing quite as strong as the smell of a man."

I gasped. Never had I thought about that aspect of a marital encounter. How would I heat water for a full bath every morning in a house where I was practically a guest?

"What shall I do to manage that?" I asked.

"Remember to take a full pitcher of water up to your room when you retire, and prepare to use it in the wash bowl the next morning. And do take a generous amount of time at your toilet tomorrow morning in order to establish the precedent that you will require that much time every morning. It might be the only time you get some peace and quiet in the day, judging by Aunt Arozana's eager anticipation of your arrival!"

I bobbed my head to acknowledge that I had taken her point and changed the subject so Nettie could join back in, all the while thinking that it was very unfortunate for me that Lily lived in Sandwich, and I had no easy access to the one dear friend who could be of great help to me as I entered the state of matrimony.

The next hour passed by very quickly. The shrieking of young cousins as they played their game of "take the flag" provided a youthful commotion which heightened my anticipation of leaving my home and traveling the half mile to the Smith household. My mother constantly disappeared into the kitchen to wipe her eyes, re-appearing with tray after tray of confectionaries as if that had been the reason she vanished. But I knew she was lamenting my depar-ture even as she wished me all the happiness a mother could wish her daughter on her wedding day. And then the time of departure was upon us.

Henry left the men and came over to me, declaring, "Well, Mrs. Smith, let's go home, shall we? Where are your bags? Time to load them up!"

Silkie and Sinbad came trotting from around the side of the house, pulling the Smith buggy with Winslow in the driver's seat. The glistening black horses were beautifully adorned with necklaces of red velvet roses, and their tails were braided as if they were travel-ing to meet President Cleveland. The entire party applauded and I was both flattered and embarrassed. Winslow beamed as he stepped down and turned to face me. I knew he had groomed the horses es-pecially for me.

"Here's your new missus, boys," Winslow informed the horses.

"Don't go giving away my horses, Father!" Henry clapped Winslow on the back in jest. "They do look pretty dandy, though. I guess that's appropriate, considering the lady who will be riding in the buggy!" Henry pumped his father's hand as though Winslow had just won first prize at the county fair.

As if on cue, Papa came out of the house with a traveling valise in each hand, both crammed with clothes I had packed. Lewis fol-lowed him with a large trunk full of books, quilts, crocheted doi-lies, and linens. The books were my familiar favorites; the household textiles were contributions from our generous guests. Henry put his arm around me and led me to my mother who stood forlornly on the doorstep, openly crying now.

"Don't worry, Mrs. Paine. I'll take good care of Eva," he assured her. "She's not moving far, you know," he chided gently. "We'll be very close by, and I am sure you'll see each other as soon as tomorrow."

"I know, Henry," Mama smiled up at him through steamy spectacles. "I know you will be very good to Eva. You'll have to forgive me—I've never married off a daughter before." She attempted to make a joke.

I gave her a quick peck on the cheek. "I *will* see you tomorrow, Mama. Please don't worry."

She nodded and quickly ducked back into the house.

Turning to my father, I said, "Good-bye, Papa. Thank you so much for everything."

He bent down to kiss me. There was a strong odor of tobacco smoke on his beard as he hugged me with an iron grip close to his chest. In a moment he let me go.

"Henry, please hand me up into the buggy," I appealed to my husband. I wanted the painful good-byes to be over.

My father was not finished, though. He reached for Henry's two hands, and held them in his own. "I expect that you will be an exemplary husband to my daughter, Henry, and treat her as she deserves to be treated," he said gruffly.

"Yes, sir," Henry looked serious. "You can count on that, sir."

At this, Papa released him, and Henry picked me up and placed me on the seat of the buggy as easily as he would a small child. He swung up on the other side and took the reins. I waved to Lewis, and Charles and Lily. I waved harder at Nettie, who nodded once soberly, the only guest not smiling at us.

"We will see you there, Eva," Mother Smith called out to us. "You two go get settled in. We'll be along soon."

Henry lightly touched the whip to Silkie's hind quarters, and we were off. Our guests fell in behind us, cheering and singing, the stronger of the little boy cousins running behind us a good distance on the sandy road before being called back by their parents. There was a roaring in my head. I reached into my handbag and pulled out my shaker of smelling salts.

"Eva, are you alright?" Henry asked from beside me.

I looked up at him. White clouds of beach plum blossoms made the road sweet and ethereal, punctuated by explosions of vivid purple lilacs in our neighbors' dooryards.

"I'm feeling a little faint."

"We'll be at the house in just a few minutes, Eva. You need to lie down."

I contemplated this. I had never been in a situation before where I had lain down in front of Henry for any reason whatsoever—not on a couch in my home, not in a field at a picnic, certainly not at the shore. I was compelled to take another strong pull of smelling salts.

"Yes, Henry. That will be fine." It was the first time I'd ever required my salts for anything besides a funeral. My emotional tizzy was quite puzzling to me, but I knew that I was in the strong, capable hands of my husband.

∼

If I could shout anything at the world, it would be this: I am the queen! I am the queen of the anthills; I am the queen of the beehives, the bird nests, the spider webs. This is *my* domain—the garden, the hen yard, the wood lot. I will guard my borders as zealously as any monarch. Be you friend or be you foe? Declare yourself, for I am most certainly able to decimate you, be you foe!

Why do I feel such confidence? Because I have met the uncertainty which has vexed me so. How fortunate I am to have a husband such as Henry. How wonderfully he guided me through the uncharted territory of the marital bedroom. I have come through my wedding night, and all is well.

Together we climbed the stairs to our new bedroom at the respectable hour of nine o'clock. It was dusk by then, even with the lengthening hours of daylight as summer approaches. Henry struck a match and lit the paraffin lamp on the bed stand and turned the light down very low. I was aware of his parents being present in the house, just two rooms down the hall from us. I silently thanked Mother Smith for leaving an empty room between ours and theirs, allowing us some privacy. We whispered to each other.

I was as frightened as a rabbit being chased by a fox. I was unable to breathe, unable to properly unbutton my silk dress. I asked Henry to help unfasten the buttons down my back. My shoulders and neck muscles were so rigid that my head ached violently.

"Eva, it's only me," Henry teased as he stood behind me and gently pushed down on my hunched shoulders.

"Mmm," I nodded and took a deep breath through my nostrils. My back was to him as he unfastened my dress. He slipped it off my shoulders, and the silk rustled to the floor at my feet. I stepped out of the pile of fabric, and picked up my wedding dress to place it on a chair.

I turned and stood before him in my corset and under slips. He ran his hands over me— from my armored bust to my cinched waist. I struggled to maintain a confident expression on my face, but my heart was beating so fast I imagined he could hear it.

"Let's get this thing off you," he whispered as he began to unlace me.

"No, no. I'll do it. If you pull too hard, the laces will break, and I'll have to rethread it later." I slowly unlaced the crisscrossed cords and felt the sweet release of pressure as my corset loosened. Henry reached for me again and removed the corset. He put his hands to my waist and examined the pattern left behind on my skin by the corset stays.

"Good Lord, look at the marks this contraption leaves on you! I don't know why you women wear these things, honestly, Eva. Your body is beautiful without it!" His hands were on my breasts. As I felt my husband's touch for the very first time upon my naked skin, I looked up into his eyes, seeking reassurance. I found it. His expression was kind and loving.

"Breathe, my dear, don't hold your breath," he murmured. He had his clothes off in a matter of seconds, and then he came back to me to remove my slips. The drawstrings were gently untied and he let the slips fall. All that remained were my lace-trimmed bloomers. I took these off and blushed in the dim light as Henry beheld the dark triangle of hair between my legs.

I dared not look at Henry below his shoulders. I knew he was standing naked next to me, and again the tension caused my head to pound. He took my hand and brought it down below his waist. I couldn't take my eyes from his. He placed my hand on his body, and for a moment, I was unaware of what I was touching. And then, the heat, the thickness and the hardness of Henry's member were all surprising and terrifying to me. I couldn't imagine how something with such dimension would ever fit inside my body. I whimpered with anxiety.

"Here, here. Now, Eva. Don't be frightened," he tried to comfort me. "This will not do. Come here, now, come and lie down on the bed with me. We will kiss each other to begin with. That is quite enough, don't you think, for our first night together?"

I nodded in relief. We lay down on the bed together, and I drew the coverlet up to our chins. Henry reached for me and pulled me against his body. I marveled at the sensitivity of my skin as it encountered his. We began to kiss, which was heaven. I've always loved Henry's blue eyes, and to be able to kiss him and look into his eyes, darker now by the flickering lamp, was divine.

Many minutes passed. Still, the kissing continued. Drenched with happiness, I tingled with inner heat. Henry passed his hands down between my legs and gently tugged on the hair there. This, I must confess, caused the most immediate response from me, and I opened my legs to him. His fingers burrowed into me, and again I was astonished, this time at the abundant wetness of my most private place and the wonderful feeling his fingers evoked.

"Let's just try, dearest," he said. "If I hurt you, we'll stop. Just tell me to stop, and I will." He slid over onto me, spreading my legs wide on either side of him. I had never been in this position before and had not imagined that it would be necessary in order to accomplish a union between husband and wife. How could I have been so naive? And then, quite naturally, I wrapped my legs around him and embraced him as much with my legs as with my arms.

What came next was impossibly mortifying and painful, at first. Carefully and slowly, Henry entered me. The pressure was unbearable for a long minute, but then the pressure vanished and only pleasure ensued. I thought that we had achieved "intercourse," but then he withdrew himself partially and thrust back inside me again. This time it was very pleasurable, and I welcomed the sensation by hugging Henry tighter. Again and again he entered me and withdrew while looking directly into my eyes, and I into his. We breathed each other's breath, we rocked in each other's arms, and when Henry spent his passion inside me, I dissolved into perfect peace with my husband and all God's universe.

Our union was accomplished with no words between us, and I know that no words in my vocabulary could ever suffice to describe the way I feel towards Henry as a result of our intimate exploration. I am truly his wife and Henry is truly my husband. Our marriage has been consummated.

~

Chapter Three
Mother Smith's House

May 23, 1886

The first few days after our wedding, I concentrated on settling into the Smith household. I worked with Henry's mother in the morning, learning the household routines she preferred. After lunch, I took the buggy to fetch more of my belongings from Mama's house. By necessity, my wrists grew stronger every day—a result of driving the two black geldings the short distance by myself. Several afternoons were necessary to transport all of my clothing; it is impossible to fit more than one dress and petticoat into a satchel. And I wanted all my books to be with me rather than on the bookcase back home. I've discovered that I cannot part with anything that has a pleasant memory attached to it.

Mama and I spent hours sorting and packing in my old bedroom. Mama suggested that perhaps I need only keep one paper from each subject I had enjoyed at Wellfleet High School. But I'd enjoyed all of my studies. Just holding a thesis in my hands and reading the first paragraph brought me directly back to the time I had researched the topic and expressed my opinion. I once thrived on exercising my intelligence in scholarly pursuits, and as I begin my domestic life, I want some evidence around me that I am indeed capable of mental expression. Mama thinks this is amusing.

"Eva, I believe you are avoiding the prospect of housekeeping," she joked with me as we packed yet another crate of books and papers. "I always thought you would make such a good school teacher, but now *that's* out of the question."

As she brought up her old refrain, I thought of the five nights I'd just spent with my new husband—nights when I never felt the urge to read into the hours of darkness. Sharing a bed with my husband had strongly affected my nocturnal reading habits.

"Mama, you're the one who's been attached to that thought. I would rather have Henry any day than be an old maid school teacher," I said.

Mama winced. "I didn't mean any harm," she said. "Henry will be a good husband for you. It's just that you possess the gift of a superior intellect, and I hope you don't lose it. But I'm sure you'll find an outlet for your fine mind, my dear." Mama buckled the straps on my last crate of books.

She sighed and looked away as I kissed her cheek. Had I not visited her every one of the five days that had passed by since the wedding? Papa also moped about as I prepared to leave. I could not be solemn, though, as I bid them good-bye. I reminded them that I was, after all, just a ten-minute walk away. Papa nodded and reached for his newspaper.

"I know, Eva," Mama said. "We are happy to have you so close by. But when I want to tell you something, or ask you a question, ten minutes away is just too far. It would take me ten minutes to walk to see you, and then ten minutes to walk home. And so you see, the remark goes unsaid." Her face was wistful.

"Mama, you are talking to me *now*. If you want to talk about something and I'm not here, jot it down so that when I visit, you'll remember to mention it."

"That's not the point," she said. "Oh, never mind, Eva. I *am* sorry to be so dreary. I'll come to the Smith's to visit you there soon. I do have to make the effort, don't I? Perhaps next week."

"Yes, do, Mama. I will be so pleased to have you. But until you're ready, I'll come see you every afternoon. Now I must get back to Mother Smith."

As I said this, Mama looked pained again, but said nothing. I climbed into the buggy and drove Silkie and Sinbad out of the yard. Tessa was not at all appreciative of being left behind. She whinnied loudly after me from her paddock, and I could hear her desperate calls half way back to the Smith house.

I have always disagreed with people who refer to God's creatures as "dumb animals." Tessa aptly demonstrated that she knew how to make her feelings known far more adamantly and publicly than my mother could. It was because of Tessa that I cried, and I arrived at the Smith homestead with red eyes. Mother Smith noticed immediately, of course, when she came out to help me carry in my belongings.

"Oh Eva, this is quite a change for you, isn't it, dear?" she asked kindly. "I remember trying to get used to my new home when I was first wed to Winslow. I sorely missed my mother. But you will make the adjustment—it is not an unpleasant change. But the change must be noted. Change does indeed take its toll."

I was grateful to Mother Smith for her sympathetic words. I left the crates on the front porch and drove the buggy out back to the barn. There I took my time unhitching the two blacks, brushing them until they glistened, and turning them out in their pasture. I washed my hands at the pump and went back to the house.

Mother Smith led me into the front parlor and pointed at a book-case. She had thoughtfully cleared some shelves for me. She then unpacked my books and arranged them on the shelf while I carried my clothes upstairs. This last load included my winter clothing and boots—which I would not be using for months. As I hung my woolen cape and put my gloves and hat into cedar drawers, I felt truly at home. I was ready for all seasons.

Henry and Winslow were both down at the wharf, preparing the *Dora Freeman* for the next trip out. My mother-in-law took advantage of this time together by offering to show me how to bake spice cookies.

"Henry can eat up a storm, and Winslow is not far behind him, so I must teach you how to bake some of their favorite treats." She motioned for me to sit down at the kitchen table.

"You see that little wooden box there, dear? That box is full of recipes. They are written in my own hand, back when I first became a bride. All passed down to me by my mother, and then improved upon through trial and error. As time went by and I was able to procure the ingredients a little easier, I noted the changes," Mother Smith said.

I nodded, knowing it was unnecessary to ask what she meant by this; she would tell me, I was certain.

"Yes, dear, you can't imagine the inconvenience of maintaining the pantry before the railroad came through," she said. "It's been sixteen years now. My goodness, where does the time go? Now I've come to depend utterly upon Ike's general store for everything, and what a convenient location he has there, right next to the railroad platform. He can order anything he wants, and it arrives in due time with no fuss.

"The packet boats were just too slow, not to mention the danger. Can you imagine sailing to Boston for winter food supplies, never knowing if you would have to endure a storm or not, but just trusting the good Lord to deliver you home with your flour, your molasses, your dry beans and salted beef for the winter? You modern young ladies have no idea what it was like before the railroad came down to us."

"You sailed to Boston by packet every year?" I asked the obligatory question.

"No, certainly not, my dear! I sailed only once, and was so ill from the passage that I sent Winslow with a list thereafter. But to think of the risks we went through just to travel from one town to the next! The stage ride from here to Provincetown made me cringe, which is another reason why I do so love the train, but please don't mention that to Henry or Winslow. They hate that railroad—they are certainly in agreement on that subject. Now watch me, Eva. I'm going to show you the secret of making soft cookies."

Mother Smith put some lard into a bowl and energetically swiped at it with a metal kitchen instrument.

"Write this down. This is called creaming. We are creaming the shortening. There now. We will add an egg, yes, one egg, and some sugar. How much sugar? I never measure it. Get me that measuring cup. How much is that? There, dear, three quarters of a cup of sugar.

"White sugar is best, although I know your mother does not abide by it. Honey just wouldn't do here, though, not to get the consistency that I want. Now, we are going to add some spices. This is where the general store is just heaven to me, I can get nutmeg and cinnamon and anise whenever I run out, and easily, too."

Mother Smith continued on in this way for perhaps ten minutes while I wrote out her instructions. I never said as many as a dozen words. I wondered how she had ever cooked alone in her kitchen all those years without the company of another woman to chat with. I thought of my mother down the road, cooking alone in her kitchen. Lewis would be out in the yard until called, and Papa would be reading in the other room, waiting for his dinner. Now that I was out of the house, perhaps Papa could be encouraged to go into the kitchen and keep Mama company. She would enjoy it if Papa read the newspaper aloud to her while she cooked. I would have to suggest this.

Next, Mother Smith showed me how to test the oven, how to put hard wood (not pine) into the stove to get it hotter, how to draft the stove to maintain the oven heat, and how to add wood when it ran low. Soon it was time to test whether the cookies were baked through.

"Take a tooth pick and poke it into a cookie and when the pick comes out clean with no cookie batter on it, immediately remove the tray from the oven." Mother Smith was happier than I had ever seen her. As we waited for the next tray of cookies to bake, she would not rest. She wanted to tell me about the laundry.

"Laundry is done on Monday. I am sure your mother does laundry on Monday, of course, everybody does. Now, you see this Eva? This is bluing. Yes, it gets the sheets very white—perhaps they should call it whiting!

"I would be most obliged if you would pump the water outside and bring it in, dear, to heat on the stove. It will be delightful to have you here, as both of the men will be out to sea again by Monday. Winslow says the weather has warmed up enough for him to go out with Henry this time.

"I cannot tell you how lonely it is when the men are out, and how difficult it has been for me to handle heavy things by myself. I do have these smaller pails here just for that purpose, as I carry less now than I used to. Don't you think it wise to carry two smaller pails, evenly balancing your body, than one large one? I think so, too.

"So, Eva, if you would please carry the wood in on Monday morning, I will fire up the stove. We'll fill up this kettle here, and then, when it is boiling, bring it out to the yard. In the winter it is too cold to do that, so I manage all the laundry here in the kitchen. But in the warm months, we will bring it outside to the laundry tubs. I have two nice copper ones—one for washing, one for rinsing. I am sure your mother does it the same way. . ."

I excused myself to go out and use the outhouse. My dear mother-in-law surprised me by having both the compulsion and the capacity to fill every second with the sound of her voice. I stayed out in the privy for a good ten minutes and read the Methodist book of hymns, which apparently Henry had placed there for consideration or memorization, I didn't know which. It certainly couldn't be there for actually singing in the privy, although the thought of that made me laugh. I was surprised the hymnal was there at all, Henry's parents being Congregationalists, but I took it as a good sign that they respected Henry's choices.

Eventually I left the privy, stopped by the pump in the yard to freshen up again, and quietly approached the kitchen door. I was curious to know if Mother Smith talked on at such speed to herself. I could not imagine speaking so quickly or consistently, without allowing or inviting a comment from a present person. And yes, the dear lady was indeed talking to herself. Actually, she was talking to the Lord.

"And I do thank you with every breath I take that dear little Eva has come to be with us. Now, I must tell her what I do when there is a need to remove blood from the sheets. I am sure her mother has a technique, but mine is undoubtedly better. This is because, thanks to you, Lord, I have a strapping son who does me the great service of cutting enough ice off the pond every winter to last me through the summer. Therefore, I am always able to put very cold ice water on spots of blood, which is the very best way to remove stains. Thank you, Lord, for dear Henry, what would I do without him?"

I now had the problem of walking into the kitchen as if I had not overheard. My face flushed the hot beet red that it quickly achieves whenever I'm embarrassed. I decided that I simply had to acknowledge hearing. Mother Smith was correct, after all. There was indeed a spot of blood on the sheet up in our bedroom, and I had been agonizing over how to discreetly wash it. But my mother-in-law knew perfectly well there would be the blood of a bride upon the sheets the first Monday after her son's wedding, and how much better that she was one step ahead of me, than for me to agonize about it!

I was suddenly overwhelmed with affection for Henry's mother, and I burst through the door to hug her.

"I am so glad that I have a mother-in-law like you, Mother Smith," I said. "No airs, just down to earth, and so wise. You are simply the best mother-in-law I could have asked for."

Mother Smith was delighted. She hugged me back, surrounding

me with her ample arms and pressing me deep into her soft bosom. I felt safe and secure. When she let me go, her smile was angelic.

"Well, well, dearie." She was out of breath. "You are most appreciated. We are going to get along just fine." She sat down and fanned herself. The cookies were ready, and I took them out of the oven with potholders—my own mother would have been proud of me.

~

The next afternoon I walked to Mama's, as I was finally finished with the transporting of my belongings and didn't need the buggy. It was a pleasant day for a walk, and Mother Smith took a nap every afternoon "to give my heart a rest," as she put it. Henry and his father were down at the wharf, which is where, I am learning, Henry is to be found every day if he is not out to sea. It was the perfect time for me to leave the Smith house and go visit Mama. My red cape was necessary to ward off a stiff breeze.

As I walked, I considered my lingering dilemma regarding the word "home." For part of me, home is still the home of my childhood, and the house where I now reside is still "the Smith house." At the end of my visits with my mother, I say, "Well, Mama, it is time for me to go back." I cannot yet say to my mother, "It is time for me to go home."

Mama was delighted to see me, as always, and we visited over a cup of tea while exchanging news. If I am living away from Mama, at least she enjoys the advantage of receiving neighborhood updates more quickly due to my daily visits. I live closer to the railroad station and post office than Mama does, and Mother Smith is much more likely to have someone stop in with a piece of news. In Paine Hollow it is taken for granted that we will hear all news over our clothes lines and backyard fences. But as a result of my new location at the head of the grapevine, my mother now receives the latest news before Aunt Elizabeth can hear it and tell her. Mama enjoys this new state of affairs.

I retold the things I had heard that day: The windy weather had caused some difficulties. The train was an hour late on its way back from Provincetown because the sand dunes had blown onto the tracks in Truro. The sand had to be shoveled off by the engineer and the conductor. The lifeguards over at Cahoon Hollow were practicing in the high surf when their lifeboat capsized, breaking Callum Atwood's leg. He will not be able to work again for several months. The Marine Benevolent Society will make a donation to the family. Carrie Longwood's goat died after Josh Smith's dog attacked her. Should we all pitch in and buy Carrie a new goat, since her sickly children cannot drink cow's milk?

Since the Smith household receives the benefit of being on the route to the post office; the Paine Hollow ladies are likely to stop by to ask Henry's mother if she has any letters to be mailed. They take that opportunity to chat a few moments about the weather and the health of anyone who is in need of prayers or assistance. Of course, the main reason why Mother Smith has received so many visitors during my first week as Henry's bride is that the ladies are curious as to how I am settling in.

"And Mama," I said, "Mother Smith always says the same thing, as if she has rehearsed it. 'Eva is settling in comfortably. It is a great pleasure to have her here. A woman living alone in a house with two men is not an easy thing!' It is as if she has been waiting to say that for so long."

"I am alone with your father and brother now, so I suppose I know just what Arozana means," my mother said with a sad look. "The quality of conversation is not the same."

I silently scolded myself for being insensitive and distracted Mama with stories about the Smith household.

"Dinner is a *very* loud affair," I said. "Both Henry and his father have quite a lot to say after being down at the wharf all day. Uncle Winslow is a bit hard of hearing—in fact, I can barely speak loudly enough for him to hear me. And so Henry speaks to him at the volume he employs when communicating with his crew during a high wind!

"Mother Smith—yes, I *am* to call her that," I said, seeing the look on my own mother's face, "Mother Smith takes it all in stride; she expects it. She doesn't say much at all through dinner, and I am sure that the men are not aware that she is simply exhausted because she has been talking to me all day long!"

"How is Arozana faring with her heart problem, Eva?" Mama asked. "It was disturbing that she had such a spell on your wedding day. But I'll allow that the emotions of the day had quite an effect."

"She seems to be fine," I said, "Though she does make the time for her little nap in the afternoon. She is quite ready for her pillow, as she puts it, after a full morning of housework. When she gets up in the late afternoon, I help her prepare and serve dinner. She and Uncle Winslow go to bed fairly early. I stay up much later with Henry. I look forward to reading the news with him—he buys a newspaper every day on his way by the depot."

"Anything of note in the *Provincetown Advocate* yesterday?" Mama looked hopeful. "By the time I get the newspapers from your Aunt Elizabeth, they are a week old."

"Well, let me think. The visitor's bureau is predicting another increase in excursionists to Provincetown this summer—coming in by railroad and steamers from New York and Boston. The Provincetown hotels that have bathing machines in the harbor are finding themselves already booked for the summer. And there is some debate regarding swimming classes for the local school children so they will be able to swim as skillfully as the city children who learn in their public pools. There is a proposal of swimming contests in speed and stamina."

"My, how things have changed," Mama said. "Swimming lessons! I can't think of two people who knew how to swim when I was a girl, and now everyone wants to know how. These summer visitors have made their impression, haven't they? You won't catch me in a bathing dress, though. I'm far too old to learn how to swim."

"You just may learn someday, Mama. They say it's very healthy for the body to exercise in salt water."

All this talk avoided the unmentionable topic of my new marital relations. How could my modest mother ask me, and how could I decently bring it up?

I am more than surprised at the ardor with which Henry embraces me every night. Even more mysterious to me is the way my body is beginning to expect him and seek him after such a short time together. As Mama and I discussed the news of the neighborhood and the greater world beyond, I wondered to myself—is this how it is with all newly married people? Do we all immediately take to each other so? Now that relations between Henry and I are allowable, am I to experience this type of intimacy every evening that my dear husband is in from the sea?

I am beginning to hope the answer is "yes." One night Henry whispered into my ear that he is blessed to have a wife as arduous as he is. In fact, the walk to Mama's had been accompanied with stinging pains from my groin area. I know it's because of the friction I now experience nightly; my body is simply unaccustomed.

I wished I could ask my mother what remedy I might use in this situation, as I would have with any other medical or health related concern. But I could not bring myself to do so. I was embarrassed at the thought. Here was the occasion where my married school friends would be the ones to ask, but no one lived close by. I would have to wait and see if I could get in a word to a friend after church on Sunday.

And yet, my modest mother surprised me. At the end of our afternoon visit, she said in an off-hand manner, as if she had forgotten to mention it, "Oh, Eva, something just arrived by post for you yesterday. Let me get if for you." She went into the little birthing room that was now used as her library and writing room and returned with a brown paper package addressed to "Miss Eva Paine." I wondered who would not have known that I was now a married lady.

As I opened the package, Mama went into the kitchen to bundle some freshly baked scones for the Smith household. I found myself holding a book titled *Tokology, A Book for Every Woman*, authored by Alice B. Stockham, M.D. I immediately realized that my mother had ordered the book for me.

Turning to the dedication page, I read, "To all women, who following the lessons herein taught, will be saved the sufferings peculiar to their sex." Reading through the chapter headings, I saw that the book addressed the subjects of conception and childbirth. There was another, slimmer volume in the package, and this was titled, *Venus, the State of Feminine Physical and Mental Health*, also by a female doctor—a Carin S. Goodhue. I blushed as I glanced over colored illustrations of female reproductive anatomy seemingly including all stages from virginal to fully pregnant to the "process" of birth.

I had seen diagrams of the human body, both female and male, in my high school anatomy class, but these illustrations were far more detailed. The table of contents promised chapters on the physically damaging evils of the corset, the benefits of fresh air and cold water baths, and the respectful attitude husbands should have towards their wives on the matter of conception. I was amazed that Mama had gone to such lengths for me.

"Wherever did you find these books?" I asked her as she came from the kitchen with the bundle of cookies.

"I ordered them from Boston a few weeks ago—I saw an advertisement in the bride's section of the *Boston Daily Globe*," she said. "I'm sorry they didn't arrive on time for your wedding day."

"Thank you, Mama." I didn't know what else to say. I hugged the books to my chest.

"May I look at them?" she asked shyly.

I handed them to her. She slowly opened the slim volume first and quickly passed through the colored illustrations, clucking her tongue.

"Well, I suppose it's better to know about those parts of the body than to leave it to the imagination and have the imaginings be incorrect," she said. Never before had I seen a picture of the female hymen or clitoris, and neither had she. Embarrassed, she closed the book before reaching the chapter on pregnancy.

"I'll keep that brown paper, Mama. Let's wrap the books again before I walk back," I said.

"That would be wise," she agreed.

Together we made sure the books were properly repackaged. I kissed Mama's cheek, thanked her, and left her.

~

The Smith house was quiet when I arrived, giving me an opportunity to go up to our bedroom and put the brown package away in my drawer. I certainly was not going to share the books with Mother Smith. That would seem a step too intimate, even though we had addressed the topic of blood upon the sheets.

I peeked into her bedroom, and she was resting comfortably upon her bed, still asleep. A deep concern overtook me. Mother Smith was not emitting the familiar snore to which I had become accustomed. I quietly tiptoed to her bedside and could discern no breath at all. Placing my hand on her cold forehead, I knew instantly that she had gone to be with the Lord.

The little smile on her face was serene. Her lips were closed, as were her eyes. The creases around her eyes and mouth were perfectly smooth and relaxed. She lay on her back under her top quilt, as she did for her afternoon naps. Her head was perfectly centered on her feather pillow. I could hear a fly buzzing in the room, but otherwise all was perfectly quiet. I surprised myself by reaching for her hand and holding it, feeling the stiff coldness. There was no question that her spirit had gone from her ample body.

"Oh, Mother Smith," I said. "You left me so soon. Happy passage to you." I stood beside her, in awe. There before me was the body of Arozana Paine Smith. This woman had always been so animated, her gestures so energetic and enthusiastic. Now she was at perfect peace. Her expression gave evidence that the occasion of death could be a pleasant one. I knelt down beside her to pray, telling her good-bye and thanking the Lord for welcoming her.

A guilty thought pushed its way into my mind. While my mother-in-law died, I had been at my mother's house receiving books on feminine health and pro-creation. I felt a stirring of self-indictment, and then I refused to accept it. I would not make the mistake of thinking that my actions were more powerful than God's will. There was nothing wrong with what I'd been doing, just as there was nothing I could have done for Mother Smith. She had died peacefully in her sleep. The Lord had taken her as he had planned.

Outside, a wagon stopped to drop Henry and his father from their day at the wharf. The men called out cheerful greetings to our horses and then went around to the back door of the house. Tears wet my face as I anticipated the pain the men would soon endure at losing this lady—this dedicated wife and mother. Perhaps the expression on her face would give them some comfort, as it had me. I patted her hair and looked at her smile one more time. "Farewell, Mother Smith," I murmured.

I looked around the tidy bedroom. A bottle of medicine stood on the bedside table beside her Bible. It came to me in a rather nonsensical manner that Arozana would not need her medicine again. Shooing the thought away and steeling myself for the sad hours and days to come, I took a deep breath and went to the top of the stairs to call down to the men.

∼

My husband's intense outpouring of grief was beyond anything I'd ever witnessed. Never had I seen a man lost in such pain. Henry cried instantly and openly from the moment he climbed the stairs and discovered for himself that his mother was indeed dead. Henry's emotions had such force that he could do nothing but let them fly.

My father-in-law was more measured and practiced in his reaction, praying his thanks over his deceased wife's body as she lay on their bed. "Thank you, dear Lord, for taking her in such a gentle and merciful manner, while she was enjoying her life and her family. I don't know what I will do without her, but I am sure you will provide the answers, dear Lord. Amen."

Even as I stood there accepting the enormous fact that my mother-in-law was gone, I mentally took stock of what I might prepare for dinner—not only for Henry and Winslow, but for the many relatives and friends that would soon be coming through our doors. I knew I could manage biscuits and stew, but not much more without Mother Smith's direction. The unwelcome truth came pushing into my mind with the urgency of an arriving train that it would be my responsibility forevermore to keep house by myself. I discretely left the men and went to the kitchen and stood there, wondering what to do first.

Henry wailed from his mother's bedroom. Winslow came down the stairs and went out the front door to give the news to a passing wagon, asking that Dr. Brown be summoned and that Mr. Snow, the undertaker, also be informed. The driver could be counted upon to stop at every house along his way, giving the news. From neighbor to neighbor, the word would reach out in several directions—to the railroad station and post office, down Paine Hollow to the shore, and north to the center of Wellfleet. Whether or not the wagon was going past the doctor's house or the undertaker's funeral parlor, both would receive the news within the hour.

I stared at the kitchen stove. I needed to bring in the wood—that was first—and then start the fire to heat the stove so I could prepare a meal. There was some leftover beef stew in the beehive cellar; I had put it down there myself at Mother Smith's request. "I'm much less spry than you are, my dear." Her voice came into my ears, the exact tone and lilt of it, as she had said these words to me so recently.

Holding my skirt with one hand, I climbed down the stout ladder on the worn rungs that had supported Mother Smith for hundreds of descents down to the cold cellar. Now she was gone, never to climb down the cellar ladder again. She had climbed the ladder to Heaven; I had to keep reminding myself of that fact. She had gone to her reward. That thought made her sudden departure a bit more bearable.

I brought in the short starter sticks from the woodpile and a handful of kindling from the brush pile. These I placed through the front burner hole and arranged them as Mother Smith had demonstrated. Then I searched about for the matches, trying to remember where Mother Smith kept them. Henry continued to wail from above. I left the kitchen and went back up the stairs and witnessed him trying to raise his mother to a sitting position. I rushed to him.

"Henry, Henry! It's of no use," I said. "She's gone. We must accept that." He looked at me, abashed, and gently released his mother back into a reclining position. He took her hand.

"Oh, she is so cold. If I had been here, I could have given Mother her medicine. If you had been here, instead of at your mother's house. . ."

"Henry, darling, she died in her sleep," I interrupted him. "There was no struggle here. There would have been no way for us to know, even if we were both downstairs in the kitchen at the time. See how peaceful she looks. It is the Lord's will, dearest." I rubbed his back as he looked down at his mother. His strong body shook with sobs. "I'm going to make you something to eat for dinner," I said.

"I'm not hungry, Eva," he managed to say.

"We'll see about that." I surprised myself with my quick reply. "You need something to eat, Henry. You can't neglect your own health. I'm going to make dinner. Your mother would want me to. Now spend some quiet time with her before everyone arrives." I left the room after steering Henry to the chair that his mother had sat in every morning to put on her stockings and shoes. I had taken my time alone with Mother Smith when I discovered her, and Henry needed his.

Downstairs, I looked out the front door at Winslow. He sat slumped on a bench facing the road.

"Can I bring you anything?" I asked him quietly, not wanting to disturb him.

"A glass of whiskey, please, Eva," he said.

"Yes, of course."

I brought it to him as quickly as possible. The whiskey bottle was kept in the medicine chest in the back pantry, and if the Smith household was anything like my father's, it only needed to be replaced every few years.

"I'll allow that I'm in enough pain to warrant this," Winslow said as I handed him the full glass.

"It will do you good," I said. Winslow's face was ashy gray, his eyes red and dry.

"We spent thirty years together," he said. "I don't know what I'll do without her." He watched two figures walk towards us on the road. "Here comes your Aunt Elizabeth and your mother. They've received word. They'll all start arriving soon. I think I'll go up to see Arozana once more."

"Send Henry down to me. Tell him I need him. I need his help." I wondered if Henry would leave his mother to let Winslow have some time alone with his wife.

"Yes, Eva. I'll tell him." He tipped up his glass and drank the contents in five swallows. He groaned as he got to his feet and walked heavily to the front door. I gave him my arm to help him up the steps and into the house, and then he grasped the banister and slowly climbed the staircase.

Mama came through the front gate with Aunt Elizabeth. They hugged me wordlessly and immediately took me out to the kitchen.

Mama quickly located the matches and lit the stove. Aunt Elizabeth opened a basket and took out muffins, a cold meat pie, a jar of beach plum preserves, and two loaves of bread. They had stopped at the houses along the road and solicited food for our supper. I sat down at the table, very calm. My mother and aunt exchanged glances and sat down with me.

"Tell us about it, Eva," Aunt Elizabeth said. "What happened?"

"She was gone when I got back from visiting you, Mama. The most peaceful expression remained on her face, and it seems as though she died in the middle of a nice dream. Or perhaps, she actually knew she was going—and could see her way into Heaven." I marveled at my composure. "I am feeling content about it for Aunt Arozana." Already I could see that in my mind I was reverting to the name I had called her all of my life and that it would be very hard for me to continue to refer to her as Mother Smith.

"But poor Henry, he is beside himself. I don't know what I should do. What *should* I do about the funeral? Is that my place, to do something?"

Mama's tears came running down her cheeks, and Aunt Elizabeth and I couldn't prevent ourselves from joining her in a crying session.

"Arozana's sisters will tend to her," Aunt Elizabeth said. "They are on their way. They will wash and dress her, and then Mr. Snow will take Arozana away. Since Winslow is a deacon at the Congregational Church, I know he will want the services of the funeral home in Wellfleet and then a proper church service on the day of her burial." Aunt Elizabeth had spoken. Being the wife of the prosperous Captain Wiley, she was up to date on all the latest social requirements and customs.

"I can't see the benefit of that—at such expense—especially when she is to be buried right here in South Wellfleet," my mother said. "I think a person should still be laid out at their own home, but this new funeral business seems to have taken hold. Unfortunately for Arozana, it is the fashionable thing to do."

"Well, that's the way it's done now, Sarah," Aunt Elizabeth said. "But we have plenty to do. We've got to get you situated as the lady of the house here, Eva. Unfortunately, it has come upon you all at once, and you will have two men to care for by yourself. It is a matter of knowing what to do when, and we will help you with that."

Mama nodded and Aunt Elizabeth continued, "We'll see to it that Henry and Winslow are well fed tonight, along with everyone else who drops by and requires feeding. You go out and tend the animals. Here comes Henry down the stairs, take him with you, Eva." She dropped her voice to a whisper and said, "Be sure to ask Henry to stack some extra firewood here at the kitchen door—we'll need it for the amount of cooking that will be necessary in the next few days."

Aunt Elizabeth hushed and she and Mama stood to greet Henry with hugs and gentle words of sympathy which he politely accepted. I was thankful that their presence had a calming affect upon him.

Henry and I went out to the barn together. There was no need for us to talk to each other. The routine chores were comforting as we carried the water and threw out the hay. As always, Henry had a treat in his pocket for the horses, and he scratched them behind the ears as I locked the chickens up for the night in their coop, safely away from the foxes. Our barn yard duties were quickly accomplished, and after washing at the pump, we embraced each other knowing we would not be alone again for hours. Henry shuddered with spasms of effort as he suppressed his tears.

A group of women walked up from Paine Hollow and went in the front door. Several men stood out in the yard, hats in hand, waiting for Winslow to come down from his bedroom. They saw Henry carrying firewood and came around the house, eager to help. Just six days earlier, these same people had come to my parents' front yard for a wedding celebration. Life was changing rapidly. But there was no slowing it; the occasion was upon us.

The house was quickly full of people, and I don't know how I functioned—I can scarcely remember what I said or what I did. Dr. Brown came in to perform the duty of declaring Arozana Paine Smith legally dead and noting that on an official certificate. Winslow came down the stairs and joined the men. I found myself repeating many times the story of finding Arozana peacefully gone. Everyone who loved her wanted to hear the story for themselves.

Arozana's sisters arrived and went quietly up the staircase. Some time went by, and then they called to me for water, which I carried up the stairs to them. I watched as the two women soberly washed Arozana's face, hands, and feet. After straightening her clothes, they decided that the undertaker could earn his money and formally dress her himself. They picked out a dress for Arozana to wear in her coffin. Because of her increasing girth, her older dresses no longer fit her. Arozana would wear the same dress she had worn to my wedding.

When Arozana was ready, Henry sent all the women out to the kitchen with me while the men moved Arozana down to the front parlor and arranged her under her quilt on the sofa. Many visited her there, wanting to be with her before the undertaker took her away. Mr. Snow came to fetch Arozana well after dark, perhaps thinking that the household would finally be calm. But it was a wrenching scene with all of us ladies crying in the flickering lamplight. An evening breeze blew into the house through the front door when it was opened wide to accommodate Arozana's transfer to the hearse. Henry had resigned himself to the departure and insisted upon helping to carry out the stretcher. I personally handed the traveling valise that contained Arozana's dress to Mr. Snow and politely requested that he have the dress pressed. I knew my mother-in-law would appreciate it.

Later that evening, after everyone had gone home, I found I

couldn't sleep. Henry urged me to go to bed, but he went outside and walked down towards the shore, braving the mosquitoes in the warm evening air. I was very aware of the emptiness left behind by Arozana's absence. For an hour I stayed in bed, tossing and turning, and wondering where my new husband was, and how he was. Winslow snored from his room, sedated by the medicinal doses from the whiskey bottle.

Unable to get any rest, I got up and lit the lamp. I carried it down the hall and entered Arozana's sewing room. After a moment's hesitation, I sat down at her prized possession, a Singer sewing machine that Winslow recently purchased for her. Arozana hadn't cared that half the women in the neighborhood called it "cheating"—she loved the efficiency of the machine as it evenly sewed a smooth seam. She had confided in me that she never had any fondness for hand-sewing and was delighted with her husband's gift. I picked up a quilting square that she'd been working on and positioned it under the needle. A warm feeling came over me, as if my mother-in-law was there with me in the room.

I moved the treadle with my foot and sewed a strip onto the log cabin block that Arozana had started. My seam wasn't as perfect as the others on the square, but I thought Arozana would be happy with my effort. And so I continued.

Henry came in at three in the morning. I heard him walking through the house downstairs and pausing in the parlor. After a few minutes, he came up the stairs and followed the light to the sewing room. I showed him that I had completed five squares. He nodded and drew me down the hall to our room. After taking immense comfort in each other, we slept.

~

CHAPTER FOUR
Uncharted Territory

In spite of a morning rain shower, Arozana Smith's funeral was very well attended. The memorial service at the First Congregational Church was a fine testimony to the wife of a favorite church deacon. The entire membership of the Wellfleet Methodist Church was also present, Reverend Moss included. Funerals create the most harmonious mingling of the two churches.

I felt close to the Lord as I sat on the front pew between Henry and his father, and we sang hymn after hymn with the blended congregations—Arozana's favorite hymns exalting the Lord's glory and wisdom. All voices rang out loudly and strongly, helping Arozana Smith's soul make the journey to a peaceful resting place while proclaiming our belief that although she would be sorely missed, she was in a better place.

Reverend Pike delivered a sincere and loving eulogy, even though it contained several factual errors about Arozana's life. Her Wellfleet neighbors were to lift her up in prayer (she lived in South Wellfleet), and the good reverend incorrectly stated Arozana's age as being seven years younger than she actually was (forty-two rather than forty-nine).

At the second inaccuracy on the part of Reverend Pike, I observed the meddlesome widow Matilda Chase counting on her fingers, presumably figuring the age Arozana had been when she gave birth to Henry, her twenty-seven year old son. A look of glee crept onto the widow's face, as if she had arrived at a startling conclusion. The story would soon be spread about as fact that Arozana had been fifteen years old when Henry was born.

We stood to sing *Amazing Grace* and the entire church swelled with resounding vocal unity. I fought away my judgment of Matilda Chase and tried to cultivate a feeling of charity towards the old widow. If I was to indulge in judging another while I sang *Amazing Grace* for my deceased mother-in-law, what kind of Christian was I?

After the hymn, the wooden pews creaked and groaned as we all sat down. Reverend Pike motioned for the pallbearers to come forward to Arozana's coffin, a signal which prompted an immediate reaction on Henry's part. The congregation sat quietly and allowed Henry his unchecked sobs of grief. My husband was well known to all present as a fearless mariner, yet here he was, shamelessly exhibiting the softer side of his character. Henry Smith did indeed have a hole in his armor that led straight to his heart.

The outpouring of emotion is a common occurrence in the Methodist church, but the Congregationalists do not express themselves so, as Winslow demonstrated with his grief-frozen face and stiffly erect posture, silent as a pillar. I looked up at the minister and stroked Henry's arm as I sat between the father and son. Reverend Pike was praying the final prayer of the service, but I could not hear him.

Then it was time to remove Arozana's coffin from the church to Mr. Snow's glass encased funeral hearse. Arozana Smith was leaving her church for the last time in a horizontal position—not chatting and laughing with her friends. I heard her voice in my mind telling me to stop thinking such thoughts, she had already left us. She was already gone.

The procession back to the South Wellfleet cemetery took a good part of the afternoon. After saying our thank-you's and farewells to the folks from Wellfleet who would not be attending the burial, we departed. The glass hearse led the way, bearing the flower laden coffin. The five-mile drive from the center of Wellfleet to our cemetery was indeed melancholy with the absence of Arozana's constant chatter. Winslow and I barely spoke as Henry drove us along behind the hearse. I wished that it was appropriate for my mother to ride with me and keep me company. The two-dozen carriages following us spread out over a quarter of a mile. Thankfully, the morning's rain shower had dampened the sandy road, and the mourners in the funeral procession did not suffer from dust clouds. If a funeral ride could be pleasant, Arozana's was.

We approached our empty church. It sat forlornly in the graveyard, all shuttered up and awaiting its fate. Winslow deemed it foolish to bury Arozana in the Wellfleet Congregational cemetery. He wanted her close by so he could easily visit her grave.

Arozana Smith was interred in the Smith family plot, at the front of the churchyard in the northeast corner. Her father, the late Captain Robert Y. Paine, rested peacefully with his wife just ten paces away, alongside some of Arozana's little sisters who did not survive their long-ago childhoods. Although Arozana bore only one child of her own, she was the ninth of twelve children born to her mother. Many of her living brothers and sisters and their spouses were present at the burying ground, along with grown nieces and nephews with families of their own.

The new Smith headstone, which had been expertly prepared by the undertaker's stonemason, not only had Arozana's name and dates carved into it, it also had Winslow's name and birth date followed by a dash and then a blank space. My composure had been sedate thus far. I had not felt the need for my smelling salts all day, but when I read the pronouncement in granite that my father-in-law would join Arozana someday, I immediately reached into my handbag for a salts bottle. I had not prepared adequately and found none there.

Mama stepped up to my side as we stood over the hole in the ground. She'd kept a close watch on me throughout the day, even as she deferred to the fact that I was on Henry's arm every minute. The pungent odor of freshly turned soil immediately instigated in me a nauseous condition. Looking down, I saw the layers of earth—the thin offering of top soil, the whitish gray sand below that, and then the damp rusty colored sand at the bottom half of the excavation. I knew Arozana was watching us from above, but I couldn't keep myself from thinking—how horrifying to be buried deep down in the dank sand, so cold and away from the light. I chastised myself, and silently repeated over and over again: *Aunt Arozana was a good woman and has gone to be with our Lord. We shall all be with her someday, God willing.*

"Here are the salts, Eva, you look at bit unsteady," Mama pulled a small glass bottle out of her purse. Her eyes were red under her spectacles. She was very sad at losing one of her oldest friends. I took the bottle from her and sniffed. The strong vapors immediately restored me to a steady position.

"I wasn't prepared to read Winslow's name, Mama," I said as Reverend Pike announced the reading of the Twenty-third Psalm. The shuffling sound of thin Bible pages filled the silence as the mourning party turned to the Old Testament.

"I know it's financially prudent to have the stone prepared for both spouses when one passes, but do we always have to be so financially prudent?" I whispered to Mama and she squeezed my hand.

"Shush now, Eva," she said.

"Will you and Papa have it done this way when one of you passes?" I whimpered at the thought.

"Of course," she said. "Shush, dear. We'll talk about this later."

Reverend Pike began the final graveside prayer in his most somber tone and all murmuring around the grave ceased as we bowed our heads in unison and joined in reciting the familiar words:

The Lord is my shepherd, I shall not want. He maketh me to lie down in green pastures; He leadeth me beside the still waters. He re-

storeth my soul. He leadeth me in the paths of righteousness for His name's sake.

I looked up at Henry towering over me—his eyes streaming again, his nose running. I handed him another of his handkerchiefs, having brought along several for the day, and then steeled myself for the next verse.

Yea, though I walk through the valley of the shadow of death, I will fear no evil, for thou art with me. . . I hid my face in my own handkerchief. I never have been able to read on to the end of the psalm once the valley of the shadow of death is mentioned. I fought to govern my emotions as I listened to the loved ones around me assure me—

I will fear no evil, for thou art with me, Thy rod and thy staff, they comfort me. Thou preparest a table before me in the presence of mine enemies, Thou annointest my head with oil, my cup runneth over. Surely goodness and mercy shall follow me all the days of my life, and I will dwell in the House of the Lord forever. Amen.

We sang another hymn for Arozana. I don't remember which, because I tried to remove my thoughts from the grave by looking out to the bay. The funeral guests would be arriving at the house immediately, and I had to be presentable. I could see the wharf and a few men out there working in the gray stillness. There was no wind. A light fog hovered out towards Billingsgate Light, and there were no sails in sight.

I directed my mind to the details at hand. Did I have enough cookies, pies, and breads at home for the folks to eat after the burial? The careful management of my emotions came apart; the thought of "home" undid me. I broke down and truly sobbed, for Aunt Arozana would never go home again. Yes, she would enter Heaven, but I knew nothing of Heaven. As a newly married couple, Henry and I made a pretty pair, I am sure, both of us bawling our eyes out as freely as two abandoned little children.

Winslow gestured to the undertaker that it was time to lower his wife's coffin—and hastily. Down into the earth went Arozana

Paine Smith. Shovels were handed to Winslow and Henry, and together they ceremoniously threw the first clods of dirt down onto the smooth wood. The sound was hollow and thudding. The shovels were passed to two of Arozana's brothers—one of them named after their prolific deceased father, Captain Robert Y. Paine, who lay so close by.

Generations of fathers and sons, many of them bearing the same first name, were buried around us. I wondered what it would be like to have the weight of generations attached to my name—the weight of all those gravestones standing there facing east, waiting for the second coming of Christ. I pictured sons and fathers and grandfathers holding hands back into the past and smiled into my handkerchief, imagining the confusion of hundreds of people bearing the same name in Heaven.

When all of the men present had contributed a shovelful of dirt to Arozana's grave, we women somberly returned to our buggies. The men soon joined us, leaving the gravediggers to finish the job properly. But Henry continued to stand over his mother's grave as our relatives and neighbors began to roll out of the cemetery gate. It became apparent that Henry was not ready to leave. I climbed down from Winslow's buggy and tugged at Henry's elbow.

"I must go to the house, Henry—we'll have guests there in a few minutes."

"Go ahead then, Eva," he said. "I'll be along soon. I just want to be sure they do a good job here." The rhythm of the two gravediggers lent a hypnotic effect. In perfect time one man took a shovelful of dirt, his shovel biting into the earth pile with a metallic sound, as the other dropped a thudding measure into the grave. The hole was half-way full, and the hollow sound of the coffin could no longer be heard.

I wanted to kiss Henry, but he would not bend down to me. I settled for taking his hand in mine and kissing the back of it. A slight nod from him told me he had received my sentiment, and I climbed into the buggy with Mama and Papa. I would ride with them, I decided. It would give me some time with Mama.

"Henry's not ready yet—he'll walk back to the house," I told my father.

"Let's go then, Tess, shall we?" Papa gently slapped the reins down on the horse's back, and Tessa walked towards the cemetery gates, pulling us gently along as if she knew we were in hallowed grounds. The buggy springs creaked loudly in the misty stillness. Winslow followed in the Smith buggy, transporting the neighborhood widows who normally walked everywhere.

I was again preoccupied with the hospitality I was to offer at the house for the next few hours. I looked back over my shoulder, hoping Henry would not tarry. He had taken a shovel from one of the gravediggers and was finishing the job of burying his mother. His back set in determination, his feet firmly planted on the side of the grave, he threw two shovels full for every one of the other man.

I was not surprised. Henry has never been one to stand on decorum when there is a job to be done. He towered above the other man, dressed in his black mourning coat and derby hat, methodically and elegantly performing this last task for his mother. I could not imagine the pain of burying a mother, since mine was sitting next to me, but I wept for Henry from the privacy of the rolling buggy. Mama dabbed at my face with her handkerchief. I looked back until the mistiness in the air dimmed the sharpness of Henry's figure.

∼

I got through the afternoon with the constant help of my mother and all of the other good ladies of the neighborhood. Nettie was there in the kitchen—very capably serving, cooking, setting the table, and then removing empty platters from the table, and replenishing again from the large selection brought by the kind souls who had begun to bake as soon as word was received that Arozana had passed on. Back and forth Nettie went from the kitchen to the dining room. I could not keep up with her, and after twenty minutes I stopped trying.

"Sit, Eva. Sit, sit, sit!" Nettie said to me several times, and at last I obeyed. The men stood out in the yard, talking and smoking and chewing tobacco. The ladies were in the dining room and front parlor. It was my duty to make conversation with the ladies—most of them good friends of Arozana's, many of them related in some way.

A few were not such good friends, but visited according to custom. These women I found most tiresome, as they had much of little consequence to say, but ironically required my utmost attention. Matilda Chase proved herself to be this type of funeral guest. She apparently presumed that her widowed status gave her the right to be impolite. With no introductory expression of sympathy, she asked,

"What will become of your mother-in-law's beautiful china, Eva?"

"That is not for me to determine," I said. My mother was sitting next to me, but her presence had not prevented Widow Chase from asking the question. Mama clucked her tongue, but said nothing. My answer did not have the desired effect of halting Widow Chase's line of inquiry.

"I've always loved that china, especially the soup tureen. If you think that Winslow would be interested in disposing of it—many times a man disposes of a wife's belongings in order to forget the pain of loss, especially when he marries again—as I say, if he makes any mention of disposing of Arozana's belongings, I would be willing to take a look at her things and offer to purchase some of them." Widow Chase quickly ended her sentence as Aunt Elizabeth entered the room.

"Matilda Chase, always at it, are you not?" Aunt Elizabeth scolded. "Leave Eva alone. What a thing to ask at a time like this! Of course, Eva will be using the china herself. Enough of that nonsense, Matilda."

I was thankful to my out-spoken aunt for her reprimand, as my mother was far too reserved to do it, and I was far too surprised by the inquiry. Widow Chase looked up at Aunt Elizabeth like a schoolgirl who had been caught cheating on an exam. She stood and rustled out of the room, her black silk whirling all about her in a great whoosh as she squeezed between the other women present.

"She didn't mean anything by it. It's just her way, Eva," Aunt Elizabeth said. She took my hand. "Of course, you are the mistress of this house now, and you will need everything here to carry on!" She looked directly into my eyes, emphasizing her point.

"Thank you, Aunt Elizabeth," I said, withdrawing my hand. I looked at Nettie, who was once again on her way back to the kitchen to fetch another plate of breads and cookies. Nettie would revel in a house outfitted like this one was, but I could not. I wondered how I would ever keep up with the housekeeping. Even though Aunt Arozana had taken a nap every afternoon, she worked hard every day. Watching my face, my mother correctly surmised my thoughts and tried to encourage me.

"You are so capable and intelligent," Mama said. "I'm sure that you will take to running this household quite efficiently."

I smiled. "I was just beginning to understand how to manage it all," I said. "But there is so much I don't know yet."

"Such as?" Aunt Elizabeth cocked her head at me like a bird.

"Well—the finances." I spoke in as low a voice as possible so as to not be overheard. "I know Aunt Arozana managed the finances of the household, but she certainly did not have the time to share them with me. Yesterday I went to the general store to buy groceries for this afternoon and Ike had me sign the book where Arozana usually signed. He told me the bill was always due on the first of the month. I know nothing of paying the bills or where the money will come from." It was inappropriate to talk of finances at a time like this, but it had to be done. I didn't know when I would have the opportunity to voice my concerns again.

"I will speak to Winslow for you," Aunt Elizabeth said. "Of course he will show you the household ledger and teach you how to keep it. Now, stop worrying, Eva. You have so many of us to call upon if you get into a pickle, and we will help you out."

Aunt Elizabeth was like that, she had no trouble speaking directly to men, due to the fact that she was the wife of Captain Wiley—one of the most successful sea captains in Paine Hollow, and also one of the most sensible, as far as we women were concerned. Captain Wiley had managed to make the leap from sail to steam that many other men had yet to make, therefore insuring his future employment with the Boston Fruit Company and the prosperous state of his household. Even now, he was out on the ocean between Jamaica and Boston with a hold full of bananas. Elizabeth Wiley would feel no qualms informing Winslow that his duty was to teach me how to keep the household books—something I would never dare mention to my grieving father-in-law, resulting in what financial tangle?

"Properly kept books are the mark of a good housekeeper, Eva, and your mind can certainly handle the arithmetic. It is very simple compared to the algebraic equations you mastered in high school."

"Thank you, Aunt Elizabeth, for your assistance in this matter. Let's do talk about something else!" I really could not concentrate on a conversation for long. "Where is Henry? Is he back from the cemetery yet?"

"He's out in the yard with the men," Mama said. "It's getting dark, and your father and I should be going home now." She rose from her chair and tightened her crocheted shawl around her shoulders, indicating that she was ready to go.

Reluctantly, I rose to hug her. Within the hour all the guests had departed, leaving behind many cards of condolence. Nettie would not consider leaving me until she had tidied the dining room and kitchen. She stowed away the remainder of the donated food before kissing me good-bye.

"Please come see me tomorrow, Nettie," I whispered to her.

She nodded that she would. Henry came in from the back yard

and sat silently in the front parlor. Nettie went and kissed him good-bye on the cheek, but he sat there exhausted, unable to speak or smile. After Nettie left it became very quiet and the clock on the mantle ticked loudly.

Winslow went out to the paddock to tend to Sinbad and Silkie. I was blessedly alone. My husband was with me, but was not with me. I could observe him, but Henry did not appear to notice me. Although together at the Smith homestead, we were separately facing the new reality of our lives. At that moment, I knew I was on the threshold of uncharted territory.

~

Late August, 1886
Domestic Life

My first three months as a sea captain's wife revealed more to me than I wished to learn. Two days after Arozana's funeral in May, Henry and his father put out to sea on the *Dora Freeman*. The men were markedly relieved to be shoving off, smiling and calling out good-byes to me as the crew raised sail and the schooner glided away from the wharf.

I understood why they were in such good spirits. The big wide ocean before them would command their complete attention and temporarily reduce the pain of life ashore. Arozana would not be so missed out on the watery territories where she had never accompanied her husband or son. "She's gone, and I have to accept that. I may as well fish with Henry," Winslow told me the morning of their departure. I knew both men wanted to leave the house—Arozana's house.

A bride for less than two weeks, my life again changed dramatically. Being alone in the Smith house was nothing short of eerie, even through the daylight hours. In the sharp stillness of vacated rooms, I learned that my time would now be measured by extreme rhythms as contrasting as the full bay at high tide is to the bare sand flats of low tide.

I was afraid to be alone through the dark hours of night. I convinced Nettie to come and stay with me. She walked over every evening, arriving at twilight to have tea with me. We chatted over our tea cups and somehow managed to laugh together. By ten o'clock, we were yawning our way to our prospective sleeping quarters—Nettie to the tiny guest room, and me to my bed—so empty without Henry. Nettie rose and left early in the morning to attend to her own chores at home.

Without Nettie, I would have run back to Mama's to sleep at night. After kindly spending five evenings with me, Nettie informed me that it was time for me to spend the night alone, as this would be my life for years to come.

"You wanted to be married, Eva. This is what a captain's wife *does*," Nettie declared. "She waits for him to come home."

"But I didn't realize I would be alone so much of the time," I said.

"Being alone in the house is the plight of most brides—until they have the company of their children. It's not every bridegroom who lives comfortably in his father's home." Nettie raised her eyebrows at me. "What did you *think* marriage would be?"

"Oh, I don't know," I said. "I suppose my notion of marriage centers on our love for each other. I can't stop thinking of Henry—I need to be with him. Nettie, you won't understand until you fall in love. It is such a strong feeling. It fills me up until I think I'll burst."

"Rubbish. You're so emotional, Eva," Nettie said. "You must be more practical. You are going to be alone a lot until your children come—or until Winslow decides not to go out with Henry. Thank heavens Henry lives here in the hollow. At least you haven't been taken away from your friends and your mother. You don't have to try to make new acquaintances in a strange neighborhood. Consider yourself fortunate."

The ever practical Nettie is such a strong tiller against my sentimental sails. I am indeed fortunate, as she says, that we are still close neighbors. I need my friend more than ever.

~

Aunt Arozana is not here, but all of her belongings are. Winslow informed me that he was not up to the task and he wanted me to store away his late wife's personal items. For some time after the men sailed away, Arozana's Bible lay open on the little table next to her reading chair, as if she might sit down any minute to study a verse. Her notebook of minutes from the Ladies Social Union rested on the top shelf of the bookcase in the hallway, ready for the next monthly meeting. Her boar's bristle hairbrush lay neatly next to her tortoise shell comb on her bedroom bureau. Her fan and opera glasses, sent to her by a friend from Boston should Arozana ever need them for a local performance, were artfully arranged on top of her desk.

Paperweights, knickknacks, mending baskets, an embroidery hoop displaying a half finished cross stitch pattern, books of poetry including well thumbed volumes by Elizabeth Barrett Browning—all of these things and more in every room emphasized the fact that I was in Aunt Arozana's house. I found myself constantly correcting my habitual expectation that she would walk through a door or call me from the kitchen at any moment.

Reluctantly, I began to pack her personal belongings and correspondence away, as Winslow had requested. But as I arranged her toilet articles in a cedar trunk, it decidedly felt as though I betrayed her. It remains a chore that will take me months to complete. In the meantime, it gives me some comfort to see Arozana's things in familiar places around the house.

Arozana's cat Polly has become a friend. It is very much against my own mother's philosophy to allow a cat to sleep in the house, but I have allowed—no, I have *encouraged*—Polly to come and sleep with me. Polly and I battled over the little matter of a bath, which I insisted upon to free her of fleas before bringing her to the bedroom. I further annoy Polly by shaking wintergreen oil on her fur to be sure the fleas do not return.

The cat misses the presence of her late mistress, and perhaps fears that I, too, might desert her. She constantly brushes against my ankles as I work in the kitchen or out in the yard. In spite of the fact that I sometimes stumble over her, Polly never leaves my side. She accompanies me when I walk to Mama's house, to the delight of the neighborhood children.

~

This summer is passing by, and Henry and his father have come home and gone back out to sea a half dozen times. Generally, they are away for two weeks and home for three days. Always there is a wonderful reunion between Henry and me, and then the sadness of his mother's absence settles upon him like a damp cloak. Winslow is very serious. I haven't seen him smile.

The fishing fleet began the mackerel season after the Fourth of July. Of course, everyone took a holiday to fire off the cannon up on Cannon Hill and picnic there on the bluff overlooking the harbor. I heard much discussion generated by the men as to whether it was more advantageous to fish for the mackerel with long lines of baited hooks or to employ a purse seine net. The majority of men in attendance favored the lines, but Henry disagreed with them. "Why abandon the nets when fish school together? Fish don't string out in a long line, so I won't be putting out a trawl." Henry was emphatic in his opinion, and I daresay, entitled to it. No amount of persuasion from the other men altered Henry's mindset, although they made a sport of trying.

I do miss Henry so when he is out. He tells me that the mackerel will swim south sometime in September, and the season will be over. Then I will see more of my husband.

The housework will *never* be done, so I plan my days by the clock, rather than by the task. When the noon hour arrives, I stop the chore at hand, have a bite to eat, and go in search of female company if company does not come to me. I begin again in the late afternoon and work my way to the end of daylight, which comes so late in the summer. The hour when the fireflies come out and hover over the shrubs is my favorite. Their flashing sparks of light signal that my day is finally over.

Many times I've been certain I would not be able to accomplish a task, and then, somehow, I was able to. I have mastered the art of stove-tending—getting the kitchen oven to stay at a constant temperature so I can bake bread. Rising at four-thirty with the roosters is now familiar to me. This enables me to mix the bread dough, let it rise, punch it down to rise again, and then bake it in the oven—all before nine in the morning when the heat of the day sets in.

I let the stove go cold through the hot summer afternoons and do laundry in the yard, this being the cooler task. I am not particular about the day of the week and on hot muggy days, doing the laundry is actually enjoyable. I am able to keep myself cool by washing the clothes with cold water, although Aunt Arozana never would have approved. I have devised a way to wring out the sheets after scrubbing them—it entails tying twine around one end of a sheet and then fastening the twine tightly to a pine tree in the yard.

Thus, the pine tree has become my laundry companion, holding one end of the sheet securely for me while I twist from the other end and wring the water onto the flowers at the base of the tree. These flowers grow healthy and vigorous, as do I. In spite of the loss of Aunt Arozana, I am a happy bride, and my chores require strength— something which I acquire more of daily. I am finding satisfaction in the strength of my body along with a startling awareness that the stronger I become, the more enjoyable my fortnightly marital relations are.

As I work, I recall how Aunt Arozana talked to herself and hold myself back from developing the same habit. However, being alone so much has enlightened me as to how that very thing could happen, so I've decided to sing. I sing my way through hours of chores and find that washing, rinsing, and hanging the laundry is accomplished more quickly when I sing. If I run out of songs, I recite poetry either silently in my head or aloud—it does not matter. I am especially fond of Longfellow's *Paul Revere's Ride*. The rhythm of the poem goes well with scrubbing laundry up and down on the scrub board. I have washed all the curtains in the house. They've been scrubbed clean to the words:

Listen my children and you shall hear of the midnight ride of Paul Revere, on the eighteenth of April, in Seventy-five; hardly a man is now alive who remembers that famous day and year.

I daresay that not another soul in Wellfleet can recite the entire poem with as much stamina as I can.

～

When Henry is out to sea, and even when he is in, I make sure I visit with Mama for at least an hour in the afternoon. Sometimes she surprises me, and walks to my kitchen door before I can walk to hers. Her house is as empty as mine. Papa and Lewis are out on the water more than they are in—Papa with the *Nautilus*, and Lewis on the *Mary Cole*. Mama and I frequently acknowledge that it is a blessing we live so close to each other.

Reading the newspapers with Mama is always a bright spot in the day. She will hear only the news that is pleasant and cringes at anything that is horrid, or even merely unpleasant. "There is too much trouble in the world," she says. My task is to scan the columns and avoid all mention of drownings, murders, hangings, fires, bankruptcies and incarcerations, and read aloud to her the items on engagements, weddings, socials, fashion, births and celebrations. She agrees to hear obituaries because, "So many of my friends are dying now, and I really have to know."

We are both excited by the reports (and accompanying illustrations) that Lady Liberty is finally standing tall in New York Harbor, ready for her October dedication. The statue is a gigantic Centennial birthday present to our country from France—more than a decade late, but fantastic all the same.

According to newspaper accounts, it has been a year since the French frigate *Isere* arrived in New York Harbor with the unassembled statue packed in 214 separate crates. Since then, an impressive pedestal has been erected by the renowned architect, Richard Morris Hunt. At last, the statue is standing tall, ready for her presentation to the American public. President Cleveland will light Lady Liberty's electric torch of freedom, which is expected to be visible twenty-five miles out to sea. Vessels from all over the world have arranged their schedules in order to sail in the grand celebration parade in New York Harbor. The advertisements on the newsprint between us on Mama's kitchen table called our imaginations into hard duty.

"What a spectacle *that* will be! What I would give to be a seagull flying over the festivities," Mama said.

"I would love to go and see the statue," I said. "New York City has never attracted me—but now I want to visit someday."

"Then you will, dear. I'm sure you will."

"But what about you—don't you want to, Mama? You're the one who mentioned it first."

"I am quite content to stay home. I wouldn't want to go unless your father sailed the *Nautilus* down. I wouldn't be comfortable sailing with anyone else."

"The train then, Mama. We could travel by rail," I said.

Mama shook her head no.

"And why not?" I pressed her. "You are still so strong and healthy. Wouldn't you like to go on an excursion with me before Henry and I start our family? Don't you feel well?"

Mama blinked and bit her lip.

"I am feeling fine, dear," she said. "It's just that Arozana is gone, and I do miss my good friend. When I married your father and came to Paine Hollow, she was so kind to me and kept me company when our men were out to sea. We always talked like this about traveling to visit a place that we'd read about, but we never left our homes to do it. It seems as though the men were always out to sea, and we were left in charge of everything. And then, when the men were home, it was even more impossible to leave. Arozana and I never did travel together."

"You do miss her, don't you, Mama? I'm so sorry you lost your friend," I said. I wondered how I would feel if I lost Nettie. "But Aunt Arozana had a bad heart, and we were lucky to have her as long as we did."

"I'm not complaining that the Lord called her home," Mama said. "I think of her often, though. Not only do I think of the places we wanted to visit together, I think of all the changes we hoped would come to pass, especially a lady's right to vote. Arozana's death is all the more reason to press for a serious agenda at our Ladies Social Union. The charity work is necessary, yes, but I'm growing impatient with the fashion shows and the entertainments that we stage.

"If the members of our social union can't find the backbone to declare that women should have the right to vote, then I don't think it's worth being a member. As a tribute to Arozana's friendship, I'm not going to rest until I have voted in a national election!" Mama made a fist and hit the table with it, although not nearly as hard as Papa does when he makes a point.

Her passion took me by surprise.

"You are *right*, Mama," I said. "We must work on suffrage with more commitment. We've been too quiet with our opinions. Let me talk to Nettie, and we'll draw up a resolution that the Ladies Social Union is in support of women's suffrage to present at our next meeting. And further, the members of our club must be able to defend this position in public. Otherwise, we are not worth our salt."

I took the newspaper back home with me and pasted the article on Lady Liberty's upcoming dedication into my scrapbook. "We'll get you the women's vote," I told her before I shut the cover on her illustration and turned to my afternoon housework.

Many dozens of times I've had conversations with my women friends that we must win the vote, but I've never discussed it with Henry. How strange that I've just assumed he would be in agreement, but the truth is, I don't really know. My father is aware of the opinion that Mama and I share, having sat and read his newspaper through our evening discussions before I was married.

The conversations were especially animated two years ago when suffragist Belva Lockwood ran as the presidential candidate for the new Equal Rights Party. "I cannot vote, but I can be voted for," was her campaign slogan which suffered daily ridicule in the newspapers. But as the first female attorney allowed into the Supreme Court to argue a case, we women knew Lockwood was intent on making a point, not on being elected. Even so, she did receive several thousand votes out of the millions cast—male votes, of course. Unfortunately, Susan B. Anthony spoke publicly against her, an action which I will never understand. But that controversy has passed until the next presidential election, and we must use this time to continue the fight for suffrage.

I have not discussed my opinion at the Smith household, being of the mind that it is not polite to discuss politics under my father-in-law's roof. But as the Smith house has become the place I call home, and I feel less like a guest and more like the mistress of the house, I will look for the opportunity to advance my opinion to my husband.

~

I rely heavily upon my writing to get me through the solitary evenings. Reading is food for the brain, but writing is the product of the thoughts I've entertained throughout the day. I have written a letter to Henry, although he will never receive it. The words flowed out of my pen onto the paper, letting me learn what my own mouth has not yet said aloud. This is my heart. But I should not burden Henry with my longings. What the good Lord wants, the good Lord will deliver.

Dearest Henry,

I do miss you immensely; it is so strange and lonely in this house without you. When you are home, you fill up the space with your masculine companionship. Polly has been my company through the evening hours—she sits at my feet and purrs. Of course, our neighbors have been very kind to me during this time of sorrow. But their sympathetic visits at afternoon tea time do little to remove the weird stillness of the evening hours.

The constant unwelcome thought that steals into my mind is that the house is as quiet as a tomb. The parlor clock loudly measures my time—I can hear it from the kitchen. I cannot escape the oppressive ticking dissection of each minute; yet, I must not forget to wind the clock. It is as if I am condemned to listen to the passing of time while you are away.

I am finding it difficult to adjust to the fact that I am the Mrs. Smith of the household. Today I answered to that title when the book peddler Blackwell came to the front door with his wagon full of leather bound samples. I do so want to order the whole Shakespearian series. However, I shall refrain.

I am hoping that we shall soon have children who will fill these empty rooms with laughter and companionship. I wonder if our last wondrous evening together before you sailed will bring forth a child, and I have indulged myself in communing with the child I imagine I carry within me. Although I dread the hours of childbirth, they will be a small price to pay for the

*years of motherhood to follow. I know you will make
a loving father and good provider to our brood. Please
return to me safely. I trust that your endeavors are
successful, as always.*

Your admiring wife, Eva

I have burnt the letter in the kitchen stove. It would be cruel of me to give it to Henry. I have not spoken to Henry of my hopes—I am very aware of the great pain he is in with the loss of his mother. The child, when it arrives, will remedy his grief. I look forward to the diversion of sweet infanthood. There it is—I do so want a family. I pray that this is the plan the Lord has prepared for Henry and me.

~

September, 1886

By necessity, I've become accustomed to the ebb and flow of a sea captain's life. There are periods of intense activity as the men prepare to leave, periods of shattering silence during the two weeks duration of their trips out, and then, just when I'm comfortable with sleeping alone, the schooners sail back into the harbor and the excitement of my husband's return is upon me again.

When the numbers are compared to last year's, the *Dora Freeman* did quite well this summer, thanks to Henry. Lewis has continued to crew on the *Mary Cole*, and she has brought in almost as many barrels of mackerel as the *Dora Freeman*.

But according to the figures Mr. Avery keeps so carefully at the Southern Wharf Company, there is little doubt that the total catch is down again this season. Our little fleet has to go further from home—up to the coast of Maine and beyond—to find the schools of mackerel they pull in.

More and more, the talk between the men is of the shoaling up of our harbor and the fact that the larger vessels can no longer easily moor inside the protection of Blackfish Creek without being stuck in the mud at low tide. Many discussions have occurred around the kitchen table between Henry and Winslow and the neighborhood men who drop by for an evening smoke when they know Henry is home.

I am becoming quite informed through all the talk. The Stubbs Boat Yard down at the head of Blackfish Creek has reduced the draft on their new schooners, and some have keels built light enough to be cranked up into the vessel when moored in shallow waters. Henry predicts a loss of stability in the new vessels once out of the protected waters of the harbor. He says shortening the masts is perhaps an option, as less sail would put less stress on a keel, but all these accommodations will reduce the speed of the vessels.

My own conclusion, though hard to accept, is that in some not too distant year ahead, our harbor will be too shallow for any schooners, and they will have to move north to join the fleet at Wellfleet harbor. The men who frequent my kitchen table have not conceded that point, as the rivalry between the fleets of South Wellfleet and Wellfleet is long and deep.

Arozana's brother, Captain Robert Paine, gave grim evidence of our harbor's troubles: "I measured the channel depth again last night. High tide on a full moon is fine, but last night was just half moon, and the channel was less than two fathoms deep. It was never less than three fathoms deep when I was a boy—I was measuring it then for my father!" A veteran seaman, Captain Paine has weathered a long career of sailing many types of vessels, from ocean-crossing clippers, to fishing schooners, to coastal traders. Uncle Robert is an avowed enemy of the railroad.

"Damned railroad, how are we going to compete with that monster?" he bellowed. "It might be necessary for crossing the western territories, but we certainly didn't need it here where we had coastal lanes aplenty and a fleet worth boasting about. I tell you, it's putting the fleet out of business!

"You want to ship from Cape Cod to Carolina? The railroad can get your cargo there faster than I can—and carry more tonnage than I could ever fit into the hold of a schooner. Those Wellfleet oyster cultivators are getting rich, they have a huge market now thanks to the railroad—you should see the train loading up in Wellfleet with barrels of oysters, but where does that leave the coastal traders?

"It's bad enough that the fish numbers are down, but I think the merchant fleet is beyond revival. It will never be the same as it was! This whole town is losing its life blood, and all because of a few rich railroad speculators who couldn't leave Cape Cod well enough alone. You'd think that with the western territories to cross, they'd be happy. But no, they had to come all the way down the cape and throw down the iron rails. We survived without the railroad, why the hell did we let it come?"

Winslow flinched, but did not reprimand his older brother-in-law on his abuse of the language.

"I don't believe we were asked," declared Henry. "I would never have leased my land to the railroad as some of your brothers did, Uncle Robert! Now every woodlot over there on the backside has been divided by the tracks, and all for what—a pittance for a ninety-nine year lease! Anyone who found a little spare cash by the agreement spent it long ago. A horse and wagon can't get over that berm they built up, leaving many woodlots high and dry. How's a man supposed to harvest his firewood with the railroad berm blocking his way?

"And you know the railroad dike has gone and cut off the Duck Creek flow down in Wellfleet, and it's shoaled up that boatyard up in there. Put them right out of business, it did, and all of Commercial Street along with them." Henry echoed and amplified his uncle's anti-railroad sentiments and then drained his coffee cup.

And so the discussion goes. A newcomer listening in would never guess that the event of the arrival of the railroad occurred years ago, when I was a little girl. None of the mariners are in favor of the obvious link that the railroad has provided to what I consider to be civilization. I never interrupt the men at their conversations, especially on this topic.

But I immensely appreciate the convenience of traveling by rail, even though I've only traveled twice with my parents to visit cousins in Provincetown. The trip over the moors and sand dunes of Truro took only a matter of hours, rather than the full day formerly required by the stagecoach. I would love to take an excursion again, and soon. However, I would not be so foolish as to announce this to the men during their smoking hour.

~

The hot weeks of summer have stretched far into September. I sew away the warmest hours of the day in the cool front parlor. Henry carried the Singer sewing machine there for me, and I happily work on a quilt when he is out to sea, even though the general opinion of the neighborhood ladies is that I am "cheating" because the quilt is not hand sewn. The root of the matter however, is the closely held notion that the quilt will suffer from the lack of fellowship it would have been blessed with had it been sewn by the hands of the neighborhood quilting group.

Whenever a sewing machine salesman turns his buggy down into Paine Hollow, the first housewife approached sends the man on his way. A sewing machine is viewed by our neighborhood housekeepers as a modern contraption which will do away with the hours of feminine social discourse that are the primary benefit of the weekly sewing circle—the resulting quilts and garments being important, but secondary.

Last spring, Winslow was caught at home alone by a persistent chap who took the Singer off the back of his buggy and gave Winslow a demonstration. When Arozana returned from her errands that day, she found the Singer sewing machine in her house, thus becoming the first lady in the neighborhood to own one. So strong is the resistance to the sewing machine that my mother never asked to enlist the Singer for help on the creation of my wedding dress, preferring to call upon the good ladies of the neighborhood sewing circle.

Sadly, I haven't learned to crochet or knit, and I am not patient enough to be successful at hand sewing. Thus, the sewing machine has provided salvation for my roaming, unemployed mind. I finished the log cabin quilt that Arozana started and put it on Winslow's bed, to his great pleasure. Now I am working on a quilt for our bed. I chose teal green, royal blue and purple as the three main colors, and find that I eagerly finish my chores every day so I can go into the cool parlor and work on the quilt.

The blend of ocean colors is soothing to me (and will be familiar to Henry), and the constant progress on the quilt assures me that I am creating something that will bring a sense of completion, unlike housework.

Besides the quilt, I have other work to do at the machine. One morning as I was piecing together a quilt square, I heard a rap at my kitchen door and found the Widower Cahoon, our community auctioneer, standing on the stoop.

"Good morning to you, Eva," he said in his singsong voice. "Would you be so kind as to consider taking on some mending for me?" His beseeching expression was enhanced by the silvery beard framing his weathered face. He went on before I could answer. "My coat here needs some repairs. I will pay you for your time, of course." Mr. Cahoon held out a dark blue coat.

I knew his coat was a quarter of a century old, having been issued to the auctioneer by the Union Army. Mr. Cahoon wore it all winter and to every formal occasion, including parades, funerals, auctions, and summer weddings.

I took it from him and examined the strained seams and the worn button holes. I found a generous seam allowance on the side seams, and I knew that even with my limited sewing experience, I could take out the seams and sew them up again, giving Mr. Cahoon the extra room he required for his expanded waistline. The faded wool was thin and worn, but I knew better than to suggest that the coat be replaced.

"This won't take me any time at all. You don't need to pay me, Mr. Cahoon," I said.

"That's not right, Eva, I cannot properly ask you to mend for me if you don't let me pay you. And I'd rather pay a seamstress to mend my clothes for me than look for a new wife." He chuckled at his own joke and opened a leather pouch, removing seventy-five cents. "If I give you this as a deposit, could you also sew on some new buttons?"

I tried to protest that I did not consider myself to be a seamstress, but he put a finger to his lips to silence me and pressed the coins into my hand. I looked down at the three quarters, and immediately thought of the train fare. If I could earn money, then I could justify planning an excursion—perhaps even to Boston, which seems to me a glittering city far beyond my reach, although many of my seafaring male relatives are familiar with her wharfs and supply companies.

And so, as surprising as it is to me, I've unexpectedly earned some money. Mr. Cahoon has happily spread the word that Mrs. Henry Smith repaired his beloved coat, resulting in people knocking on the door several times a week to drop off more mending. I silently thank Winslow every day for his well-intentioned purchase of the marvelous Singer sewing machine, and I thank Providence for giving me the hours alone without interruptions to learn how to properly operate the device.

The operating manual is very detailed, and I've begun using the special attachment provided for smocking and gathering. A dress is so easy to whip up—the long skirt seams sewn in a matter of minutes, rather than the hours it takes to stitch by hand.

I've been so engrossed with the sewing machine that Nettie was forced to come and find me because she had not seen me for several days.

"Eva, do you ever take a walk anymore? I haven't seen you lately," she said as soon as she walked into my parlor, her tone demanding an answer.

"I was just down at Mama's yesterday! I did stop by your door, but you were out." I rose to hug her.

She was perspiring from the walk and little beads of sweat showed on her face. I went to get her a wet washcloth to cool off with.

"Come into the kitchen, Nettie, and have some tea with me." A gallon jar of sun tea sat on the back porch rail, brewing gently in the warm rays. I brought the jar in and took some ice from the ice box. We sat down to a refreshing drink of peppermint tea over ice. Nettie looked around the kitchen.

"Why, I do believe you are putting your stamp on the premises, Mrs. Smith," she teased. "I love your quilted potholders hanging there on the hook. I didn't think it was possible, but you are truly becoming the model housekeeper."

"Matrimony has a way of shortening the path to that end quite quickly," I said. "And with Aunt Arozana gone—"

"I know, Eva. I just meant that you actually enjoy being in charge of the house."

"Yes, I do enjoy it," I said. "Although I have to admit I've had to throw out more than a few loaves of bread that didn't rise properly, and laundry is not my favorite chore. I particularly hate to iron, and I've burned the back of Henry's white shirt. Now I'll have to rip it out and replace it before he gets back in. Mama was always so efficient that I didn't realize I had so much to learn!" This admittance sounded strange to my ears. "But Henry and his father work so hard out on the water that it's only fair I work hard here at home," I said.

"Speaking of which, I have some news for you," Nettie said. "I have accepted a position as housekeeper for Deacon Bentley."

I pictured old Deacon Bentley in my mind. The feeble man is in his eighties and still manages to arrive at church every Sunday, come rain or shine. He stations himself at the crossroads of Paine Hollow and the county road and stops every conveyance rolling towards the Wellfleet churches until he finds one that has seating for him. Deacon Bentley does not mind riding to town with Methodists, but he is a very devout parishioner of the First Congregational Church of Wellfleet—very solemn and serious in his intonations during the church service, even though he can no longer hear Reverend Pike's sermon.

"Oh, no," I said. "You're not going to be spending your time in Deacon Bentley's house, are you? You will suffocate in his house—it is so closed up and stuffy." I heard the horror in my own voice.

"I choose to do this," Nettie said. "It's work I have taken for pay. Deacon Bentley needs someone to cook and clean for him, and Dr. Brown recommended me for the position."

"You will never meet anyone if you become Deacon Bentley's housekeeper," I protested.

Nettie made a face at me. "I have told you time and time again that I don't want to be married," Nettie said. "I don't *want* a husband—or children, for that matter. I can be quite content just putting things in order for other people and being paid for it. You do all that I will be doing and more, and you don't get paid for it. You just have to do it."

"Oh, Nettie," I exclaimed. "How can you say that? I love keeping house for my husband. Being married is wonderful. I only want the same thing for you—this bond of closeness and understanding between a man and a woman. You will not get that by keeping house for an old man, pardon me for saying so."

"Eva, be still now. I will be happy. I *am* happy. I look forward to tackling the deacon's house. I don't think anyone has been in there to do much since his wife died. I will have Thursdays off, and I will still have my social life in the evening. I'll continue to be secretary and treasurer of the Ladies' Social Union. Please, Eva, be happy with me. I enjoy the prospect of actually earning some money."

"What will you do with money? It seems as though you have everything you need provided for you by your parents!" I had no idea why I threw this unkind remark at Nettie. I suppose I was still upset that my spunky friend was planning to disappear behind the doors of Deacon Bentley's house.

"Who wouldn't want their own money—to buy their own books, to buy fabric for a new dress now and then, or to save for the future?" Nettie was impatient with me, I could see it. And now I was beginning to feel uncomfortable, as I had a secret that I should be sharing with her, my best friend.

"All right, Nettie. You're right," I conceded. "Of course a woman should have some money of her own. Come with me, I want to show you something. I'm afraid I haven't been forthcoming with you."

I brought her to the front parlor and opened the closet door. There was a neat pile of folded clothing in a laundry basket. I pointed to it.

"This mending was dropped off by the men folk who have no women in their homes to keep their clothes in order." I closed the closet door, and then opened a trunk set against the wall. "And here—bolts of fabric brought to me just yesterday by Captain Horace Doane's wife, all the way from Wellfleet center. She has four children and an infant and no time to sew for the new school year. Here are the patterns she brought me for the dresses and breeches."

Nettie's mouth hung open. "Eva, how will you ever get this done? Just months ago, you were helpless in the matter of sewing your own wedding dress."

"Helpless then, but I did observe how all the pieces fit together. Even though it took six women to finish the dress for me, I could now put it together in three days by myself. The Singer is just a wonder. I love it. And I can earn some money, too." I grinned in delight. I wanted Nettie to share my high regard for the sewing machine, even though I was breaking with neighborhood tradition. I sat down at the machine and put a scrap piece of folded fabric under the pressure foot.

"Watch," I commanded her. I put my foot on the treadle and rocked it back and forth, simultaneously turning the silver wheel with my hand to help get it started. The cable from the treadle turned the wheel, which raised the needle up and down. The needle reached the end of the seam in seconds.

"Now, reverse." I lifted a shiny lever to show Nettie how the sewing machine could stitch backwards. "This locks the seam and keeps it from unraveling." I clipped the thread, and handed the cloth to Nettie for examination.

"Pull on the seam," I said.

She did, and opened it to examine the stitches.

"How can the stitches be so tight?" she asked.

"There are two pieces of thread, one you see here coming from the top of the machine and passing through the needle, and one thread coming up from the bobbin, which is under the pressure foot plate. These threads lock together on every stitch. And I can make the stitches shorter or longer by adjusting this lever, and I can make them looser or tighter by turning this knob."

"Eva, how did you ever learn all of this?"

"I read the manual. And stitched and ripped and stitched and ripped until I got it right! It's not hard when you have time on your hands. When Henry's out, I sew for hours. It passes the time, and I love to see the results!" I showed her a child's blue silk dress and white pinafore hanging in the closest—complete with French smocking across the bodice.

"A special attachment," I said as she fingered the even rows of puckers. "This dress is a surprise for little five-year old Rebecca Townsend. She will look so pretty in it. I made it for practice from some scraps left over from my wedding dress. And now, here is the best part."

I opened the bottom drawer of the desk and took out a small wooden box. Together we looked inside at the accumulation of coin and paper money.

"That is almost ten dollars. I have suddenly become a seamstress. I am suddenly earning money." I said.

"What does Henry think?" Nettie asked.

"Henry says that he is happy if I am happy while he is gone. He knows I'm earning money, but he doesn't know how much. To tell you the truth, I am surprised by how much I've taken in just this week—at least three dollars."

Nettie was impressed. "You did well to figure this machine out. Look at this complicated manual—these diagrams, they are so confusing," she said.

"Not at all, Nettie. You could do it, too," I encouraged her. "If I were you, I would save for a machine. Come on, sit down, and I will give you a lesson. But you can come and use this one anytime, really."

I spent the rest of the afternoon teaching Nettie how to make a log cabin quilt square on the machine. She then went further and sewed on a backing, creating a sachet pillowcase. When she got ready to go home, she held the pillowcase in her hands and marveled at the straight seams and durable outcome.

"Spread the word, Nettie," I encouraged her. "We women have to step into the machine age along with the men. Because of this sewing machine, I will soon be able to take a trip to Boston. And I want you to come, too. I'll ask Henry and see if he wants to come with us. Even if he doesn't, you and I will go to the Museum of Fine Arts. I've always wanted to visit the museum."

Nettie smiled broadly.

"Aunt Arozana would be so proud of what you are doing with her machine. What are you going to spend all your money on? You'll earn far more than enough to cover train fares and museum admissions."

"Along with a few little extras that I want for myself and a little more for the offering plate at church, I'd like to propose a fundraiser to the Ladies Social Union for the cause of winning the women's vote,"

I said. "I think it's high time we helped to *fund* Susan B. Anthony. It's wonderful that we passed the resolution to publicly support her at the last meeting, but we could go further. Miss Anthony is always on the lecture circuit, and travel is expensive. Besides just voicing my support, I've decided to open my pocketbook. If I start the fund with a donation, that gesture may get the other ladies thinking in the direction of financially supporting Miss Anthony, rather than just expecting her to get the job done for us."

"Yes, an initial donation would get some attention," Nettie said. "I wish I had the courage that Miss Anthony has to speak in public on women's suffrage. She certainly deserves more than lip service in the way of support. She's been at it for as long as I can remember. I'll make sure to put you on the agenda for the next meeting so you can speak to this yourself. Your example will be a good start, Eva, and for those who can't financially donate, they can lend a hand at the fundraising event."

"Mama actually suggested the idea to me. I can't take the credit for it."

"Your mother! That doesn't sound like Aunt Sarah at all."

"It's true," I said. "Mama's had her dander up ever since we read the news that the Statue of Liberty is finally being dedicated this October. You have to admit that it's an ironic situation that the whole country is clamoring to celebrate a female statue representing liberty when females don't even have the right to vote. Mama says we will never have it unless we develop the spine to support the cause right here in our own little social union."

"Agreed," Nettie said. "We have to do more than just make resolutions. I'll begin to research the best way to correspond with Miss Anthony and order some of her pamphlets for the club. We could take a vote on a monthly donation pledge to Miss Anthony."

"Thank you, Nettie," I said. "You're so efficient. And I do wish you luck with Deacon Bentley." I grimaced as I said the words.

"Silly Eva," Nettie said. "If I were married, as you seem to so desire, I would have far less time to be your efficient secretary and treasurer—in fact, I might have no time at all."

I knew she was teasing me. A husband and children could never stop Nettie from getting a lot done. She is the most efficient person that I know, and I envy her for that. I also envy the fact that she knows her own mind and has no struggle with her decisions.

After Nettie gathered her belongings and said her good-byes, I returned to the sewing machine. I sat down to another dress for Rebecca Townsend. Clive Townsend has been so kind to my mother through the years in letting her know exactly when my father sails in. I am happy to practice my new skills by outfitting his youngest daughter with the dresses she needs for church and her first year of primary school.

I have an ulterior motive. I will be proficient at sewing children's clothing when the time comes for me to sew for my own. The good Lord has not yet gifted me with pregnancy. All in good time, I am sure. However, I cannot say that I am patient. It is becoming a concern to me that Henry and I have frequent relations with no result. But, we have been married for only four months. I have no call to be so concerned. Henry is not concerned. I will not be concerned.

~

CHAPTER FIVE
Seventy Times Seven

September 24, 1886
Disappointment

The suddenness of the end of romance is startling. Does romance return? I am alone in my sewing room—very busy, purposefully. It is the first time I have designed an avoidance of my husband.

Two nights ago, Henry sailed into the harbor in a frightful mood. The *Dora Freeman* had snapped her main mast in a squall, and she limped home with only the jibs and foresail canvas to push her on her way. The unfortunate event occurred while the first mate was on watch and Henry slept below. Henry did not tell me about the incident when he came home. He greeted me with frigid silence, but he left his log book on the kitchen table, awaiting delivery to the owner of the *Dora Freeman*. I turned the pages back from the end until I found the source of the trouble.

> *September 22, 1886: Daybreak commences with freshening breezes. We are heading southeast off Nantucket, following a mackerel school. Seine net has been filled twice this morning, ten barrels filled. Noon—a change in the wind from southwest to southeast. Light chop increasing to heavy chop ends our fishing today. All hands employed with clearing the decks and prepar-*

ing to sail home. Mate Pierce to bring her home on his watch. 7PM. Squall weather encountered while heading northwest; left my berth to arrive on deck to gale force winds at thirty knots. Main mast snapped before main sail could be lowered. Lost mast and main sail overboard in order to save vessel. Lines had to be cut. Squall passed over by 8PM. Midnight: Have put in at Nantucket Harbor to offload mackerel and make preparations to sail home with one mast. So ends these twenty-four hours.

Master Henry W. Smith

From the sharp exchanges between Henry and his father regarding "the fool," I have heard Henry's opinion that Mr. Pierce did not head into the wind quickly enough when the squall came up. The mate has been let go, I am sure, but the damages are severe, and the vessel's owner is none too pleased that the anticipated profits from the catch will be going towards repairs. A day was lost at Nantucket Harbor, preparing the *Dora Freeman* for her limp home. Now she is being refitted with a new mast over at Stubbs Boatyard. Henry wonders if he will keep his position as master.

I must breathe deeply and proceed calmly, trying to influence Henry with intelligent concern. I believe this is what I should do, although it has not helped the relations between us thus far. Henry hardly seems to notice my presence unless he is bellowing for something he cannot find. And there he is, calling to me again.

~

I am unsettled, and I frequently find myself with pencil in hand, writing out my thoughts, because I don't want to discuss Henry's foul moods with anyone. Perhaps I've erred by acquiescing to the Disagreeable Henry, as I've named that part of him in my mind, in a manner that was sure to continue his behavior. One does not let a bad dog get away with unfriendly behavior, or a bad horse, for that matter.

Young wives (and old wives, too, I have observed) are in the habit of responding to their husbands' tempers by becoming too accommodating. I do believe this has been my mistake. Perhaps I should simply refuse to acknowledge Henry's foul moods, just as a lady refuses to acknowledge a drunkard on the railroad platform.

But knowing what I should do and being able to carry that out are two different matters. Henry is certainly capable of resurrecting the anger my mother remembered him exercising as a boy. I must go back and acknowledge the incident that discouraged me just before Henry left on this ill fated voyage.

~

There is a place for everything in this house. By the end of the summer, there was no question that one of Arozana's prime functions had been to keep track of every possession and item that resides in the Smith household—her own possessions, Winslow's possessions, and especially Henry's possessions. Henry does not put his belongings away in their assigned places; he sets them down on top of whatever furniture crosses his path as he strides from one room to the next, performing a never-ending list of tasks that he must complete in order to set out on a voyage.

What Arozana did so well was to follow after Henry at a respectful distance when he entered the house and pick up anything and everything that Henry set down. Then, she would put things away in their intended places: keys to key hooks; hat to the hat peg; boots to the back shed; books to the bookshelf; tools to the back kitchen tool cabinet; scissors to the top desk drawer; wallet to the shelf near the grandfather clock in the hallway. When Henry wanted an item, it was always where he expected it to be.

The trouble is, I had no inkling after the short time I spent with Aunt Arozana that I should follow her example. I had no conception of how dependent Henry really was upon the mother hen behavior that Arozana so enjoyed, and I don't believe Henry did, either. Further, I didn't know all the locations or places were items should be or had been placed for years. When I put the scissors in the kitchen drawer instead of in the top desk drawer, I found out through Winslow's unexpected impatience that things, indeed, do have their proper place.

Winslow called to me with a stern voice early one morning as I was making beds, "Eva, *where* are the scissors?" He had looked for them in their habitual location, which I had unwittingly changed. I rushed down the stairs to find the scissors for him, thinking that the strength of his emotion had much to do with the fact that he was in mourning for his wife. Quickly, I rushed to the kitchen and handed the scissors to Winslow, assuming that all would be well now.

"Thank you, Eva, but they belong *here*." He was unappreciative of my effort. I turned to Henry in amazement, but he nodded a solemn agreement. Thus I learned to be aware of the expected locations of household items that the two men live their lives by, all pre-established for decades by my dear late mother-in-law.

If I harbored an assumption that I was the new mistress of the house, and therefore would be respected as such by the men, I was wrong. Because the men have strongly indicated that they wish nothing to change, I struggle to keep house for Henry and his father by trying to replicate the way Aunt Arozana did it.

Under the circumstances, I've done rather well at this task, especially in the case of following around after Winslow. He is neat and tidy, and he almost always puts things back where they belong. I watched him to learn the expected location of all items. He also takes meticulous care of his own possessions.

Henry, my own husband, has proven to be the harder one to please. If I do not get directly on Henry's trail from the moment he enters the house, I will miss seeing where he flings down his possessions as he walks through.

The evening before his departure on the unfortunate fishing trip, Henry misplaced his wallet. Together, Henry and I searched high and low for the missing item which held his identification papers and money from the boat's owner should Henry need to go ashore for supplies while away from homeport. As he searched, Henry became more and more agitated, pulling drawers out and spilling them on the floor. He scattered papers and documents from one end of his desk to the other with a sweep of his arm as I stood by, incredulous. In minutes, the room was in a shambles.

"Henry, Henry, please, let me look," I tried to help him. "I will look for the wallet, you get ready for tomorrow."

I knew I could find the wallet if only Henry would calm down.

"I *need* that wallet, Eva, or I won't be going anywhere!" His face was red.

I began to search a bookcase, but he grabbed my right wrist to move me away so he could look. I jumped away from him, and he let go his vise-like grip. I grabbed onto my wrist with my left hand, wincing in pain. He looked at my face and grew all the more angry.

"Eva, I'm sorry, but you are in my way," he shouted at me. "You can't seem to keep this house in order. I will find what I need. Go to bed," he ordered in a stern voice, as if I was a deck hand.

I left the room. I did not want to go to bed; I could not go to bed. I went through the back door and out to the hand pump in the yard. There I pumped cold water over my wrist as angry tears dripped down my face. How could I be in this position? I wanted the comfort of my own girlhood bedroom, where no man entered in. I wanted to be gone from the Smith homestead that very moment. I had done nothing wrong, and there was no good reason for me to be treated in such a manner. Aunt Arozana had played a cruel trick on me, training her son in this way and then leaving me to deal with him and her husband. *For better or for worse*—I promised just months ago.

I heard Henry rummaging loudly through the house. I watched him through the window from the safety of the yard, thinking to myself that I could just run down the road and be at my old home in a very short time. It took everything not to do it. I held tightly to the rough trunk of the pine tree where I'd washed dozens of loads of clothes for Henry and his father.

Finally Henry went to the bottom of the stairs. "Eva," he shouted, "I found it."

The soft lamplight glowing from within made the house appear as unreal as a stage setting. Did I want to enter upon that stage again? No, I did not, but I had no choice. Slowly, the angry protests left my mind and my sobbing subsided. I had not cried so hard since I was a little girl.

Henry continued to move around in the house, packing for his voyage. Winslow had already retired to his room, wisely getting out of Henry's way when the search for the wallet began. Soon Henry himself climbed the stairs. In a matter of seconds, he was back down them again and out in the yard, frantically looking for me. By the moonlight, he found me sitting at the well, my eyes puffy and swollen. His demeanor changed instantaneously.

"I am so sorry, Eva. Please excuse my terrible temper." He picked me up as if I were a little child and sat down on the bench with me on his lap. He stroked my hair and held me to his chest. I couldn't say anything for a while, shuddering with the remnants of my crying fit.

"Where did you find it?" I had to ask.

"In the pantry," he said. "I must have put it down there when I went in to get one of your cookies earlier today."

I sobbed again, in spite of my resolve not to do so.

"I am really sorry, Eva. Can you forgive me?" Henry asked me this with his most gentle voice. I knew I couldn't forgive him yet, not truly. I was still so upset, and my throbbing wrist reminded me of the unreasonable anger my husband had displayed. But I thought that I would be able to forgive him soon, as I should. Seventy times seven—that is what the Lord Jesus recommended as the number of times we should forgive someone a transgression, according to the Gospel of Matthew.

"Yes, Henry, I do forgive you," I said. "It's a worrisome time for you right now as you prepare to go out." As I said it, I knew I'd said too much and should not have given him an excuse to act so terribly towards me.

"That's my girl," He patted my head again and tried to take my hand. I whimpered in pain.

"What's the matter?"

"My wrist hurts. I think it may be sprained."

"Did I do that?" he asked. "How did I do that? You are as tender as a child, Eva. You are as delicate as a flower. We've got to build you up." He took me by the other hand and said, "Come up to bed. I won't be seeing you for a fortnight. Let's just forget about this and start anew."

I didn't reply. I thought of the laundry and how I wouldn't be able to do it for several days with a sprained wrist. We went into the kitchen through the back door.

"I need a bandage, Henry. Help me with that before we go up."

Henry demonstrated his prowess with medical situations. We found a swath of linen in Arozana's box of medical supplies. Henry wrapped my wrist to keep it stationary for the night and then made a cold compress with a dish towel and ice. We walked through the house together, blowing out the lamps as we went. I tried not to look at the condition of the rooms as we passed through; they were chaotic and disorderly beyond belief, from the kitchen to the front parlor. It would take me days to sort things out so I could receive company through the front door.

We climbed the stairs, and Henry helped me undress. I concentrated on keeping my right hand and wrist away from him so he wouldn't hurt it further. I thought of a peaceful pond in the woods I know of, the beautiful layers of transparent blues and greens. In this way, I kept myself from crying while I allowed him to enter me and rock himself to contentment. He soon snored soundly beside me. I could not sleep.

I was greatly relieved when Henry left early the next morning. But now he is back, and with this broken mast affair, in a worse mood than ever. I do hope it lifts soon. I wonder how long the "worse" can last with Henry. I am ready for the "better" again. In the meantime, I am completing many sewing tasks.

～

October, 1886

Astonishingly, I've met with much success in my new enterprise. Here I am, happily sewing the hours away. This windfall is timely, as Mr. Avery has released the final numbers of the fishing season, and it's confirmed beyond any doubt that far fewer barrels of mackerel were taken this past summer than previously.

I point out to Henry, if he is in a mood to listen to me, that the mackerel can swim where they want to. To my mind, there is nothing to prevent them from abandoning their annual expected migration from their mysterious southern location to the northeast waters in the spring, and back south again in the fall. But Henry states that the mackerel will always swim the same route, even though they have the big wide ocean to swim. He says that the mighty schools have been fished out and blames the Gloucester fleet. His opinion is one to be respected, as Henry has once again earned the title of "High-Liner." The *Dora Freeman* brought in the most money for the vessel owner and crew members, and thus for our own household. Henry is proud of his success but does not mention it in public. Other captains and crews were not so fortunate.

Since the numbers were published, the general morale of the whole village has been one of discouragement. Much talk has gone on about the *death of the industry*. Many families have left already, moving closer to Boston and factory employment. I can't imagine

Henry doing anything like that, ever. Even if the fish disappear totally, I know he could never permanently remove himself from the sea.

Now that I have been Henry's wife for five months, I know he anticipates each voyage with every fiber in his body. His life is a cycle of preparing to leave, being out there on the water, sailing triumphantly home, and preparing for the next voyage.

The weather is still mild for October, and he wants to go out for cod, he says, before the vessels are pulled ashore for the winter. We have no Grand Banks schooners here in our little harbor, but Henry says there is no need to sail as far as the Banks—he will find the cod off the back shore as they migrate south for the winter. And so, he and Winslow and my father and my brother Lewis are going cod fishing on the *Nautilus* for the pure fun of it, I know. Of course, they are saying it is for the purposes of bringing in some cod fish for the family to put by for the winter, and to make a little money as well.

Practicing my developing household arithmetic, I have pointed out to Henry that it will cost more money to stock the *Nautilus* galley with vitals for four hungry men than it would cost to simply buy the cod fish from someone else, but Henry won't hear of that. They have to eat anyway, he says, whether here at home or out on the water. Tomorrow they are off to round Provincetown and head east of Truro off Highland Light. And since they are so adamant to have their fun, I have a little plan of my own. I am going to Boston by train.

The sewing money I've earned has not only paid for train tickets to Boston and allowed me to be more generous with my donations to the church and the Ladies Social Union; it has also been a welcome addition to the household budget. I reason that if I truly believe that women are equal to men, as I do espouse at every Ladies Social Union meeting, then I must act more like my male counterpart when it comes to money and use it for household expense and maintenance.

Therefore, I have decided to put two thirds of my earnings towards the household expenses and keep one third for myself. In this way, I am giving equal shares to the other two members of the household. After all, Henry and Winslow put all of their income after expenses towards the household.

I luckily find that I am not attracted to all the fashion finery—jewelry and ribbons and imported laces and silks, nor the extravagant household goods illustrated in the mail order catalogs— the fancy furniture, the latest ironstone dinnerware patterns, the crystal vases, the bedspreads, the drapes. This house is so full of things that must be cared for and put away that I do not want more. Further, living here in South Wellfleet, I think that it will be some time before we are electrified. Many of the things that are available to the public now would not function here, as we have no electric power to connect to. I am happy with my kerosene oil lamps and my treadle sewing machine. Besides, electricity will bring with it a monthly bill to be paid.

Books are my weakness. Mr. Blackwell, the astute book salesman, knows that I am frequently alone and have money of my own to spend. One lonely rainy day, I made the mistake of buying a book from him when I thought that a new book would cheer me. I kept it out of Henry's sight, as he says that Jane Austen was romantic and ridiculous, but I immensely enjoyed reading *Pride and Prejudice* once again, as this is the third time I have read it. I could have borrowed a copy from Miss Gross, my former English teacher. I was perhaps a bit hasty in purchasing it, but I do plan to lend it out as frequently as asked. But how wonderful that I do not have to ask for what I want; I can buy it myself from my earnings.

I have purchased train tickets for Nettie as well. We are going to visit with our former schoolmate, Annabelle Holbrook Crandle, who has moved to Boston as the new wife of a young banker. We are to take tea together at the Museum of Fine Arts in Copley Square, and I am so very excited. Having read many accounts of city life,

I am curious to experience Boston myself. My brown serge suit is nothing fancy, but it fits wonderfully. Mama says I cut quite a figure in it, and so I shall not be ashamed to wear it.

Nettie and I are to stay overnight at the rooms of Deacon Bentley's sister, arranged by Nettie. And Mama is to come feed and water the horses and chickens while we are away. Henry thinks this is all a bit excessive, but he has not protested too much; he is so anxious to get out to the cod. It is a beautiful October with no hard frost yet, and I am looking forward to seeing the swan boats in the Boston Public Gardens. Perhaps it is a good thing that I have not yet conceived, as I would never consider traveling if I were in the expectant condition.

Every month, I anxiously hope and pray that my menses will not visit me, but it always does. If Henry is in, of course he knows that I am in such a state. He is quite tender with me during that week, and readily forfeits our evening bedtime habit of marital relations. He does take notice of my discomfort, as I can barely uncurl myself to get out of bed in the morning.

At first, it was extremely embarrassing to have to spend the night with my husband in bed next to me during this time. I wished I had a separate bedroom to go to so I could suffer alone. I am mortified when Henry gets a glimpse of blood on the sheets should the padding not hold through the night. But he takes it much better than I do, laughing and saying that it is all part of life—he has seen plenty of blood before. He rubs my back, and has brought smooth warm stones to me, heated on the wood stove.

"How did you know this would help?" I asked him after I first experienced the comforting warmth. I had never heard of the remedy.

Of course, he knew because his mother had used warm stones.

"You can't live in a house with a woman all your life and not know when she's having her time of the month," he said. "Mother suffered terribly, and she would always send me to the kitchen for the stones while she lay upon the couch. You know she didn't have a daughter to help her—it was me."

Henry does have his finer points. I have just been visited by my menses, which although disappointing, is very timely. I shall not have to worry that it will come upon me as I travel to Boston. I cannot imagine how women simultaneously handle traveling and dealing with the extreme toilet and mounds of extra laundry. Men certainly do have a much easier time of traveling, with none of the anxious concerns that women do as we plan around the ebb and flow of our own interior tides.

~

October 15, 1886
An Excursion

I have been to Boston, and think that perhaps I will not go again, as I was unhappy for days upon my return home. The culture in Boston was so stimulating that when I turned my thoughts towards Paine Hollow, my existence seemed as modest as a brown moth. But I found a sharp edge of rudeness in my friend Annabelle's new city manners.

I must concentrate on my life here at home and be exceedingly grateful for my blessings. This conclusion is underscored by the fact that although Annabelle Holbrook Crandle was hospitable to Nettie and me in sharing her new world, she was publicly inconsiderate in her remarks to me regarding my marriage to Henry. Apparently, Annabelle's new station in life as a banker's wife has caused her to become very arrogant and opinionated, and she forgets the town from which she springs. It is distressing. I am sending Annabelle the proper thank you correspondence, of course, and will post it tomorrow so I can put her out of my mind.

~

To be sure, the sights of Boston were gratifying beyond my imagination. The many churches and halls that sheltered our country's revolution one hundred and ten years ago are inspirational, even as the city grows around them and new buildings dwarf the seminal structures where John Adams, John Hancock, Paul Revere, and Robert Treat Paine—a distant ancestor—once held forth.

The paintings at the Museum of Fine Arts astonished me. I had no previous notion that a painting could be so large and at the same time so perfectly detailed. The vibrant colors and perspectives of so many gifted artists and sculptors were overwhelming.

I chose John Singleton Copley as my favorite. The man was a genius in depicting colonial scenes with great accuracy, and he also painted the most realistic life sized portraits. I looked into the eyes of Paul Revere. I almost curtsied for British General Thomas Gage and his wife—who was dressed in a coral red gown while reclining on a royal blue sofa—both long dead, but looking as present as viewing them through a mirror. One wealthy subject, a Mrs. Daniel Denison Rogers, wore a pearl gray silk gown and the most amazing plumed hat which threatened to fly off her head in the breeze that blew her scarf out in a graceful swirl. To be so beautifully captured in oils is to be memorialized in the kindest way.

Annabelle and her new husband, the successful banker Robert Crandle, kindly treated Nettie and me to an evening symphony at the Boston Music Hall. I am at a complete loss to describe on paper the heavenly sounds of a full orchestra. The combined effort of fifty gifted musicians transported me. I closed my eyes to listen as we sat in our balcony seats. I thus avoided openly staring at the ornately bejeweled women seated nearby with their attending gentlemen dressed in formal regalia. It was all so grand that I hardly dared to look around me.

Never have I felt that I would like to have more than what my neighbors possess here in South Wellfleet. Never have I begrudged those Wellfleetians who have prospered: our banana importer and founder of the Boston Fruit Company, Lorenzo Dow Baker; my distant cousins, the Young's, who have stepped into the banking business; or Isaac Rich, God rest his soul, my mother's late cousin—street fishmonger turned seafood businessman—so successful that he left a founding fortune to the Boston Wesleyan University. Our little vicinity here on Cape Cod is nothing to be ashamed of. We have done well by the world.

But I must confess that I am envious of the cultural atmosphere of Boston. The reality of it startled me. I have read all about it on the printed pages of the newspapers, but to experience it, to smell it, to hear it, to see it in all of its vibrancy—I have now experienced envy. I know that my life with Henry will not include many days in the city, or any kind of life that approaches that electric excitement.

But the stinging remark that Annabelle made at the art museum is an unpleasant memory so strong that it clamors for my attention over all the other experiences of my visit. It will eventually fade from my memory, and I shall only remember the beautifully vaulting roof of the gallery and the charming accompaniment of pianoforte as we ate confectionaries that melted in our mouths.

Annabelle wore the most fetching maroon velvet dress and jacket which caused her to be as beautiful as the paintings we viewed. With her low décolleté, I dare say she garnered as many looks from the ladies and gentlemen that viewed with us as the paintings themselves did, and I go a bit further to offer the opinion that this was exactly what she was hoping for. We sat on the couch in the museum foyer, teacups and saucers balanced on our knees.

"So tell me, ladies," Annabelle said in an animated manner she has adopted, "What is the latest news? Nettie, how about you—have you attracted any prospective suitors worthy of your attention?"

"I am sorry that I have nothing that you would regard as newsworthy to report," Nettie told her. "As Eva knows, I am not interested in marriage, I'm not in pursuit of anyone, and I'm certainly not encouraging anyone who may be in pursuit of me."

"Oh, Nettie. What will become of you?" asked Annabelle, crinkling her face as if she had bit into a lemon.

I had to giggle, having heard this from Nettie many times before.

"I don't know what will become of me, Annabelle," Nettie said in her declarative way, "But no one knows that in advance about themselves. Whatever becomes of me, it will be by my own actions and decisions.

"What I do know is what will *not* become of me. I will not be a wife to a demanding and unappreciative lout, and I will not spend my evenings toiling to catch up on all the work of a family household. I am quite content to spend the hours I have alone reading or tending to my knitting and sewing." Nettie added a spoonful of white sugar to her tea. Her teaspoon made a tinkling sound against the china cup as she stirred.

"And regarding my position as housekeeper for Deacon Bentley, it is quite enjoyable. The place is cheerful and sunny, and he is very appreciative. I leave him in the late afternoon when he is content. I return in the morning, and he is happy to see me. And I am paid enough so that I have all that I need. I enjoy living with my mother and father, and am really quite happy. "

"Such a simple life, Nettie," Annabelle said. "You were brilliant in high school, and Eva right along beside you. I always admired both of you, and missed you when your class graduated. You two scholars from South Wellfleet brought something to the Wellfleet High School that my class couldn't replicate—the class of '82 was a hard act to follow. You could have so much more than what little South Wellfleet has to offer—don't you ever want more?" Annabelle dramatically flung her arms out, as if to embrace the museum and the city around it.

"Boston society is so exciting," she continued. "Robert's cousin, Miss Lydia Crandle, is patron to one of the most frequented salons on Newbury Street, and I've met so many brilliant feminine thinkers. Both of you would do very well in the discussions—far better then I ever will."

"Thank you for the compliments, Annabelle," Nettie said. "But I don't think I could live in Boston. It's far too chaotic."

"Why Nettie, of course you could, you have no husband to hold you back as Eva does. It would be so enjoyable if you would move here and join me on the social rounds. We just had Susan B. Anthony come speak at the salon, and her speech inflamed us! We American women *must* continue to pursue the vote. How could we be so backwards in this country that former slaves have the vote, but educated women do not, unless they live out in those godless western territories? My friends, you would both be so useful in this pursuit!" Annabelle lowered her chin dramatically as if to share a confidence, but kept right on at the same volume.

"Next week we are traveling down to New York City for the unveiling of the Statue of Liberty. We aim to protest vehemently on the women's vote issue, and what better venue? We have hired our own launch to take us out into the harbor."

"We are involved, Annabelle," I had to chime in. Envy shot through me when Annabelle mentioned the Statue of Liberty, and I couldn't let her think that only women from Boston had this cause in their hearts.

"The South Wellfleet Ladies Social Union has created a suffrage fund, and we are currently sending donations to Miss Anthony. We plan to indefinitely donate a percentage of the admission fees from our entertainments. And we'd love to see any literature that you have from her talk at your salon," I said.

Annabelle's brow crumpled into a scowl and she ignored my request.

"Of course, we raise funds as well," she said. "Some of these Bostonian ladies place hundreds of dollars on a weekly basis at the disposal of the cause. You will never be able to compete with that from South Wellfleet."

I could not bear the implication that Nettie and I were lesser persons due to Annabelle's meteoric rise in fortune and her prestigious new relations on Newbury Street.

"I don't think that the point is to compete—I'm sure Miss Anthony appreciates all the support she receives, no matter what the amount. If we are all working on the same cause, what difference does it make if some can donate more money? I think it's marvelous that women are donating a hundred dollars at a time, and all the more so if it is their husband's money! After all, every man has a mother." I spoke in a pleasant tone, but I wanted to make an impression on Annabelle.

"Nettie and I earn our own money, be it modest or not, and we donate a portion of it to Miss Anthony's fund. If we all do what we can, we will eventually persevere." I tried to make my voice light, but I was not practiced in the art of engaging in a political conversation in a public place, and my face was burning red. I was certain that the museum patrons seated on the adjacent couches were judging my every word.

Annabelle seized her advantage.

"Eva, you would have been so much more useful to the cause had you not gone and married your *cousin*!" she loudly declared. "Such a provincial custom, with possibly disastrous consequences for your future children."

I was stricken. The conversation of other patrons buzzed in my ears, and I heard a roaring sound, as if ocean waves were breaking outside upon the museum steps. My corset was far too constricting and I could not get a breath.

"That was a very unkind and untrue remark, Annabelle," Nettie adeptly evaluated the remark before responding to it. "The truth is that Henry and Eva are *not* cousins. They are second cousins, and there is a generation of separation between the two distinctions. For your clarification, this means that between them, Eva and Henry share one set of great-grandparents out of the eight sets between them." Nettie talked in a low voice, but it was loud enough for any eavesdropper to catch her words.

"This is a common and safe type of union—one I am sure you will find prevalent in the most privileged of families in Boston society. So do be careful to whom you pronounce your opinions, my dear, as you do not know how your new friends are related. You may be insulting the very people you wish to impress!" Nettie finished calmly, as if she was tutoring a young student and hoping for the best results.

"Of course you're right, Nettie," Annabelle exclaimed. "I certainly meant no harm, Eva." She smoothly went on. "I'm sure you and Henry will be happily blessed with many healthy children."

She stood and fluffed her velvet skirt.

"Let's take a buggy down to the Public Gardens." Annabelle smiled at us as though no insult had been passed. "You must see the park before sunset. The maples are all blazing golden this time of year. And then it will be time for us to go our separate ways to refresh for the symphony this evening."

Annabelle took my elbow as we left the museum and went down the steps to Copley Square. I distracted myself by taking in the massive silhouette of the Boston Public Library across the square from us and thinking that the entire population of the town of Wellfleet would easily fit inside the building. I wondered at the thousands of books the library could accommodate and wished I had the time to thumb through the card indexes. Annabelle was speaking into my ear.

"Don't be cross with me, Eva, I meant no harm. Please don't tell anyone what I said—it was unkind of me."

"It's forgotten, Annabelle," I said. "We all say things we don't mean from time to time."

I surmised she did not want the story that she had been so insulting to me told around her hometown. I assured her I would never mention it, because I certainly would not.

But through her rudeness, Annabelle had alerted me as to what other acquaintances could be thinking. Why would Annabelle be the only one to hold that opinion? Was there some modicum of truth to the notion that Henry and I should never have married? Would our familial relationship negatively affect the health of our children? Or would the Lord punish me and prevent me from conceiving? Were we naïve country folk?

The questions swirled around in my head. I reminded myself that before our marriage, I had consulted Reverend Moss on the matter, and he had assured me that all was well. But judging the simplicity of Wellfleet "society" and Wellfleet "experts" from the distance of the Boston Public Gardens, I worried that perhaps Reverend Moss was incorrect. I fought off the invading shame and concentrated on the sights before me: the statues, the walkways, the strolling Bostonians, and our magnificent Capitol Building just to the east of us up on Beacon Hill— the brilliant dome completely gilded in gold leaf, I wondered at what expense to the taxpayers. Nettie and Annabelle and I circled the pond, crossed a bridge, and found the famed swan boats drawn up out of the water, waiting to be dismantled for winter storage. I was disappointed.

I could only buy a post card of the idyllic scene the little barges create during the temperate months. The post card illustrates a swan boat carrying six garden benches of passengers, all lined up in a row. A boatman sits back at the stern, operating a bicycle-like contraption which is cleverly shielded between two immense wooden swans. The glassy surface of the artificial pond provides the perfect environment for the amusing craft. The overcrowded swan boat wouldn't last two minutes in the waves of Wellfleet Harbor. We *sail* across the harbor for a picnic on Billingsgate Island. We have no use for swan boats.

Looking down through the water, I saw that the depth was quite shallow, and ducks had clouded the water with their manure. I shuddered at the thought of falling in. I am accustomed to clear blue ponds—so clean that we cut the ice in the winter and use it to cool our drinks all summer.

The remainder of our visit was tainted by the conversation at the art museum. My enjoyment of the trip would have been tremendous had that incident never occurred. With effort, I can recall the obligatory conversations with Annabelle and her husband at the Boston Music Hall symphony concert, the overnight accommodations with Dame Bentley, and the train ride home with Nettie. I had overlooked the stuffy air in the coach on the way up to Boston, but on the way home, the cigar smoke and sloshing tobacco spittoons turned my stomach. With great relief, I quickly alighted from the coach onto the South Wellfleet platform and breathed deeply of the salty fresh air.

I will not obsess upon Annabelle's sentiment that I have been ignorant in marrying my Henry. Oh, she has hurt me. True, I've called Henry my cousin, as we all call each other "cousin" here in Paine Hollow. But Henry is not my cousin at all. He is the son of my father's cousin Arozana. Henry is my second cousin, and as the minister assured us, there is no sin or stain in such a relationship.

∾

CHAPTER SIX
An Icy Winter

January, 1887

On Christmas Day of 1886, I managed to roast a decent chicken for our meal, but we were all somber as we remembered Arozana in the blessing. Mama and Papa and Lewis came to my table, which was a very nice concession on Mama's part. She wanted to honor me in my home, she said, on my first Christmas as a wife.

Henry surprised me with the new edition of *Poor Richard's Almanack*, as he said it would help me with all aspects of managing our home. I surprised him and his father with new woolen pants, patterned after their worn ones. For Mama, I made a quilted velvet lap robe to keep her cozy in the sleigh. She exclaimed it was almost too fine to use and then immediately spread it on her lap. For Papa and Lewis, I made wool vests—blue for Papa and green for Lewis. Henry complimented me, and said he would like one, too.

Before dinner, fair weather allowed us to attend our respective church services. Lewis drove Mama and Papa and Winslow to the Congregational Church, while Henry and I took our sleigh to the Methodist Church—just a stone's throw away. All the good people of Wellfleet left their Christmas dinners baking to celebrate the birth of Jesus Christ in the church of their choice. It was uplifting to join our congregation in good cheer and sing the lively Christmas hymns at full volume. Hark, the herald! Angels sing! Glory to the newborn King!

Mama told me after the services that there were periods of time throughout the morning when the Methodist organ music infiltrated the Congregational Church.

"It is good that there are such happy Christians on the Lord's birthday," she commented.

"Yes, Mama, that is why I love the Methodist Church! Won't you come with me next time? I know you would love the music," I teased her.

"Oh, I couldn't, dear. Your father would *not* understand. Our pew is at the Congregational Church."

Of course, her answer is always the same. She is immune to my constant campaign.

Since Christmas, it has turned out very cold, and we have received two feet of snow followed by an icy freezing. The severe January weather has kept me housebound for days. I long to walk down to Mama's house, but the bitter wind prevents it. I dread going out into the yard to feed and water the animals. I need better boots. The men have their foul weather gear and oiled boots, but I am afraid that my boots are not standing up to the icy world outside my kitchen door. The horses have been quarantined inside their stalls. It is far too slippery in their paddock to chance a leg injury. Therefore, Henry and I both shovel manure daily to keep the stalls clean.

Henry has carried the Singer back upstairs so I may take advantage of the heat rising from the kitchen stove. He positioned the machine over the heat grate, and my feet are warm when I sew. That is always a happy task for me.

The schooners have been relieved of their masts since the beginning of November and are drawn up on the shore to escape the marauding icebergs that crunch up on the beaches. Samuel Higgins is the talk of the hollow. He was remiss in not pulling his craft, the *Delilah,* up above the high tide mark, and the ice has caught her and been playing with her all over Blackfish Creek. *Delilah* has now been pushed out towards Lieutenant's Island and is a comical sight sitting askew up on top of the ice field.

Henry walks down to the shore every day to meet with Papa and check on the *Nautilus*. Not being an owner of his own vessel, this gives Henry something to do besides cutting ice on the pond or splitting wood. The *Nautilus* is safe until spring, drawn up into her winter napping position. But there have been years when the ice has come right up onto the beach with a full moon tide and destroyed the piers and stored vessels. Papa will continue to fret about his precious boat until the ice goes out in late March.

With winter upon us, Lewis has taken the train to Boston and rented a room at a boarding house. He's been hired to deliver for a bakery and is quite happy in the city. I am both surprised and proud of my younger brother's ability to make such a quick decision and then act upon it. It is another surprising revelation to me—I always thought Lewis would do as I have done and stay here in the hollow. To his credit, his horizons stretch further.

I think of my brother's position in Boston compared to the life led by Annabelle Crandle. Lewis was one of Annabelle's classmates in high school, but I doubt Annabelle will acknowledge him when he delivers bread to her back door in the elegant new Back Bay neighborhood. Lewis writes to us that he finds the driver's life exciting, as guiding a team of horses through the crowded city streets is a constant challenge. But I am sure he will be back with the warm weather to sail out again with Papa.

Some vessel owners have sent their schooners to Virginia for the winter, not wanting to tempt the winter ice field. Until the ice melts, there will be no position available here for Henry as master of a fishing vessel.

~

My kitchen is frequently filled with the blue haze of pipe tobacco as land bound seamen stop by to have a smoke with Winslow and Henry. I bake several loaves of corn bread every morning and serve the men thick slices with butter accompanied by my strong tea. The never ending conversation continues to be the lamenting of the diminishing numbers of fish, and thus the diminishing numbers of schooners in our harbor, and thus the diminishing number of seagoing positions available.

I have heard and heard again of the wonderful days of plenty in the sixties when, in spite of the war, Winslow remembers the fleets from Wellfleet and South Wellfleet brought the number of local fishing schooners to one hundred vessels, employing more than a thousand men and boys: *The combined fleet from Wellfleet was second only to Gloucester, surpassing both Provincetown and New Bedford.* Winslow has drilled this statement into my consciousness.

"We were too busy pulling in fish to go a-soldiering," Winslow extols any nodding visitor who will listen to his stories in exchange for my corn bread and tea. "The town selectmen voted to hire other men to take our places in the Union Army, because we supported the entire economy of Wellfleet. That's how bountiful the fish were, and how important the fishermen were!

"It's nothing like that anymore. This past year, only a couple dozen vessels total sailed out from both harbors. But I remember the days when you could stand on shore to watch the fleet sail by, and it would take an hour of your time."

"And there's the writing on the wall," is Henry's standard rejoinder to his father's lament. "Why, just a few years ago, our schooners took in more than 25,000 barrels of mackerel, and this year the take was not even a quarter of that. That's a hell of a note!"

"Henry, watch your language!" Winslow is always the proper speaker, taking his position as a deacon of the Congregational Church with him wherever he goes, including to the kitchen table. No one can accuse my father-in-law of being a hypocrite.

"Son," Winslow says, "You are going to have to make some adjustments in your expectations. There will come a day in the very near future when there will be sorry few mackerel to go after. You've got to consider other possibilities now and be ahead of the crowd in making your choices. You could take out excursion boats in the summer—there are more and more visitors here wanting to be sailed to Billingsgate and Provincetown."

The retired mariners sitting around the table shift in their chairs and nod in solemn agreement as they puff on their pipes. These weather-beaten sea captains were once well known in ports around the world. During the reign of the clipper ships, some thirty years ago, they made the China run in record times. But steam ships have taken over their routes, leaving behind these men so skilled in harnessing the international winds and managing large crews of muscled sailors. These old "uncles" recognize the adjustments Henry will have to make in order to continue to follow the sea. They provide a wise audience for Henry and Winslow's constant argument, and I am glad they visit.

"I will never sail those city folks around," Henry cries out. "You could never get me to take their money."

"Well, then, you'll soon be running down south for oysters, because like it or not, the mackerel are not going to last forever, and there are other ways you can make a good living. Most of the men are oystering in the spring now, and it's a good way to spend the time until the fish come back up. There's good money it."

I've learned that Winslow is the practical one of the two, and Henry is the emotive son.

"Father, you know I'm not an oyster man. I have no grant out there on the flats to spread the Chesapeake oysters over—I am a sea captain!"

"I'm saying you can *sail* down and fetch oyster seed for the Wellfleet grant owners," Winslow says. "There's a great demand for oysters in the market, more so now that they're shipping them by rail out across the country."

"Don't remind me of that railroad. If it weren't for the railroad, we would still be fine."

"That is not true, Henry," Winslow says. "The mackerel will be fished out soon, regardless. The railroad brings other opportunity. You have to be able to change with the times. I never thought you would have such difficulty seeing it. Maybe it's just too big a challenge for you to have to learn to do something else, since you're still the High Liner, but those seines are going to come up empty in the not too distant future."

"Confound it!" cries Henry. "I'm going out to split wood." He rises abruptly from the table, nods curtly to the puffing uncles, and stomps out the backdoor.

This conversation, or some variation thereof, has occurred a half a dozen times this month. But soon we will go through the discussion yet again, I am sure.

~

During these months when Henry is in from the sea, I cannot help but think of the opportunity presented to Henry to sign on with the Boston Fruit Company and make the Jamaica run for Lorenzo Dow Baker. The wealthiest and most generous member of the Methodist Church, Captain Baker made his offer one Sunday before he departed for his winter home in Jamaica.

Henry politely declined, declaring, "I thank you kindly, Captain Baker, but I believe the only way to navigate the ocean is under sail. I have not made the leap to steam engines, as you have!"

"But Captain Smith," Captain Baker said, "I know you would do quite well with a steam powered vessel. I could put you on as a mate in-training with your neighbor Captain Wiley, and you would find that you have nothing to fear, especially on the new steam schooner I had built in Bath. She's almost two hundred feet long and has engines powerful enough to push her at ten knots, *and* she's got three masts of auxiliary sails."

Captain Baker failed to mention the name of his latest vessel; it was the talk of the town—the *L.D. Baker*. My uncle, Captain Wiley, commanded the giant that was large enough to accommodate 20,000 bunches of bananas and had cabins for twelve paying passengers.

"I once felt as you do, and loved nothing but the sail," Captain Baker said. "I still own my first schooner for sentimental reasons. But, nothing beats the power of a steam boiler against a strong headwind. And your missus would certainly enjoy a voyage to the warm island of Jamaica once you become captain to one of my fleet."

I stood silently by my husband's side, anticipating Henry's answer.

"No, my Eva belongs at home while I am out to sea. I know a ship's master may take his wife with him, but I wouldn't be one of those. I prefer to keep Eva safe from the harsh conditions found out on the water." Henry looked down at me and asked, "Isn't that right, my dear?"

"Yes, Henry," I said, while smiling sweetly at Captain Baker, trying to convey appreciation for his kindness.

I do imagine that a voyage to a warmer climate could be an enjoyable thing. But, thus far, Aunt Elizabeth has not accompanied *her* husband, the good Captain Wiley, to Jamaica, and therefore, it would be far too premature for me to entertain the thought. I do wonder what remark I could make, though, that would cause Henry to reconsider the standing offer from Captain Baker. I am aware that Captain Baker does not make these offers to every fishing schooner captain in town, of which there are many.

And so, since my husband is unwilling to consider the idea of submitting to a training voyage under Captain Wiley on the *L.D. Baker*, Henry is home.

Sometimes he is as icy as the weather. Going into town for church these past few weeks has been out of the question, and if we did have a day when we could travel, the church is usually colder inside than out, as the hot air from the coal furnace rises up to the vaulted ceiling and never enters our pew.

~

Henry and his father have had a terrible quarrel. As soon as the shouting began, I went to the sewing room up over the kitchen and remained there for an hour after the event.

The trouble appears to stem from the fact that this is the first winter without Arozana and now that she is gone, Henry wants to save fuel and keep the house at a cooler temperature. He attempted to shut off the front parlor and not use the parlor stove. That end of the house has been very cold, and I have had to move the geraniums to the kitchen window sill.

Winslow, however, wants the house to be as warm as it has always been. He has complained about it in various ways that Henry has not acknowledged—little remarks about his aches and pains with which I have sympathized, but Henry has not even deigned to hear.

Today Winslow unlocked the door to the parlor and went in and started the coal stove. By mid-day, the woodwork had lost its cold and clammy feeling, and the whole house was warm and cozy. Henry was furious.

"It's going to cost a lot of money to keep the house heated like this!" He shouted at his father. "Mother is gone, and there is no need for it any longer."

"Henry, I like the house to be warm. This is still my house. I will have it warm."

"Well, how do you think we're going to pay for this foolish waste of fuel?" Henry bellowed out. "Money doesn't come easily this time of year."

"That's why we save our money during the summer," Winslow said. "Think of your wife, Henry. Eva is not used to living in a house where you can see your breath during the winter months. Do you want her to get sick?"

"Don't bring her into this! She is my wife, and she will agree with me!" Henry roared back. I kept the treadle going on the sewing machine. I did not want to eavesdrop; I did not want to hear these words. I hoped Henry did not mean them.

"Henry Smith, you listen to me," Winslow said. "This is my house, and I will be warm. Yes, you are my only son, and yes, someday you will inherit this house and it will be yours. But in the meantime, I am not dead yet, and I say the whole house will be heated. If you don't like that, you can go and find yourself another place to live." Winslow's voice rose to the loudest volume I had ever heard him use. But he did not sound angry, only as if he were simply announcing the truth.

"Fine, then! We will spend money as if it was water. Have it your way!" Henry slammed his way through the house and went out the back door into the wood shed. Within minutes, he came back into the kitchen and dropped a load of firewood next to the cook stove. Out the door he went again and then back in with another load. It was an astounding amount of firewood he was bringing into the house. Where would we stack it all? Thankfully he turned his attention elsewhere and went to the parlor at the front of the house, where his father sat in front of the coal stove.

"Hand me that bucket," Henry demanded. He came back through the house below me and out the back door again. Then he made several trips back and forth to the front parlor, and I heard the coal hitting the storage bin as he poured it from the scuttle. I dreaded the thought of the black dust he was raising and the time it would take me to clean the house as a result.

Obviously, the men both miss Arozana dreadfully, and the commotion has nothing to do with the cost of fuel. I am embarrassed to be a witness to the struggle. Henry sorely needs a task—a job to keep him busy. I pray to the Lord for relief. It is apparent that some work has to be presented to my husband, or I will be very unhappy for the remainder of the winter. With Henry so opposed to any suggestions from anyone, I know he will have to work out the answers for himself, and I hope it happens soon.

～

Through the month of February, I was in the presence of my husband every night, except for one. Henry took the train up to Barnstable to hear a Methodist speaker. I did not go with him, as once again, my time of the month was upon me. Further, in light of Henry's dislike for the railroad, I was relieved to let him go by himself so I did not have to listen to his grumbling.

In spite of frequent marital relations, I have not conceived. The darkness of winter has kept me burning the lamps from late afternoon into the evening. I like to join Winslow and Henry by the coal stove after dinner while we read the newspapers together. Winslow goes to bed by eight o-clock. After Winslow goes up, I kiss Henry good-night and tell him to come to bed soon—I will sew until then. My sewing room is adjacent to Winslow's room, and the convenient location of the floor vent right over the kitchen stove cheers my feet as I treadle away. Soon, Winslow is snoring. I then carry my lamp into our cold bedroom, and Henry hears me from below. He is up the stairs within minutes.

In this way, we are able to have frequent marital encounters even though we live with my father-in-law. If I thought for one minute that Winslow could hear the squeaking of our bedsprings, I would not be able to enjoy my husband's advances. Henry does understand this and has even joked to me about it.

"You put Father to sleep with the sound of the sewing machine, Eva, the same way a baby goes to sleep with the clickity-clack of the train," he said.

"I haven't had that pleasure yet, Henry, of seeing our baby fall to sleep on a train," I replied.

"We will continue to work on that, dear wife," he assured me.

And so we have. I do look forward to our private evenings together, when once we have warmed the frozen sheets and created our cave under the quilts, we delight in each other until sweet sleep falls upon us. Our intimacy makes all the cares of the day worth enduring. And one day soon, I know I shall discover that I am with child. I do thank the Lord that in his wisdom, he made the act of attempting procreation enjoyable. I am so blessed.

~

I believe that the good Lord created beautiful creatures to teach us the inevitability of loss. Mama's horse, loyal Tessa, has died. What a sad thing it is, to recall her proud stance, her expressive brown eyes, and the sheer bulky hugeness of her love.

Pound for pound, Henry can never love me as much; it is pure impossibility. I cannot believe that I am thinking of her in this irrational way—she was an animal, not a person. But, Tessa loved me for the person I am, never dissatisfied with me, always just wanting my presence, my attention—me as I am, with no adjustments.

Clever as she was, she opened her own stall door latch and ventured out onto the frozen pasture where she slipped on the ice. Papa told me that he heard terrified whinnying and looked out the kitchen window to see Tess down on the ground, struggling to get up.

He had to shoot her immediately—there was no helping her broken foreleg. There will be much crying in the hollow today between Mama and me. I am quite glad that Henry was at the post office when Papa walked over wearing his ice cleats to tell me the news.

"Not Tessa! Our beautiful Tess!" I cried out. My knees deserted me and I collapsed as Papa reached out to catch me.

How sentimental of me. Tess was a horse. Lord, forgive me for my weakness. I have my healthy husband. Henry has not been one of the men to die this year out on the wild ocean. He is alive and well. As are my brother, my father, and my father-in-law. Looking at the families around me, there is hardly a friend or relative that is as fortunate as I am.

The problem for Papa will be the burial of Tess. She is huge, of course, and the ground is frozen. I hesitated to ask where she was, and when I finally got up the courage, it was a contest to get the information out of Papa.

He had to have Clive Townsend's team come up and drag Tessa over to the side of the pasture. Papa has covered her with a tarp next to the location of the eventual hole that will be dug for her. I must go and see her one last time, even in her cold and frozen state. Otherwise, I will not quite believe that she is really dead.

~

Henry and I walked down to my parent's house, leaving Sinbad and Silkie locked safely in their stalls. Henry held my arm all the way to keep me from falling. The familiar road transported us through a crystal forest of ice-encased trees, while the polar air caused our breath to form tiny clouds at each exhale. We passed the pond where the neighborhood children gaily skated. The very ice that was the cause of so much pleasure and laughter on the pond had also caused a dear horse to go down in her pasture. I imagined myself shouting at the children, *Stop having fun. Tessa is dead.* Of course, I did not.

I couldn't go in to see Mama until we found Tessa at the end of the pasture, down near the shore. Henry pulled back the tarp for me, and there was Tess in all her reddish-golden glory. She lay peacefully on her side. The late afternoon sun glinted off her thick winter fur, and her red mane lifted gently on the cold wind. My father, I think, knowing that I was coming to pay Tess a visit, had closed her eyes.

I took my mittens off and felt her frozen shoulder and neck. Finally, I touched her soft pink muzzle. Again, Papa had insured I would not witness any vile expression of death—he had tied a cord around her muzzle to keep her mouth closed and her tongue in place.

Papa loved Tess as much as I did, and perhaps he had tied this little death halter for his own benefit as much as for mine.

Tears stung my eyes and froze on my cheeks. There was a small bullet hole at her temple, but no blood, as I'm sure Papa had wiped it away. I pitied my father for having to shoot Tess, and cried just imagining the moment of his decision—his act of mercy. Her broken foreleg was frozen into an awkward position, indicating the severity of the break.

A point of bone protruded above her fetlock. This was what I needed to see; I knew there had been absolutely no hope for Tess. My hands went to the break as if I could somehow set the bone by kneading it back into position. My poor, dear Tessa. I felt Henry's hand under my elbow, and then he brought me back up from my knees and gave me my mittens.

"That's enough, Eva," he said quietly. He wiped my wet cheek with his own handkerchief and then carefully pulled the canvas tarp over Tessa's head. Together we replaced the ballast stones around the perimeter of the tarp.

How quickly the event had transpired. Tessa's hoof prints were everywhere in the paddock, frozen into the snow, demonstrating the routes she favored back and forth across the field. But she would never take another step.

The ice pack in the bay absorbed the sunset's golden light. Henry and I stood and stared at the fantastic frozen scene, our faces stinging in the wind. Familiar humps of land loomed up out of the ice— the south end of Indian Neck and the north end of Lieutenant's Island were to our right and our left; before us the frozen seascape stretched to Billingsgate—miles across Wellfleet Harbor. We heard a dog barking, protesting the cold and wanting to be let into a warm kitchen, no doubt.

"Henry, this is so beautiful—I can imagine that Heaven might look like this. Except it would be warm. Don't you think?" I looked up at him. "Will Tessa be in Heaven when we get there?"

Henry gave me a worried look. I instantly regretted my selfish grief for Tessa; Henry had not yet recovered from the loss of his mother, and I was indulging myself in wondering if there were animals in Heaven.

"The wind's turning," he told me.

"You're so attuned to the wind, while I don't even notice which way it blows."

"My dear, noticing when the wind changes is one my main responsibilities when I'm out to sea," he said. "You see the tree tops bending? It was blowing from the northwest all day, and now it's swung around to the north. We should probably expect a storm."

I shivered at the thought of more wind and snow.

"We must see my parents before we walk home," I said.

In the fast falling light, we stopped at the house for tea. Mama burst into tears when I came through her kitchen door. Papa and Henry immediately retired to the woodshed to smoke their pipes. I believe the men can take only so much of weeping women before they remove and distract themselves, afraid that they too might break down.

Tessa will be missed for a very long time; her familiar whinnying calls ring in my mind as I think about her. Papa has made inquiries through a horse dealer in Barnstable, and even now, is waiting for Tessa's replacement to arrive. He is a Morgan gelding trained to the harness with many years ahead of him, as long as he doesn't fall on the ice. It hardly seems fair that Tessa is to be replaced so quickly, but a buggy must have a horse.

～

The calendar says spring is here, and with it, the promising smell of damp soil has emerged from beneath the melting snow. Clouds of cold fog hover near the ground, unless there is wind. And the wind is sometimes quite strong, blowing through the trees at night so the naked branches screech against the house outside our bedroom window.

Henry's father has taken ill with spring influenza. Winslow has been in bed with a high fever for three days. My husband tells me that he has never known his father to take to his bed.

As soon as she heard, Mama came over to advise me on the care of an invalid, and was quite satisfied to learn I was providing the constant hot tea and gruel required to insure Winslow's recovery. She recommended cold wet sheets as well as the frequent application of a cold cloth on the forehead to keep the fever down. Winslow would just as soon have no attention at all, and tries to wave me away, even in his near delirium. Several times he has called out for Arozana. I haven't the heart to remind him that she is gone.

I find that I like the nursing, except for the disposal of bodily waste. Of course, Winslow cannot make it out to the outhouse. Nor can he use his chamber pot. I have had to locate the bedpan in Arozana's medicine closet, and find myself to be quite squeamish. Not only am I squeamish; Winslow is as well.

He insisted that Henry be the one to help him onto the bed pan, declaring that he did not want to put me through the immodesty of attending to him "in that way." But Henry, in turn, insisted that I be the one. And so, I have been pressed into service. Even with a fever, Winslow is modest, and we have contrived a way to keep his body draped with the sheet while he performs the act. I then slide the bedpan out, cover it immediately with a towel, and run it downstairs and out to the privy. A kettle of water constantly boils on the kitchen stove, and I bring the kettle out to the yard and pour it over the bedpan before I will allow it back into the house.

This is the first encounter I have had with the "in sickness" portion of my marriage vows, and I am surprised to find that the invalid I am caring for is not my husband, but my father-in-law. Henry tells me he is happy that I am here—he can't imagine attending to his father. "It is women's work," he says. "And you are very good at it, Eva."

I am happy when Henry is happy.

We have been married for almost a full year now, and I believe I have experienced the full range of my husband's emotions. I do hope that he feels happiness as intensely as he feels his grief, his anger, his discouragement. But I have to give him time; it has been a very hard year, after all. He will soon be out on his beloved ocean again, which will bring him satisfaction, if not contentment. Luckily, I find my measure of satisfaction at the sewing machine and contentment in Henry's arms.

~

Part Two

CHAPTER SEVEN
Pleasant Point

Summer, 1888

I have been Henry's wife for more than two years, and still I am without child. I live my life and wait for the day that I discover I am to be a mother. I tend to the house for Winslow and Henry. I sew, read, and write. I bought myself a new fountain pen at Ike's store, thanks to the payments I've received for several bathing dresses. I am delighted with the way the words flow smoothly out of the pen with no need to stop and dip in the ink jar.

Since my marriage, I've left thousands of hours of sewing behind me: five quilts, thirteen dresses, thirty-four traveling ensembles, twenty-three swimming dresses and eight wedding gowns. But these products of my industry have not kept me company the way my journal does, and so I do not sew during every spare minute. *Know thyself,* Socrates counseled, and through my ink I examine my own submerged feelings. Henry's opinion that I practice "self-indulgent scribbling" is not so strong that I lay aside my pen; indeed, the habit rewards me with perspective and patience.

Another summer is upon us. The mosquitoes are very discouraging, and it is difficult to be outdoors when the tide is high, as the dreadful insects swarm up out of the salt marshes and feast on me, raising huge welts on my skin. The South Wellfleet General Store carries on a brisk trade in punk sticks which we all light and carry about with us whenever we are outside. Ike says he can hardly keep them in stock and encourages me to buy a dozen at a time so I won't run short. The summer folks snap them up as soon as they get off the train, so Ike wants to be sure that we "locals" (as the summer visitors call us) have a chance at them.

The worst time is from late afternoon into early evening. The punk smoke barely keeps the mosquitoes away long enough for me to walk to Mama's house. Consequently, I am walking very quickly these days. The men have their cigars, and that seems to be somewhat effective against the pests, or at least the men use that for a convenient excuse to smoke more.

~

Henry is out fishing, of course. But I daresay this will be the last summer Henry goes out mackereling. He encountered great difficulties securing a position this season, and the months of April and May were tense and fretful as he searched for a vessel to command. This is the second summer that Henry is sailing from Commercial Wharf at the mouth of Duck Creek in Wellfleet. It is now impossible for him to find employment here in South Wellfleet. The Southern Wharf Company has closed its doors, and they may not open again. It is perhaps a good thing that Henry does not own his own boat. I know he would try forever to follow the elusive schools of fish.

To compound the problem of a reduced catch, our neighborhood has endured the shoaling up of Blackfish Creek. The channel is now so shallow that schooners cannot easily come or go. No longer do we congregate on the wharf to enjoy the spring send-off meal—sadly, those happy times have come to an abrupt end.

Somehow, Henry still manages to find fish. He easily contracts a small crew of young men to go out with him, but he no longer fishes alongside a fleet of neighbors. I do worry and have implored him to fish in sight of other vessels—even if they hail from Provincetown or Gloucester—for safety's sake.

But he will have none of it. "The Lord watches out for me, so why do I need anyone else?" is his standard retort.

Wellfleet center is suffering as much as we are here in Paine Hollow. Many of the businesses on Commercial Street have closed up shop for the last time due to the greatly reduced call for the cooper's barrels, the joiner's services, the replacement of masts and sails, or the provisioning of crews. I make no exaggeration when I state that there are now more fishing vessels decaying in abandonment on the shores and inlets of the Wellfleet waters than there are out to sea. The newspapers are full of accusations that the valiant fishermen of Wellfleet and other coastal ports of Massachusetts have "fished out" the once mighty schools of mackerel and caught almost every cod from the bottom. In spite of the near hysteria of some of the men, I am not worried. I know the Lord will provide.

The *Nautilus* still moors out in our cove, even though she lies over on her side in the mud at every low tide. She hasn't been here much this summer, as Papa and Lewis have made a dozen runs to Norfolk, Virginia, and back again, delivering ice from our ice houses to that port and returning to Wellfleet with immature oysters. As of yet, Henry refuses to consider the business of spreading Chesapeake oysters on the Wellfleet flats to fatten up and sweeten for market. "That's a landlubber's job," he says. I've pointed out that the men who have taken to it are making a good living. He dismisses this with a wave of his hand.

~

As far as housekeeping is concerned, I am one of the luckiest ladies in Paine Hollow. Money is harder to come by now than it was the year we were first married. But last summer, before finances became so tight, we had the foresight to modernize the house as much as our means would allow. Henry hired a plumbing company to in-stall a bathtub and vanity sink in what was formerly the small guest bedroom. How I love my bathroom and running water!

In spite of the expense, I met Henry's suggestion that we modernize with enthusiasm. Winslow had no quarrel with the plan, as Henry and I paid the entire cost—me with my sewing funds, and Henry with his shares from two fishing trips.

Henry's suggestion was initiated by the embarrassment I'd suffered every Saturday evening as my father-in-law began his weekly preparations for Sunday morning church. Winslow's routine was to carry in the tin tub from the shed, place it in the middle of the kitchen floor, fill it with hot water from the kettles, and proceed to strip down and take a bath.

Once the tub appeared, I vacated the kitchen for at least an hour and went to my sewing room until Winslow's bath was finished. But then it was Henry's turn, and only after Winslow had gone to bed would I venture to take my turn. Being the sole female in the house can be extremely awkward. I readily assented to the notion of a more private bath, as Henry knew I would. I did feel rather important as a wage earner, knowing that my financial contribution would make the renovation a reality. By lamplight, I sewed far into the summer nights, taking in many more orders than I should have in order to pay the bill in full rather than carrying any debt.

The installation of the fixtures was a rather lengthy process. First, the water tower was erected, which is fed by the new windmill that spins at every breeze and pumps the water up into the tower from the well. Next, pipes were installed to carry water from the tower into the house, and more pipes to drain the water away into another requirement of interior plumbing—an underground cesspool. The kitchen sink also benefited, and now has a new faucet next to the hand pump. Winslow could not bear to part with the brass hand pump Arozana had used, and so the old remains next to the new. The whole project was quite time consuming and for weeks workmen were on the property with their drills and equipment and booming voices.

"You cannot have a proper bathtub, Eva, if we don't have plumbing," was Henry's response when I complained that the invasion of the plumbers was far more overwhelming than I could ever have anticipated. The men ran up and down the stairs yelling back and forth to one another on the progress of the drilling. I have newfound respect for those men in the plumbing profession; they must turn their drills hundreds of times to bore their way through one beam. It frequently took the better part of an hour to drill a single hole. Of course, Henry was out to sea for much of the project, and only saw great progress when he came in every few weeks. Winslow and I endured the worst of it together. I spent hours sweeping up sawdust and dirt tracked in on the workmen's boots. But it was a small price to pay for the final result.

The Saturday night bath ritual is now far more pleasant. The white cast iron bathtub is my pride and joy. It sits upon four claw-footed legs, and when I take a bath, I am as satisfied as Cleopatra, Queen of the Nile. It is a delight to turn on the faucet and have water come pouring through the spout into the tub—and after the bath, also a delight to pull the plug and let the water drain down through the pipes, gurgling all through the house like the gutters in a rain storm. The bathtub could not fit up the staircase, a dilemma which required the removal of a window so the tub could be hauled up to the second floor by block and tackle and then swung into the house. The replacement window is much larger, and as a result, the new bathroom is pleasantly full of sun during the day, making it one of my favorite rooms.

We could not afford to modernize to the extent of installing a central coal furnace that would heat and transport hot water. We did consider the flushing water closet, but when we learned that the diameter of the drain pipe for that convenience was almost as wide as my hand, and that the pipe would run down through the corner of the dining room, we decided against it for now. I couldn't bear the thought of the extra domestic upheaval if we had been able to afford it—the chaos caused by the tub installation had been quite enough for me, and I was eager to get the house back in order.

Our house will be modernized further, but not this year. Henry grouses that this fishing season has not been his most lucrative. And so, we continue to grace our outhouse with our presence and to heat hot water on the wood stove in the kitchen.

During the summer months, the water from the tower is a tepid temperature, and only one kettle of boiling water is required to make a comfortable bath. But in the winter, the water in the tower must be drained or it will freeze and burst the tower, and so we revert to the old metal tub in the kitchen. When this happened last winter, I must admit that I was already so acclimated to the convenience and privacy of the upstairs bath that I had almost forgotten the frustration of the kitchen bath. I do appreciate the difference, and feel very fortunate to be one of the first ladies in Paine Hollow to have running water.

~

After all these years as a captain's wife, Mama has been to sea. This past spring, when it was very damp and foggy, Mama surprised us all by agreeing to sail south to Norfolk with Papa and Lewis. She endured seasickness on the voyage due to the strong April winds and waves, but to her great delight, she found Virginia's spring weather to be warm and hospitable. While Lewis bunked on the *Nautilus* in Norfolk Harbor, Mama and Papa took a room at a guesthouse for a month. Mama wrote little cards to me describing the beautiful flowers and birds that surrounded the front porch.

> *My dear Eva, I have almost forgotten the misery of the*
> *voyage. The cultivated flowers here are so very cheer-*
> *ful. I wish that you were with me on this beautiful ve-*

randa, enjoying the buzzing of the bees as they visit each blossom—it will be months before the bees are this busy on Cape Cod. I have informed your father that I will be returning home via the railroad. I will forevermore view the Atlantic Ocean from the shore. Give my regards to Henry and Winslow.

Love, Mother

I missed her terribly during that month. Since their return, Mama and Papa have talked of leasing a house down in Virginia for the coming winter. If they do so, the hollow will be a very different place for me. But what a blessing for my parents to be in warm Virginia for the winter—two Yankees from the north enjoying Dixie! I can't quite imagine Mama being away from her kitchen for so long. But for now, I take advantage of every moment I can spend with her, knowing that in five months time she may be off on an extended adventure with Papa. They certainly deserve it.

~

Summer, 1888

On my melancholy days, I have taken to walking the three miles to the backshore. The summer days without Henry are long, and I finish the housework by noon. I want to be out in the bright sunlight seeking the cooling breezes off the Atlantic. I find that the mosquitoes do not follow me to the ocean—they favor the marshes of the bay over the broad expanses of the ocean beach.

It is always inspiring to stand on the brink of the dunes and look down far below at the smooth sandy beach and rolling surf and then way out to the curved horizon where the ocean meets the sky. Offshore, a parade of vessels featuring white sails or billowing smokestacks pass by as they round Cape Cod on their way north or south. The view is so vast, it makes any troubles I may have seem small in comparison.

Sometimes I arrive at the top of the dune when the men from the Cahoon Hollow Life Saving Station are out at drill, practicing getting their lifeboat down the steep dune or into and out of the surf. The summer waves have no fury compared to the breakers of a winter Nor-Easter, yet Captain Daniel Cole likes to keep the men in shape, and hardly a day goes by when he doesn't have them practicing a drill.

There are more summer visitors out on the beach this year than ever before. Whimsical cottages that look like they couldn't hold up against a stiff breeze have sprung up on both the bay beaches and the ocean bluffs, and in June, women and their children arrived by the trainload to spend the summer. It is strange to see the city boys playing the days away. All the local boys of nine and older—those who still live here and have not moved with their families to areas where their parents can find employment—are out on vessels or the sand flats learning the ways of the sea or the oyster beds. The city girls are also quite vigorous and athletic—they heartily enjoy running and playing on the open beaches.

If these folks only knew of the number of terrible shipwrecks that have caused loss of life through the dangerous winter months, they might be a bit more somber in the presence of the mighty Atlantic. To many residents, the ocean beach is still considered a graveyard. We've observed the horror of shipwreck so many times. When I was a tiny girl, before the railroad brought the summer visitors, no children played at the backshore as it was considered disrespectful to the dead.

It makes me laugh behind my hand, though, to see the antics of these visiting children. They have such fun running in and out of the waves as their mothers struggle to appear dignified and keep them under some type of control at the same time. And that's where the governesses are employed; these people have the means to hire a young woman to run after the children if Mama is unable or unwilling.

I sit upon the dune reading a book or writing in my journal, as I have no children of my own to tend to, and it would not do to sit alone blatantly observing others. Every few weeks, my dear school friend Lily comes by train from Plymouth to visit her mother. She and Charles have two children now—with a new baby due any time. Lily finds it impossible to bring the children to the ocean in her condition, but allows me to take them in the buggy, and so I have spent several pleasant afternoons chasing little ones near the surf's edge. But Lily hasn't come to visit since the end of July; she is too close to her delivery time.

My Nettie is too busy to come to the ocean with me. She has taken Deacon Bentley into her own house to care for him. Nettie has rented her extra bedrooms to several summer boarders, whom she waits on hand and foot. Nettie's father and mother have moved to Maryland due to Ebenezer's permanent and increasingly demanding position as an oyster shipping agent for Atwood & Company. Nettie is now in charge of the house, as her older brothers have also recently moved from the Cape to find employment. The neighborhood is losing more people every month.

Nettie has taken on the summer boarders in order to pay the property taxes and the winter coal bill, and she actually enjoys the management of all concerned. I would find it very difficult to invite strangers to sleep in my home, but Nettie tells me that if she doesn't immediately feel comfortable upon meeting a prospective guest, she regretfully informs them that she has no room available.

As the first wave of summer residents disembarked at the railroad platform in June, the promise of money passing over the till noticeably affected the demeanor of our grocer. Ike smiles a lot more from behind his counter at the general store, and he has suddenly taken to telling the most outrageous yarns, to the point of claiming that scallops sometimes grow on trees and that we have a resident witch who lives in the dunes. I believe this keeps the children coming back for another tale and another sale of candy or chewing gum.

I understand Ike's fondness for the summer folk—most local residents went "on account" during the hard winter, and we are just now paying off last January's purchases. I certainly have been watching my pennies much more diligently this past year and am not the customer I would like to be.

Winslow is no longer out on the water making a share of a catch, as he couldn't see sailing from Wellfleet. "If I can't launch from my own home wharf, I'm not going. I'm too old to make a change," he told Henry. When Winslow made the announcement, Henry very kindly bought him a small catboat, the *Zephyr*, from a family that was leaving town for the textile mills of Manchester, New Hampshire. The price was quite reasonable, as Henry promised the former owners they could take the *Zephyr* out whenever they returned to Paine Hollow for a visit, but we have not heard from them.

And so, this is the second summer that Winslow has stayed home with me. He sometimes sails visitors on day excursions out across the bay to Billingsgate Island. He is not feeling as strong as he used to, and it is perfectly respectable at his age that he decided not to go out to sea with Henry. The *Zephyr* keeps Winslow happy and out on the water during the day and home in his own comfortable bed at night.

This small loss of income on Winslow's part has made my seamstress earnings all the more important and less likely to be applied to unnecessary items or jaunts. Therefore, I am always scrimping and don't spend as much as I used to at Ike's store. But I do make a point of stopping by and saying hello to him when I get my mail on the way home from the back shore, because he has been very kind in recommending me to the summer ladies who inquire about seamstress services.

The character of the general store has changed quite dramatically. Although Henry and I do not have enough money to go on a holiday, I find that I am living in holiday land. Ike's storefront is adorned with flags and pinwheels and whirly-gigs that blow and clatter in the breeze. Inside, Ike makes sure that he has fanciful items in stock: all colors of parasols for the summer ladies; penny candies, kites, tops and balls for the children; picture cards to send off every day by the afternoon mail; and—most important to me—the fine lightweight wool that the ladies prefer for their bathing dresses. I take several fitting appointments a week and have designed a simple pattern that I can work up in one evening, as these visiting ladies are in no mood to wait long for their bathing dresses once they lay their eyes upon the ocean beach.

Ike also sets in a supply of "city quality remedies," as he calls them, and a new shelf behind the counter is dedicated to colorful patented pill bottles which guarantee to solve a nervous headache or an upset digestive system. I prefer my own herbal teas, but I notice that the pill bottles are favored by the summer visitors.

~

I met a new friend on the first of August. As I stopped by the store on my way home from the ocean beach that day, Ike winked at me and said, "And here comes the most sought after seamstress in town, if she'd only come in from the dunes."

I could see he was putting on airs for a dainty lady who was engrossed in choosing a new sunshade for herself. She stood in front of the store mirror, trying on one wide brimmed hat after another.

"In this beautiful weather, I have to leave my sewing machine every now and then," I said. I looked down at my dusty skirt and shoes. I certainly did not look like a seamstress and hoped that Ike's customer hadn't overheard. Ike brought down a yellow parasol from the display overhead and popped it open for me.

"Can I interest you in a parasol to shield your pretty face with as you sit out there under the glaring sun, Eva? You want to preserve your beauty for your husband, don't you?"

He spun the parasol, creating a golden blur. I had to laugh, as Ike is never so animated through the long, cold winter months. He is truly a different person in the summer, as I suppose we all are.

"It's too late for me, Ike," I said. "I'm afraid I'm as brown as shoe leather. And it would be impossible for me to hold a parasol over my head when I tend to the laundry and the garden. But thank you for the sentiment. I'll take a quart of milk, though." As I counted out coins for the glass bottle that Ike fetched from the ice box, the young lady came up behind me.

"And I'll take that parasol, sir, if this good woman doesn't want it," she said. "If I don't do something, I'll get freckles all over my face in this sun." She passed Ike some crisp new bills.

The wedding ring on her left hand sported the largest ruby I've ever seen. She wore a white percale dress with a navy blue tie around her neck, simulating the British sailor look touted as the ultimate in excursion fashion by Godey's Lady's Book. I saw that the hem of her skirt was as dusty as mine was—it would have to be if she walked anywhere at all—and her white kid shoes were similarly abused. Her complexion was as smooth as cream, which made an eye-catching contrast with her unruly red hair. Ringlets that had escaped her hair pins fell down her back in charming disarray.

As she made her purchase, I wondered if I would have let myself brown in the sun so if I was not married. But Henry does not mind at all that I have a brown face. In fact, I don't think he even notices, as his is far more weather-beaten than mine. Henry is always enthusiastic to see me when he comes home, and then he is just as enthusiastic to leave on the next trip out. He has become very predictable.

The lady noticed me eyeing her dusty hem. "I've had to walk, as you can see," she said, fluffing her skirt. "Your roads are like sugar—I feel as though I am walking through quicksand. Boston's brick sidewalks have spoiled me, I'm afraid."

"Yes, the sand is a challenge," I agreed. "The barometer is falling, though, and when it rains later this afternoon, the sand will become hard packed and the dust will disappear. Then it's easier going, especially for the horses."

I must have sounded like an excursion guide making these explanations to this obviously wealthy lady. It was her turn to look me over, making note of my short-sleeved blouse, my tanned arms, my dusty brown shoes, and my dun colored skirt.

"Now I see why you people wear that color so much," she said. "Why, it's actually dust colored. It hides the dust."

She made this declaration as though she had discovered the cure for influenza. I smiled at her. She was charming in spite of her ignorance.

"Yes, that's one reason." I didn't bother to say that the price per yard was also very much less than the delicate fabric she was wearing, or that the housework I am accustomed to demands a fabric of strong constitution. I offered my hand to her.

"My name is Eva Smith. Mrs. Henry Smith. We live over at the top of Paine Hollow."

She looked at my hand for a moment before she reached out to take it.

"I'm pleased to make your acquaintance, Eva," she said. "I am Mrs. Richard Bolton—please call me Carrie." She smiled. "We've taken a cottage over at Pleasant Point for the month of August to escape the dreadful city heat. Richard has just boarded the afternoon train to return to Boston, leaving me here with our two sons and the housekeeper. I'm walking back now—would you keep me company as far as your house?"

"It would be my pleasure," I said, pleased to have been asked.

I couldn't help feeling that Mrs. Richard Bolton was curious to see what sort of house I live in, and I didn't mind letting her see it—from the outside. I'm proud to live at the Smith house. It is a welcoming home. The cheerful front door is painted a sea blue color that contrasts pleasingly in the summer sun with the bright white clapboards. My pink roses are in full bloom all along the fence and up over the arbor that frames the door, thanks to my diligent watering every morning and every evening, and I am happy to show them off.

We walked through the sand, sharing the shade of the yellow parasol and avoiding the horse droppings in the road. I soon fell under Carrie's spell. I didn't know if I liked her, but I found her exceedingly interesting. Her conversation was frank, witty and disarming all at once.

Carrie had been in residence at Pleasant Point for only a few days, and she had already formed her opinions. According to Carrie, South Wellfleet was full of intelligent people who simply did not want to venture out into the "real" world.

"You Cape Codders are attached to your land and your homesteads far more than what is good for you," she declared.

I pointed out that many families had recently taken their leave and moved to more populated areas, but she ignored me and continued with her evaluation.

"Cape Codders are thrifty and know how to stretch a nickel into a quarter. You border on prudish. Well, maybe not *you*, Eva, but the other people I've met. Your church services are far too long. But the newspapers are packed with all sorts of neighborhood gossip along with the national news.

"Now, there is a real contradiction. How can a community of prudish churchgoers be so interested in gossip? Why are the names of the guests at the summer guesthouses published in the newspaper? Why is every foray out of town by any citizen noted in the columns?"

Carrie peppered me with questions, and I couldn't answer fast enough.

"I don't really know, except that it's always been the case that we are very interested in the comings and goings of our neighbors and visitors. We see no harm in it."

"Oh, that charming little building there, is that the schoolhouse?"

Carrie pointed to the two story building where I had learned my sums and grammar.

"Yes, that's the Pond Hill School. All the neighborhood children attend school here before going on to high school in Wellfleet. Many of the children from our district go on to receive their high school diploma, and I'm proud to say I was one of them."

"And all from that little building," Carrie said.

"My house is the next one up the road, so you could say that I've come full circle. I've never thought of it that way, but here I am, living next to the school of my childhood."

As we walked up to the gate of the Smith homestead, I saw my house through the evaluating eyes of a stranger.

Carrie complimented the roses at the gate, and the "charming" brick path that wandered from the front gate, around the cedar tree, and finally to the front steps. Silkie and Sinbad stood with their heads over their paddock fence to greet us, and Carrie was impressed by their glistening black coats. She gave them each a peppermint candy, in spite of my protests that it might not agree with their digestion. She waved her hand at me and laughed.

"They will be fine. I make sure I give our horses at home a peppermint at least once a day. You see how much they love it?"

It was true; the horses crunched the hard candy and asked for more by stretching their necks far over the fence rail. But I was adamant, and Carrie took her leave, laughing and twirling her yellow parasol.

~

I have since walked over to see Carrie Bolton at her Pleasant Point retreat, bringing with me a basket of molasses cookies which her boys enthusiastically swooped down upon. Carrie was in the yard when I arrived, snipping at a rose bush with a pair of clippers. I noticed her white kid gloves trimmed with little buttons on the sides, just a bit worn and apparently demoted to gardening gloves, even though they were of better quality than the pair I wear to church. She had lost her battle with the sun, and a heavy sprinkling of freckles crossed her nose and cheeks.

Her little sons, Richie and Tommy, are two years apart. Both take after their mother with brilliant carrot colored hair, eyes the color of ripe blueberries, and a generous crop of freckles.

"Here's your dose of double trouble," Carrie quipped as the boys jumped around me, clamoring for the cookies. "Boys, please say hello properly to Mrs. Smith before you eat any cookies."

Without waiting to see if this might occur, she turned to me. "I was trying for a girl the second time, though it didn't happen, as you can see, Eva. But I am done—I will have no more children. It is such an effort, and really ruins the waistline, not to mention the bosom. Of course, I had a wet nurse in, but I can't tell you the pain I went through as I waited for my milk to dry up. It was extraordinary, and I had a week of sopping wet clothing to endure."

I was so taken aback by the disclosure of all this information that I could not think of a thing to say, and so I said nothing. It seemed an absurd way of talking about bearing children, and to hear Carrie discuss it right in front of her boys, nine and seven years of age! But the boys either did not listen to their mother or had heard these sentiments before, because I could see no reaction on their faces. It took me several minutes to recover. I could not imagine myself sharing this sort of conversation with anyone but a very close friend, and then, in very private circumstances. Perhaps I *am* prudish.

Carrie and I sat on a bench perched on the brow of the sandy bluff, overlooking the sapphire harbor below. The tide was high and several small sailboats tacked leisurely back and forth between Pleasant Point and the north end of Lieutenant's Island.

Richie and Tommy raced around the cottage, shouting and playing tag and stopping in front of our bench every other revolution to request another cookie. Tommy had set up whirly gigs around the perimeter of the yard, and they all spun and clattered in the wind. Richie tormented Tommy by pretending to push one over, and Tommy shrieked in protest to his mother.

"Richie, *please* act your age," Carrie scolded. "You are the older brother. Do not upset Tommy that way, or you will be locked in your bedroom with your arithmetic book for the afternoon." Carrie looked bored, and her threat of punishment did nothing to deter Richie.

I thought the punishment ridiculous and a very good method of teaching a boy to hate arithmetic. Much better to have him do something that he disliked already, such as scrubbing the outhouse. However, I saw that Carrie had no intention of carrying out her threat. She sat next to me on the bench, asking me the names of landmarks and seamarks out in the sparkling bay before us. I gave her a local geography lesson.

I told her our small harbor of Blackfish Creek is embraced by Indian Neck to the north and Lieutenant's Island to the south. Mill Island is over to the south as well, and then just across Blackfish Creek sits the silent Southern Wharf Company. Carrie and I watched two young men trying to sail their boat around the Campbell's' fish weir. They continuously came up against the circular structure and brushed into the net as they tried desperately to tack away from it. Mr. Campbell had recently complained to Winslow about the mysterious holes in his net, and for good reason. A rip allows the captured fish to swim away. Now I could see the cause of the rips—inexperienced sailors. Unlike Ike at the General Store, Mr. Campbell does not benefit from the summer residents.

I pointed out Great Island way off on the horizon, across the great Wellfleet Harbor, and just south of that, Billingsgate Lighthouse on the eroding Billingsgate Island, once home to a small fishing village before the waves washed away acres of land.

"Many of Billingsgate's houses have been floated across the harbor to Wellfleet," I told Carrie, "Only the lighthouse keeper's home is occupied now. My father's cousin, Thomas Jefferson Paine, lives out there all by himself," I said. "And before you ask, yes, he was named after President Jefferson, being born a few years after Jefferson died. We can sail out to visit him someday—Winslow will take us on the *Zephyr*. You would like that, Carrie. We'll bring Uncle Thomas some sweets, and the boys can climb up the lighthouse."

"Yes, Eva. Yes to anything, if you think these boys would be manageable," Carrie agreed.

I assured her that between three adults, we should be able to handle two boys. We sat quietly, contemplating the peaceful view before us. In six hours time, it would be low tide, presenting an entirely different view from Carrie's cottage. The anchored vessels would be over on their sides, their masts pointing this way or that, depending on the angle at which each boat rested. Horses wearing wooden bog boots on their front hoofs would pull wagons out onto the flats to collect the trapped fish from the weirs, and the exposed sand and mud of the harbor floor would treat the eye to a flat golden landscape—so very different from the blue water and white sails now before us. A barefoot army of summer folks and local residents would advance together across the sand with their buckets and clam rakes to scratch up dinner from below the surface.

It was an impressive view for a summer cottage. I could walk to the shore any day, but to see the bay from the kitchen windows! But of course, the location was so impractical. I thought of the blowing sands of winter, which would require the windows to be boarded over.

Uncomfortable with the pause in our conversation, I ventured to ask a frank question.

"Carrie, how can you say that you are *done* having children? How does a couple go about deciding that?" I was amazed at myself for having asked—I hardly knew Carrie.

She blushed just the slightest bit and looked down at her gloved hands. She still held the pruning clippers, and she worked them open and closed, as if snipping at some imaginary weed.

"Well, Richard has his mistress," she said. "Yes, Eva, don't gasp; it's common knowledge in Boston's Back Bay that Richard Bolton has a mistress. That is the price I pay for being married to a wealthy businessman who travels the world over.

"And I am rather glad of it. Richard is a big bore, and so tiresome. I am very *happy* that he does not bother me with that sweaty business anymore. I am *happy* to be the wife with two sons. As long as he supports me in style, I will tolerate the mistress.

"But I have my proof put away in a safe deposit box, should he ever decide to try to divorce me. Richard has always been careless, and I found love letters from his amour several years ago." Carrie rattled off the information to me as though she had recited it many times.

"Oh, my goodness, Carrie, you take it all so well. I never would have guessed you were enduring these circumstances." I was truly sorry that I had asked such a personal question, as I was unprepared for the alarming answer.

"Don't act so shocked, Eva. I am well supported, and what would I do otherwise? I would be destitute. I certainly wouldn't be sitting here with you, enjoying this heavenly sea breeze. I'd be perspiring up in the sweltering city somewhere.

"I spend Richard's money and I enjoy myself without him here on Cape Cod. He comes to see us on the weekends and plays with the boys, and that is about all the time I wish to share with him. I am glad to see him go."

"And he no longer loves you? You are so pretty and lively! That is sad to hear." I could not bear the thought of a husband's love dying.

"My dear, Richard is attracted to every woman who flirts with him! It is I who am no longer attracted to Richard. I will not let him be near me—we sleep in separate beds at home, and have for quite some time." Carrie rose from the bench and snipped at some marigolds that grew along the fence, collecting a bouquet of them. Their bright golden heads contrasted brilliantly against the blue sky, as did Carrie.

"You appear so sure of yourself," I said, "And yet, you are living in a marriage that you dislike. Even so, you seem happy." I tried to fathom the complexities of Carrie's relationship, only because she had been so forthcoming in sharing them with me.

"I *am* happy," she stated. "I have everything I want, except for a husband that I can love. But that is rarely attainable, I've observed. To me, the purpose of my marriage is to raise these two little boys, and to try to enjoy myself while I'm at it.

"And that's what I'm doing! I am raising two sons, and I hope that I can adequately influence their unruly natures. They require all of my energy and can be quite trying. Thank goodness they are old enough to go to school now—I can't explain to you the exhaustion I felt before they were off to school. And, two children are quite enough, thank you." She smiled and looked pointedly at me.

"And what about you, Eva Smith? I haven't asked *you* any questions. Tell me about yourself." Carrie waited for me to reply as I hesitated.

"I am hoping for a child," I said slowly, "But it has been more than two years now, with no result. I am so very discouraged." I hadn't shared my unhappiness with any of my old friends. This was my first admittance of disappointment, except for the inevitable conversations with my mother.

"If you want a child, you must have a husband who is home to help you make one," she teased. "You say Captain Smith is out to sea more than he is in—are you expecting an immaculate conception?"

"Henry is home all winter long," I answered. I stopped speaking as the boys came skidding to a halt next to us, their bare feet grubby with sand.

"These are your last two cookies," Carrie said as she handed out the molasses balls. "Mrs. Coughlin will be irked to death if you don't eat the dinner she is preparing for you right now in that hot little kitchen. Now, off with you!" Carrie turned towards me again.

"Well, Eva, there are plenty of children in this world who need a mother!" she said. "I can take you to the New England Home for Little Wanderers in Boston, where I occasionally volunteer at fundraisers, and you and your Henry can pick out a child! That would be one lucky child. Lord knows, the orphanage is so overcrowded that children are loaded onto railroad cars and sent out all over the country to be displayed on railroad platforms until some farm family takes them home as an extra pair of hands."

"Yes, I know, Carrie," I said. "It's not as though I haven't thought about it. We have our share of orphans living under the roofs of relatives and friends—we are no strangers to orphans here. We all have adopted cousins, if not brothers and sisters. But I want a child with Henry. We love each other. We want a child of our own." Listening to myself, I sounded almost pitiful.

"Once you stop fretting, you will conceive," Carrie stated emphatically. "I've seen it happen over and over again that once a family adopts a child, the wife becomes pregnant. Then she's got double trouble, like I do. Don't *think* about conceiving. Just enjoy each other, if you've still got a spark going."

"Oh, Carrie, we do enjoy each other, very much," I told her. "It's just that when the weather is fair, Henry is gone to sea so much of the time, and then he's home for just a few short days.

"All this time without him—I'm lonely. I want more excitement; I want more noise and activity and laughing voices around me. I find myself living with an old man—not that I don't love Winslow—but I need something more. A child of my own would fill that void. Do you see what I mean?"

The rambunctious boys came to a stop in front of us again.

"Mother, may I please have another cookie?" Richie was overly polite, precisely enunciating his words. He stood with his hands clasped behind his back, chest out, chin high in the air.

Tommy followed suit. "Yes, please, Mother?"

"What do you say to Mrs. Smith?" Carrie prompted them. She appeared to have forgotten that she had just declared an end to the cookies.

"Thank-you, Mrs. Smith," they both piped in unison.

"Anything else you'd like to tell her?" Carrie clearly enjoyed the interaction, and the postponement of the next treat.

Tommy turned to me. "The cookies are delicious, Mrs. Smith." He was earnest, but the gap in his mouth where he had just lost his front tooth made me giggle behind my hand.

"Yes, Mrs. Smith, please be so kind as to give our mother your recipe," Richie said.

"Very good, then," Carrie said, "Here is another for each of you, and that is the last one for now. And I really mean it this time. Off with you boys. Shoo, shoo." She took a fan out of her apron pocket and fanned the air towards the boys, as though they were pesky flies.

"Can we go down to play in the water?" Richie asked, his mouth full of cookie.

"Yes, but you've got to change your clothes. And wait for me! I'll not have you down there by yourself. Go change into your bathing clothes, now."

As Carrie spoke to her sons, I sat and looked at the blue horizon, wondering when Henry would be back. I soon bade Carrie farewell and walked home.

Henry is out there in the water somewhere, far away from me. I often wonder if Henry thinks of me as many times during the day as I think of him. I hope so, but knowing Henry, it's doubtful. Carrie does not realize that my husband has a mistress also, and she is the sea. But I knew that was the case from the start.

~

I've tried to take Carrie Bolton's advice to stop my perpetual fretting for a baby of my own. There are many children in the neighborhood to play with. This week, in the spirit of being imaginative, I held a tea party for the little girls with the double purpose of visiting with them and their mothers. It was such fun to have them arrive at my front door all dressed up and looking forward to a special cake or cookie and the chance to properly pour the tea for the adults.

Of course, they all call me "Auntie," which is very nice. And Laurie Young's little Abigail, who is just now walking at fourteen months old, paid me the greatest of compliments. She was careening around the room trying to keep her balance, and when I called out to her with my arms open, she came laughing to me. I was so delighted. She is a precious child.

Carrie was invited, and she wisely sent the boys off for an afternoon sail with Winslow, insisting upon paying the full adult excursion fee for each of them. Winslow has no fear of the boys; he said that the raising of Henry gave him plenty of practice. Carrie was so enchanted with the little girls of Paine Hollow that she promised them all a tea at her cottage next week. I was very pleased that the neighborhood ladies took to Carrie and she to them. My tea was a great success.

Henry was in for three enjoyable days. I told him about my new acquaintance with Carrie, but I did not make a great effort to introduce them, as I am not sure if he would appreciate her frank opinions and wry sense of humor, or understand why I do.

Nettie stopped by on a rare day out, and she convinced Henry and me to go to Provincetown with her on a little holiday. She had read in the *Provincetown Advocate* that the photography studio there has acquired new props to attract the summer folk. "Let's go and be as carefree as all the tourists," Nettie pleaded with us.

Henry was feeling satisfied as a result of a full catch on his last trip out, and he surprised me by readily accepting Nettie's invitation. Lewis had been helping Henry with a new roof for the privy, and he put down his hammer and washed up so he could come along with us.

We caught the morning train and enjoyed the scenic ride through the pastures and dunes of Truro. The bright sunlight reflected off the bay and lit my heart as well as the landscape. We arrived in bustling Provincetown at the noon hour. The steamboat from Boston had just docked, and passengers streamed off the wharf in a festive rush. The narrow board sidewalks were crowded with men wearing straw boater hats and women brandishing parasols, while the children ran down the middle of the sandy streets. Every curio shop and food concessionaire had a line at its door.

Nettie, Lewis, Henry and I spent several pleasant hours mingling with the tourist crowd before it was time to board the train again for the relaxing ride home. As a result of that fanciful afternoon, my new photograph album contains several irreverent pictures of the four of us posing together in the most theatrical hats imaginable. It was fun to watch Lewis enjoying himself; I don't think we've laughed so much as brother and sister since we were children. The holiday atmosphere did us all a world of good.

A change came over Henry when he realized that very few of the people on the Provincetown sidewalks, if any, knew who he was. My dear husband thoroughly appreciated the sense of being anonymous—which brought forth his sense of humor. He postured as dramatically as any stage actor I've seen. I know he was playing to the crowd that gathered as we were posed by the photographer.

The photographer extended a true bargain price to us after several parties registered for sittings as a result of our shenanigans. Before we were done, I insisted we also have serious portraits taken. I now have a photograph of Henry inside my gold locket. And he tucked one of Nettie and one of me into his wallet. Henry says that when he is out to sea and he looks at our photographs, it will comfort him to know that I have such a good friend in Nettie.

It is certainly not for lack of trying that Henry and I are childless. I have gone so far as to secretly send away for Lydia Pinkham's Vegetable Compound, about which much is written in the newspapers. "It is impossible for a woman, after a faithful course of treatment, to continue to suffer with weakness of the uterus." I've frequently read this proclamation in the advertisement columns of the *Provincetown Advocate*. I have applied the compound daily as directed, with no result.

Upon writing to Lydia Pinkham herself, I soon received a note back from her. "You must not have used the potion long enough, dear lady. I recommend that you try it for another six months, and you are sure to see results. These things take time."

Having used the product for a year already, I am not inclined to spend more money on it. My mother has raised the possibility that the Lord intends for me to develop the virtue of patience by delaying the gift of conception. I certainly hope this is not the case, but the Lord does work in mysterious ways.

Winslow is getting on in age; these past two years without his wife have aged him by a decade. When he's not down at the shore, he sits in his chair reading. It's been a curious development in my life that as Henry's wife, I would have an exclusive relationship with Winslow, and spend far more time with Winslow than with Henry.

I am absolutely at ease when I am alone with Winslow. It occurs to me that I am never alone in the house with Henry, because his father is always here. And there is always an undercurrent of tension between them.

I wonder what my life with Henry would be like if we could spend a considerable amount of time alone together, as I do with Winslow. Of course, this will not happen unless Henry and I move into a house of our own, and neither Henry nor Winslow seems to be inclined to favor that. Winslow is quite content with me acting as his housekeeper.

I don't have to make unnecessary conversation with Winslow, and he doesn't feel the need to entertain me. However, he makes it clear that he is appreciative of everything I do. He seats himself at the table at suppertime well before I have the meal ready, and he reads his newspaper until it is time to eat. On these warm summer days, the sun shines across the bay until after seven, and I have a difficult time bringing myself inside to cook, but cook I must, as Winslow is hungry. He barely notices what I give him for supper, be it soup or meat pie or fish or vegetables.

Winslow does have a sweet tooth, and this I indulge. He waits for and then savors the sweets. I must bake a cake every third day, and I put two thirds of it away as soon as it cools. Dessert seems to be his solace in life, that and the word of the Lord. He first reads the Bible, and then the newspaper, exclaiming over one catastrophe or another. Another drowning! Another death from childbirth! Another bankruptcy! Another vessel lost at sea!

"Come out to the kitchen and read to me, Winslow," I now call to him if he is slow to arrive on his own when I cook.

He has never wanted me to call him Father Smith, or Mr. Smith, or Papa. "Winslow will do," he insisted to me from the beginning of my marriage to his son. Our relationship is mutually satisfying; Winslow has a cook and housekeeper, and I have a reader.

"Eva, listen to this from the Provincetown column in *The Advocate*:

> *As the steamer* Empire State *left Railroad Wharf on Tuesday afternoon, the band played "The Girl I Left Behind Me." Under ordinary circumstances this would have been very touching and the selection very appropriate, but on this particular afternoon the leader of the band was not aware that the girls, boys and crew*

members were over at the Truro Highlands, and that
Provincetown was indeed a deserted village. Something
over 260 excursionists paid their respects and quarters
to the lighthouse keeper at Highland Light."

"Truro is attracting a good share of the excursionists," I say. I don't have to say a lot, because I have learned from experience that Winslow will go on and read the next column to me.

"Yes, why do they expect that because the steamer ties up in Provincetown, the passengers will remain *there* spending money all day," Winslow says. "And, here's something interesting. Seems as though they can't keep the tourists out of the churches on Sunday. Listen to this editorial:

The Sunday Question—No Question at All. To every
question, there is a right and a wrong side, and the
Sunday excursion question is not exempted. On all
moral questions, the Bible has been, and is, the only
standard. We do not see, therefore, the necessity of a
prolonged discussion of this question. The word of God
expressly declares it to be the duty of man to 'Remember
the Sabbath Day to keep it holy.' If the moral side of this
question is to decide it, (and we do not see any other
side worthy of consideration), how can anyone in the
face of this clear and explicit declaration contend for
Sunday excursion? A musty formula of the past, the
tourists say—this is called Puritanism. But what of it?
The time is far over when conscientious people will be
afraid of that word. There is no other law that marks
out the proper observance of the Sabbath. It is the day
that God claims for Himself, and if we acknowledge
the right of the Lord to claim anything from man, He
certainly has the right. And the strongest argument I

*know of to answer those in favor of Sunday excursions
into the churches is, 'Thus sayeth the Lord'."*

Winslow ends his reading of the editorial with great emphasis on the last phrase.

"Yes, I do agree with the editor's opinion there," I say. "I cannot imagine a crowd of sight-seeing gawkers trouncing through the church in the middle of the Sunday service. How rude! There should be no controversy there!"

"Exactly, Eva, exactly."

It is comfortable when my father-in-law and I agree upon a religious question, and here was something that a Congregationalist and a Methodist could agree upon. We are always careful to speak about what we do agree upon, rather than what we don't, particularly when it comes to religion. There is no winning an argument about religion, and the Lord Jesus himself counseled against entering into one.

~

September has always been my favorite month, with its crisp sunny days and clear star-filled nights cold enough to subdue the mosquitoes. The humidity of August is gone. The horizon line has become sharp and the royal blue color of the bay more intense. But this year, I note an unfamiliar emptiness inside me that became apparent when our summer residents departed.

When they first arrived in June, perhaps they stepped off the train with no one to greet them. But after spending the season in South Wellfleet, heart felt goodbyes were exchanged between many new friends.

I drove the beguiling Carrie Bolton and her two sons to the station. All the wagons for hire had already been engaged when Carrie tried to make an arrangement, and so Silkie and Sinbad were pressed into duty. We found the platform full of noisy people and overstuffed trunks. The exodus declared to us that summer was ending.

"I will miss this fresh air," Carrie said, as she looked up at the white cumulus clouds. "And I will especially miss the bright stars at night. Here, it seems as though I could reach out and touch them. But back to Boston we must go.

"Richie, put your shoes on. You have to wear your shoes to board the train. Oh, I've laced this corset too tightly—it's really going to bother me today."

"I don't want to get on the train, Mother!" Richie's red hair was disheveled, his shirt was untucked, and he held a sand toad in his hand.

"Richie, put that toad down, put your shoes on, and go get your brother out of that store. I imagine Ike has entranced Tommy with another story. Here comes the train, now hurry!" Carrie turned to her loyal housekeeper. "Mrs. Coughlin, I give up. Please see if you can get these boys under control."

Mrs. Coughlin grabbed a squawking Richie by his ear and marched him into the general store in search of Tommy. Carrie ignored Richie's protests and turned to me.

"I'm so happy that we met each other, Eva," she said. "We'll have a good time when you come visit me. I look forward to repaying you for your kindness. And you like my boys! Of course, they will be in school, so we'll have time for some sightseeing during the day without them. Promise me, now." She hugged me.

I nodded in agreement, and we stepped back from the noisy engine as it came puffing to a stop at the platform.

"Damn corset," she said. "Sorry, Eva." She darted a look at me, knowing I disapproved of her cussing. "I haven't worn this one all summer, and now I don't know how I ever put up with it. I'm going to wear my soft corset from now on—I don't care what anyone says. I'll just look a little plumper, that's all. I can't breathe."

"Be sure to sit up very straight and you'll get used to it," I said. "And I do promise to come see you, Carrie—as soon as I can."

I miss Carrie's lively humor now that she is gone. Planning a visit to Boston gives me something to look forward to. It is suddenly very quiet here.

~

CHAPTER EIGHT
Strong People

September 15, 1888

School is back in session. Every morning the neighborhood children walk to my end of Paine Hollow, because the conveyance that delivers them to the center of Wellfleet stops here. The urchins, who've been running and shrieking through the neighborhood all summer, have been transformed by their starched dresses and shirts. Feet, that have been barefoot all summer, are confined to the tightness of new leather shoes, and the children sometimes wince when they run.

The boys pull at their collars if they have grown more than their mothers anticipated—as boys will over the summer. The girls are dressed as finely as they can manage; the majority of them wear dresses that I have made. Many fitting sessions have been endured by fidgeting girls as I measured and pinned the bodices of their new frocks. I feel a great sense of accomplishment when I see the girls wearing their dresses. It is a fine delegation of young ladies from Paine Hollow—impressive, to be sure, to the teachers and student body of Wellfleet.

For the first time, the grammar school students are joining the high school students on their daily trek to Wellfleet center. This turn of events was precipitated by the economically distressed town treasury. In a hastily called August meeting, the Wellfleet school board decided that it is too costly to hire teachers for the district grammar schools and ordered the school houses closed. All students will henceforth be taught together in one consolidated location in Wellfleet center.

The people of Paine Hollow were shocked by this news, and there were many dismayed mothers conversing over back fences. It is true that the population of the town is not growing; in fact, quite the opposite is true, and at an alarming rate. I wonder what hope there is for our future if we lose many more of our residents. We assumed that the neighborhood schoolhouses would always be open for the next class session, but it is not to be.

And so, the Pond Hill School, located within shouting distance of our house, sits silent. Before I was born, my Grandfather Nathan sailed to Maine for a load of lumber so the schoolhouse could be built by the Paine Hollow men in a neighborhood "raising." It is hard to accept the fact that the school bell may not ring again. I was so expectant that some day my own little one would be walking down the road to his or her lessons. And I miss the shrieks of laughter that came drifting across the yard during the noon hour recess.

Although it is sad for the adults to see our schoolhouse closed, I believe the change to be very exciting for the children. The high school has always been located in the center of Wellfleet, and now the students of every age will ride together to school. From the start, the younger students will have so many more friends, and a music teacher has been employed to give music lessons.

The eager students wait for their ride to school just outside my front gate. I cherish the opportunity this gives me to talk to them every day and receive their version of the daily neighborhood news. The children tell me who is coming to visit from away, who is sick, what new contraption or convenience has been added to a household, who is sailing out, and who is expected in.

We know the wagon is coming well before we see it, as Sinbad and Silkie neigh out the news that horses are approaching. Quite soon after that, the four draft horses come into view, pulling into their harnesses against the deep sandy ruts of the road. The driver, Mr. Poole, being the large man that he is, temporarily shields the passengers from me. But as the long wagon stops at my gate, I get a good view of the students sitting in the eight rows of seats. They have become accustomed to seeing me in the morning, waiting with the pupils from Paine Hollow. This morning, I was loudly greeted.

"Good morning, Mrs. Smith," the riders called out in singsong unison, which led to hysterical giggles from the girls and lopsided grins from the boys.

"It's their new game, Eva," Mr. Poole said to me from high up on his seat. "They are calling out to everyone they see today. It seems that the school principal has trained them to address him in this way, and so they're practicing on everyone we pass."

When the students return in the late afternoon, after enduring a hot day in the classroom and the dusty ride home, they often come into the yard to get a drink of water from our well. I am grateful I can say that I have children in my life, if only for a few minutes on each end of school days. Between their departure and return, I have settled into a comfortable routine.

September gives me sunny days—to do laundry on Monday; to clean stalls on Tuesday; to take the horses into town for marketing and the library on Wednesdays; to visit the sick with Mama on Thursdays; and to can the last fruits and vegetables from the garden on Fridays.

And then it is the end of the week—Saturday is for receiving company; Sunday is for church followed by a dinner of roasted chicken or cod. Of course, every day I make the beds, cook, tend to Winslow, and scurry after Henry when he is home.

~

October 10, 1888

The weather has been perfect for so long that I am beginning to take it for granted—sunny, dry, and calm with a steady barometer. Winslow has surprised us all. He has suddenly found the desire and strength to take a trip out on the water with Henry. I think he reasons that winter will soon be upon us, with all its attending aches and pains, and he wants to get out and do something while he feels good. Winslow joked with me that he will earn his keep by catching a few cod to put up for the winter, and so he is off with Henry after meticulously waterproofing his oilskins, which he hadn't used for months.

It is very quiet here in the house, except in the morning. The children are quite lively as they wait for their ride to school. They do thoroughly enjoy being together—it is evident in their games and songs.

Today little William Jenkins sought me out between games of tag to give me the news that his older sister Clara is feeling poorly and would like to see me. He said Clara has had several fainting spells, and she cannot keep her food down. I promised William that I will go and visit Clara today, and so I shall, after I muck out the stalls.

Simple arithmetic informs me that two horses produce twice as much manure as my dear old Tess once did, and then I had a brother at home to help with the mucking out. Since marrying Henry and taking on the care of his two beauties, I have developed the muscular arms of a boy with all of my shoveling.

I do envy the students their days at school. How I wish I could relive my own school days! During the hours that I shovel manure, I recite Shakespearian sonnets and plays to keep myself from thinking that I have wasted my education. The horses seem to enjoy it and stay close by until I have completed my chore.

$\sim$

I finished with the stalls later than I anticipated. After raking clean wood shavings into place, a full bath was necessary to prevent me from smelling like a stable myself.

With Winslow away from the house, I indulged myself with a rare, mid-day bath. Lying in the water, with the sun streaming through the window and outlining every curve of my body, I entertained the thought that Henry would enjoy viewing me in my natural state.

The bathtub is large enough for both of us to bathe together, but I must never suggest it. Once the notion is introduced, Henry might well insist upon trying it. That would simply be impossible because of Winslow. I don't think the day will ever come when Henry and I are alone here at the house. It's Winslow's home, after all. Although I love it here, I daydream of Henry and I owning a home of our own. I do not wish Henry to prematurely inherit this house. Winslow deserves a long and happy life.

∼

After my necessary mid-day bath, I decided to walk to the depot and collect the morning mail for Mama, since I was going down into the hollow to visit with Clara Jenkins.

It was not unusual that I found our informal town crier, the irksome Matilda Chase, gossiping to the stationmaster. The episode in the parlor after Arozana's funeral, at which time Matilda requested that I sell Arozana's treasured china to her, has caused me to generally disregard anything I hear coming from Matilda's lips, and I exchange only the most superficial of greetings with her.

Matilda was talking loudly to the stationmaster about Clara Jenkins. Several times she insisted that Clara had "stumbled." Blood surged to my face, and I was passionately engaged before I could think the better of it.

"Matilda Chase, whatever are you talking about? What right do you have to judge another? Perhaps you should take the log out of your own eye before you complain about the splinter in someone else's!"

She turned to me slowly, with a smile on her face. Mr. Newcomb said nothing, but bobbed his head towards me.

"Why Eva, how nice to see you," Matilda said. "I was going to stop by your house for tea soon. I haven't seen you lately, and we have so much to talk about, don't we? I was merely stating that Clara Jenkins is not well, and I wouldn't be surprised if she was with child."

"Well, you would be wrong, Matilda," I snapped. "Clara is no more with child than you are. So please, kindly refrain from spreading vicious rumors."

"Eva Smith, are you calling me vicious? That is not done in polite society. I am highly insulted!" Matilda struck a pose of indignation, her nose pointing skyward. Mr. Newcomb lowered his gaze and moved a step away from us, clearing his throat.

"I am not calling you vicious," I said evenly. "But I *am* calling that rumor vicious, and it would be best if you didn't spread it. And as for polite society, I find that it is sometimes the most hypocritical. We have no right at all to judge others."

I turned to the station master. "I'll take my mother's mail along with my own, please, Mr. Newcomb," I said.

He ducked into the tiny post office, and in that moment, Matilda delivered a hissing remark.

"I think you are very sensitive, Eva, because *you* have been unable to produce any offspring. However, it is sometimes too easy for other women to conceive."

Matilda was satisfied—she had both stung me and made it clear she was not going to veer from her current course on Clara. I clamped my jaw shut. Mr. Newcomb reappeared with several envelopes. I took the mail, nodded my thanks, and walked away as quickly as I could, wishing I had taken the buggy.

I was at Mama's within the half hour. Curiously, her buggy was waiting in the yard with Duke harnessed between the traces. I went through the kitchen door and told Mama what had just happened on the station platform. Her wrinkled brow conveyed the news before she spoke. She came around the table and looked me in the eye.

"I am afraid that Clara is at least two months along with child," Mama said, putting her hand gently on my shoulder.

I exhaled. I hadn't noticed that I'd been holding my breath.

"Who is the father?" I asked. I expected to hear of a secret lover who would soon step forward to marry Clara, and then proclaim a premature birth of their first child. My mother looked down and bit her lip.

"Clara was at Nettie's house last night, crying for hours. She was inconsolable. She finally told Nettie it was her own father, Captain Jenkins." Mama said the words slowly.

I gasped and sat down, staring at her in disbelief. She made some mental adjustment and continued more matter-of-factly.

"Nettie and I have decided Clara must leave." Mama nodded out towards the waiting buggy. She looked utterly sad, her face slack with the loss of its usual smile.

I felt faint. I could not accept the thought of Captain Jenkins impregnating his own daughter, my dear little friend Clara.

"How could this happen, Mama? I don't understand."

"I'm afraid Clara's tendency to look like her mother did as a young woman has dealt Clara a great disservice. In his grief, and with the help of that demon rum he brings back from Jamaica, Captain Jenkins has apparently visited Clara's bedroom in a drunken and violent state. She confided last night that ever since her sixteenth birthday, her father has been quite difficult upon returning home from the sea. Clara has been living in horrid shame. She says she wants to die."

I shuddered. "Captain Jenkins has always been well respected," I said. "This is very difficult to hear. Matilda was right, then. That miserable woman—she is so smug. Clara's reputation will be ruined in a matter of hours. And Matilda has no idea about the worst of it.

Just wait until she gets wind of that horrid bit of information. Where is Clara now? I want to see her."

"She finally went home last night, but she's back at Nettie's right now. Nettie is preparing her for the train ride to Boston," Mama said. She paused and then continued, "Captain Jenkins has plans of his own for Clara. He has told her that she is going crazy and has threatened to send her to a sanitarium."

Mama moved about the kitchen, gathering a basket of food. "I believe he suspects that Clara is pregnant, and he wants to remove her. We must act immediately or she will be incarcerated in Boston as an uncontrollable daughter, and her life will be over. Of course, Captain Jenkins will never admit his own part in her pregnancy; he will claim to know nothing about that, no doubt." Mama calmly conveyed the serious consequences that Clara would soon face if we did not move quickly.

"How will Clara get to the train station without being noticed?" I asked.

"I'm driving her down. I was just getting ready to come to your house first to borrow a dress for her. I'm so glad you've come, Eva. This blue calico you're wearing is perfect. Everyone knows this dress is your favorite. And we'll use my parasol to hide Clara's face. You two both have dark hair—that's going to help. Could you please change out of your dress, Eva, and put on one of mine?

"Yes, of course, Mama. But how is Clara going to manage on her own?"

"Miss Gross, your favorite high school teacher, has agreed to travel with Clara. She's already on her way to the station. With her no-nonsense manner, she'll be the perfect companion for Clara. Miss Gross will buy a ticket for the next stop up—Eastham—where half of her family resides. I will buy another ticket for Eastham and give it to Clara. In Eastham, Miss Gross will get off and buy two tickets for Barnstable and then re-board the train. Then in Barnstable, she'll buy two for Boston. Clara won't have to get off the train at all until she reaches the city.

"The folks down at the station platform won't know the final destination of either traveler. With luck, Clara will be mistaken for you, and Captain Jenkins won't realize that Clara has left the neighborhood for quite some time. By then, hopefully she'll have arrived safely in Boston. But I'm afraid they still need a place to stay overnight, and a kind soul to direct Clara to a trustworthy pharmacist."

"I want to go with her," I said.

"You can't, Eva. Clara will be dressed as you for her own safety. You said that Matilda Chase is down on the platform? She just saw you wearing this dress. Rest assured, Matilda will incorrectly herald it to the world that you have left on the train, and that's what we want."

"Oh, yes. That's right. I can't reason properly," I said. I marveled that my mother could.

"You could easily travel back from Eastham by buggy, thus explaining your reappearance here later this evening," she said.

"And what then, in Boston?" I could barely bring myself to ask my next question. "Is Clara going to keep her baby?"

"No, dear. She is not." Mama knew this would be hard for me to hear. She spoke softly. "Clara cannot bear the thought of having a child that is both her offspring and her sibling, and who can blame her? The sin is her father's, not hers. And of course, we all know that the life of any woman who bears a child out of wedlock is a very hard fate to endure.

"As it is, Clara will have to travel west to get a fresh start—once she has regained her health and stamina. But in the meantime, Nettie and I are thinking that perhaps Clara and Miss Gross might stay with Annabelle Holbrook Crandle. Annabelle will remember Clara, even though Clara was four years behind her in school. And Annabelle would never turn Miss Gross away."

"No, Mama, that's not a good plan, and I'm surprised that Nettie would think it was," I said. "We had quite the conversation with Annabelle when we visited with her two years ago. Annabelle has a diminishing opinion of Wellfleet, and Clara's situation will simply solidify her sentiments and do Clara no good at all.

"But I'll write Clara a letter to bring to Carrie Bolton. I know Carrie would be happy to help Clara, and she has the resources to do it. Carrie is the one."

"Yes, you're right," Mama nodded in agreement.

I thought of our men—Henry and Winslow, Papa and Lewis—all out to sea and oblivious to the developments in the neighborhood. I silently thanked the Lord they were away so we could act as we saw fit. The men would undoubtedly complicate the situation, considering their respect for the good Captain Jenkins.

I changed my blue dress for one of Mama's calicos, and we left Duke stomping at flies as we walked quickly across the road to Nettie's house. We let ourselves in through the kitchen door so the boarders wouldn't see us and climbed the back stairs to Nettie's room. Clara sat on the bed, white as a gravestone, while Nettie stood over her brushing Clara's hair. When Clara saw me, she burst into tears.

"Oh, Eva," she said, "I'm so sorry." She cried softly, like a mewing kitten.

"There is no reason for you to be sorry, Clara," I said. "You haven't done anything wrong. Everything is going to be all right." I sounded more certain than I felt.

"But I don't want to leave."

"I'm afraid there is no other solution, Clara," Mama said. "You must escape this situation, and you'll have a better life somewhere else. You *must* go." Her words were adamant, though kindly spoken.

"But I'll miss everyone. Little William. All of my friends. I feel so sick. I don't want to travel. Who will help me?"

Nettie took her hand. "Miss Gross is going to Boston with you.

She will take care of you on the train." Nettie answered Clara reassuringly, but looked over at me, concern showing in her eyes.

"Clara, listen to me," I said. "Do you remember the lady with the bright red hair who made us all laugh? Mrs. Bolton, who leased that new cottage up on Pleasant Point last summer? She lives in Boston, and she's going to help you. I need some stationary, Nettie, and an envelope, please."

I sat down at Nettie's desk and began to write while Nettie twisted Clara's hair up into the same style that I wear every day. Mama held out my blue dress and helped Clara into it. Clara stood limply, allowing herself to be dressed like an invalid. I wrote to Carrie, insisting that she help Clara as if she were me, and telling her I would be in Boston quite soon to visit with her and the boys.

Mama checked the clock again and calculated her exact departure time. "We have half an hour until the train arrives. Duke is difficult to hold back—he'll make the mile to the station quickly. But I don't want to arrive a minute too soon, as that would provide an opportunity for observers to make unwelcome inquiries."

Clara stiffened. "Oh, I can't do this," she groaned.

"Shhh," Nettie tried to calm her. "You can do it, because the alternative is so much worse. Now get your strength up, Clara. You're going to be fine." She handed Clara a glass of water.

We all watched the clock on Nettie's dresser. With fifteen minutes to go before the train arrived, Mama and I went down the steep stairs in front of Clara, and Nettie followed behind her. I hugged Clara and kissed her good-bye, and Nettie and Mama took her elbows and helped her walk across the road to Mama's yard. Watching from behind, I had the strange feeling that I was watching myself walk away—my dress fit Clara so perfectly.

Nettie returned immediately, and then Mama drove by, firmly holding the lines. Clara sat on the seat beside her, her face hidden behind the sunbonnet and parasol. Nettie and I watched the buggy disappear up the road in a cloud of dust. Duke was excited to finally be trotting after his long wait.

"Clara will never come back, will she?" I looked at Nettie, who seemed wilted and drawn.

"No, I hope not," Nettie said, "Because if she does, that means her father found her." She took a deep breath. "Let's get back in the house, Eva. You've got to stay here with me for at least a few hours, and then walk home through the woods. Don't answer your door for the rest of the day. If I'm asked, I'll say Clara visited me earlier this morning, and when she left, I assumed she was going home."

"And if I'm asked, I never saw her. I went to Eastham on the afternoon train to get a book from their public library and rode back with a delivery wagon that was coming this way."

"Agreed," said Nettie.

I was uncomfortable about our planned deception, no matter what protection it offered Clara. But then I thought about the great wrong Clara had been done by her own father and the continuation of the injustice by the likes of Matilda Chase.

The sound of the train whistle as it arrived at the station sent shivers through me. I felt cold, although it was a warm day. Nettie brought a pot of hot tea up to the bedroom. We were silent as we sipped from our teacups.

Later, I walked home on a path through the woods, avoiding the road. I cried harder than I have ever cried in my life. I cried for the baby Clara would not have and the baby I could not have. I cried for Little William. I cried for Captain Jenkins. When I arrived in my own dooryard, I locked the front door and went upstairs. When the children came home from school and knocked at my door, I was very quiet. "She's not home," I heard them conclude amongst themselves. Looking down from my bedroom window, I noticed how Little William looked sweet and small compared to his schoolmates. All I can do is pray that William's life will not be as difficult as his sister's.

I do not understand the mysterious ways of our Lord, and I am quite angry with him that he has allowed this to happen to Clara—a fine young woman who has done her very best to raise William since their mother died two years ago. Why all this pain? However, the good Lord promises not to send more hardship than one can endure, and so he must hold the opinion that we are very strong people.

~

December 28, 1888

Silkie and Sinbad are as furry as bears with their winter coats. I did not blanket them this fall as I wanted their coats to grow in thick so they will be warm through the cruel winter ahead. We have received several heavy snows since Thanksgiving, and the sleigh has been pulled out of the shed and put to good use. Henry polished the rust off the runners and buffed the leather seats. Now the hard packed snow on the road presents a shining ribbon which we glide over on our way to town, and we get there a good deal sooner than we do when the roads are soft and sandy.

Mama and Papa will not be traveling to Virginia this winter as they had hoped. One of Mama's favorite cousins has taken ill, and Mama refuses to leave. Lewis has been in the hollow through December, but he is cheerfully off to Boston come January to drive the bakery delivery wagons once again.

We have just finished with the Christmas season which brought with it the pleasure of putting on our annual church bazaar. The shrinking size of the congregations of both churches has caused a pleasant truce; this year we joined together and hosted one bazaar at the Congregational Church instead of competing with one another. This does seem to be so much more in keeping with the season, after all. And for once, Mama and I could attend the same church event without argument.

Since there is no need yet for St. Nicolas to visit our house, I enjoyed volunteering with Nettie to prepare the bazaar. A report from the Wellfleet Ladies Aid Bulletin noted that:

> *The combined efforts of the ladies of our two Protestant churches produced the most brilliant Christmas Bazaar yet! A large fish bowl afloat with gold fish was the center piece of the hall, surrounded by banks of flowers fresh off the train. Pettiness was put away, and the proceeds evenly split between the Methodist and Congregational Churches at the suggestion of Miss Nettie Paine. It seems as though Christians do better when joining together than when professing their own denomination to be the better one.*

~

Looking back at 1888, it has been a year of grappling with hard realities. There is a sparkling bright spot of note, though, and that is the addition of a new friend, thanks to the acquaintance that I've made with Carrie Bolton. I had an unforgettable visit with her in November. Through frequent correspondence, she prevailed upon me to keep my promise, and she kindly extended the invitation to bring Henry and Nettie along.

My excursion to Boston just after Thanksgiving seems a distant memory, although it occurred only a month ago. I went by myself, as Nettie declined, and Henry literally snorted at the idea of visiting a female friend of mine. He declared that I would be perfectly safe on the train by myself, and so I was.

Carrie Bolton certainly proved to be the ambitious hostess, meeting me at the Boston train station and whirling me through the city in her chauffeured hansom, drawn by a high stepping Tennessee walker. I was immediately awed by the new mansions rising in the expanding neighborhood of Back Bay, Boston—the land there having so recently been claimed from the flats of the Charles River, it seemed to me it must still be wet and unstable.

The Bolton's red brick town house is no exception to the wealth on display. The mansion and its charming back courtyard are located within blocks of the street address of Annabelle Holbrook Crandle. Carrie and Annabelle live closer to each other than I do to Nettie, but they have never met, even though they may have passed each other a dozen times on the sidewalks of their neighborhood. I find the layers of human interaction in the city to be staggering. So many social circles to belong to, so many groups of friends! Truth be told, I did not wish to see Annabelle again, and therefore did not let her know I was in her neighborhood. Lord, forgive me for ignoring my manners.

Carrie's home is beautifully appointed. To her great credit, Carrie manages to be unpretentious in character, even though she lives in opulent surroundings. Her heavy furniture, sumptuous bedding, lavish paintings, and thick draperies are all imported from Europe. The scale of room measurement is much larger than what I am accustomed to. Her guest bedroom is larger than my front parlor and dining room combined. When I retired in the evening, it was as though I was sleeping in a great cavern.

Plush carpeting, marble work around the wide doorways and fireplaces, the sweeping curve of the staircase, tiled baths with hot and cold running water, theatrically high ceilings—all contributed to the high brow atmosphere of the mansion, but Carrie resides there every day with no thought that it is unusual. I marveled at the fact that this lady was perfectly happy all summer long living in a tiny cottage graced with none of her accustomed luxuries or conveniences.

Carrie introduced me to her domestic help as though I was an important dignitary, and my every whim was anticipated, from hot wet hand towels at meal time to the lighting of the gas lights in my bedroom at dusk. Carrie runs a full house-keeping staff, from head housekeeper to maid to cook to livery men to stable groom. Mrs. Coughlin holds the very important responsibility of overseeing the boys in every aspect of their day, including meals, laundry, schoolwork, and athletic schedules. Richie and Tommy leave the house early in the morning, chaperoned by Mrs. Coughlin. She returns to the house until it is time for her to meet them and walk them home from school at dusk, and they arrive at home hungry and excited.

"I barely see them when school is in session," Carrie told me. "I see their instructors more—the boys are constantly in trouble. I know you long to be a mother, Eva, but count your blessings.

"I must be down at the academy offices at least once a week, straightening out some row that either Richie or Tommy has instigated. It's a wonder the academy keeps them, but then again, we do give heavily to the annual building fund." Carrie takes every opportunity to caution me against longing for children.

I didn't see any sign of Carrie's husband, Richard, and did not ask about him, unsure as to what their current arrangement might be. I knew Carrie would tell me soon enough.

Outside the mansion, the brick sidewalks were covered with soggy brown leaves that had fallen from the elms and maples, and the cobblestone streets were louder than I remembered, full of the din of passing horse drawn conveyances and the occasional honking motor car. Once again, I found myself exhilarated by the sights and sounds of the city.

My fear of not owning the proper city attire proved to be unfounded. The fashion plates I study in *Godey's Lady's Book* (the extravagant but useful monthly publication I pay for with my seamstress earnings) have kept me abreast of the latest fashion trends. My wardrobe competed surprisingly well with Carrie's beautiful clothing. A forest green silk that I had just completed afforded me fashion, convenience, and a figure flattering style. Carrie kindly complimented my dress and then boasted about me to her friends at the "Women Only" dinner party she held in my honor.

To my surprise, the admiration of the ladies was sincere. I received several generous orders for similar "winter traveling dresses" and measured the ladies after dessert. I assured the ladies that if their measurements were taken after the meal, the dresses would be all the more comfortable to wear on excursion.

With little coaxing, I explained my technique of adding a lightweight wool petticoat to the dress's construction. The resulting padding on the hips causes the waist to appear all the smaller. The feature most appreciated however, was my simple design of centering a wide band of crème colored silk down the front of the bodice from the neckline to the waist. The silk is five inches wide at the neck, and narrows to two inches wide at the waist, thus visually creating a narrowing bodice. This light inset of silk, outlined by the darker silk on either side, hints that one might still have a waist after endless cakes and cookies, or childbirth—whatever the case may be. The desired effect is achieved without having to cinch one's corset so tightly that travel is uncomfortable, and sitting in a carriage or a railway coach is actually tolerable.

"My friends, after all these years of gasping for breath, I am looking for comfort. And with Eva's design, I don't have to sacrifice a flattering presentation," Carrie complimented me. Following her lead, her guests brought out their beaded purses.

I was quite flattered by the orders, and with the ladies' deposits I was able to purchase quality fabrics in the garment district. I've promised the dresses by mid-January. I could have them finished earlier, but something made me want to appear very much in demand as a seamstress, and presumably working my way through other similar orders.

More importantly, I wanted to finish the dresses with the knowledge that my work is of the finest quality, and that is the true reason I asked for so much time. I do appreciate Arozana's sewing machine more and more. I think of how surprised she would be if she knew of the dress orders I've received from the wealthy matrons of Boston, and further, how I am able to financially support the household through the long cold winter.

~

My one mistake at Carrie's dinner party was that during a conversational lull, I broke the silence by bringing up my indebtedness to her. "I must thank you again, Carrie, for assisting my neighbor in her journey west this past October."

"The powders did their work," Carrie said, "And Clara was ready to travel two weeks after arriving in Boston. She is now happily visiting with my sister in Missouri. Such a pretty girl, and so capable. She got along famously with my boys."

"What did you mean by that—the powders?"

"Preventive powders, certainly you've heard of them, Eva? The obstacle was eliminated, and Clara's system is once again fully functional." Carrie said this as though discussing Clara's victory over a sore throat or bout of the flu.

"I can't say that I *have* heard of them, Carrie." Aware of several pairs of eyes upon me at my end of the crystal laden table, I blushed upon realizing that a much deeper level of discussion had been quickly reached.

Up until this moment, I had purposely avoided discussing Clara's state of health with Carrie. I had not wished to hear the details; I had prayed to the Lord that kindness and mercy would be received by Clara in her time of need and left the resolution in the Lord's hands.

Now my mind rushed about, confirming for me that I had the opposite desire—one of giving birth to a child, not of preventing it—and therefore had never before discussed an aborting powder. My potion of choice, Lydia Pinkham's Remedy, promises "a baby in every bottle," but as of yet, has not delivered. Through my experience with Clara, I was now painfully aware that there are compelling reasons not to bring a child into the world, and methods by which to accomplish this, but had not anticipated that it was an appropriate topic of discussion at a cosmopolitan ladies' dinner party.

"Yes, yes, Madame Restell's Powders have always been the best for that sort of thing," Mrs. Horace Marshon, a wealthy dowager, emphatically stated. "Although the expense and the inconvenience of acquisition are quite daunting now, ever since the potion was made illegal by that dreadful politician, Comstock."

Mrs. Marshon, my mother's contemporary, was expensively dressed. The number of jewels she wore on her hands and around her wide neck would have brought enough money to buy every house in Paine Hollow, from the schoolhouse to the shore line.

"Madame Restell has been dead for ten years now, driven to her own death by that odious Comstock. What does that man know of the trials and tribulations of women?" Mrs. Marshon made a face as if she had tasted pickle brine. "But one can still request her remedy to be formulated if you patronize a sympathetic pharmacist. It's a shame that only the wealthy can afford it—by the look of the squalor and disease in that slum down near the harbor, the poor have a much greater need."

Mrs. Marshon held up her hand to indicate she was not done speaking, spooned some chocolate pudding into her mouth, and quickly swallowed before continuing. The twelve women seated at the table respectfully waited.

"Some years ago I stocked my medicine cabinet with an ample supply of the powder. My niece recently had call to use some. She found she was late just before she and her husband and children were to leave on their winter Mediterranean tour. It just wouldn't do to be in such a state on an ocean crossing, and now she is the picture of health, and happily making the final arrangements for their voyage."

Mrs. Marshon then made the most revealing comment of all. She lowered her voice and confided in the most theatrical manner, "My own dear Horace is simply too frisky for both of us, and I am afraid that if I did not occasionally partake of the powders myself, I would still be bearing children and have a dozen of them underfoot—if I were still alive to tell the story, that is."

The talkative lady quite enjoyed the fact that I was wide eyed in mortification. She pressed on.

"Hear, hear, ladies, let us toast to the good Madame Restell! She's provided self determination to many a desperate woman, may she rest in peace," Mrs. Marshon cried out with great fervor.

All of the ladies, myself included, held up glasses to the deceased abortionist who had formulated and marketed the most efficient obstruction-eliminating powder available.

I was light-headed, imagining what my friends in Paine Hollow would have thought of such sentiments. But after all, it was our own Clara who had so desperately needed the abortive powders. I opened my mouth, but nothing came out. I tried to clear my mind so I could converse.

"What is it, Eva?" Mrs. Marshon watched me from across the table.

"But what do you make of the fact that our great feminist, Miss Anthony, who has worked so tirelessly to win the women's vote, writes vehemently against abortion?" I asked.

Mrs. Marshon laughed loudly. Then she put down her dessert spoon in preparation for another speech.

"Yes, yes, the idealistic Miss Susan B. Anthony, who rails against abortion as unsafe and dangerous for women, and therefore she is against it. Well, it is all in who you engage as a practitioner.

"Of course there are those who pose as experts in every branch of the medical profession, and then wreak havoc upon their patients. But I have this to say to Miss Anthony, and I will say it to her face if ever I have the chance: You have obviously never known the terror of an unwanted pregnancy, Miss Anthony. You have never been married. Childbirth is many times more dangerous than abortion, as you would know if you had ever delivered a child. You have no idea what goes on between husband and wife, and more importantly, how often. Therefore, you have no idea of the possible frequency of pregnancy in spite of all human precautions.

"And so, Miss Anthony, although you have fought long and hard for the women's vote, in the area of motherhood, please let every women choose for herself. It is bad enough that the law is against us, without you barging in where a lady should know on her own whether or not it is the right time for her to bring an infant into the world." Mrs. Marshon thumped her hand on the table to emphasize her point. She raised her eyebrows at me from across the table, challenging me to an answer.

"Hear, hear!" The ladies raised their glasses again. I did not raise my own; I simply nodded at Mrs. Marshon, satisfied that my question had been answered. I was no longer confused. There was a long pause as the ladies waited to see what my response might be.

"I see what you're saying, Mrs. Marshon, thank you," I said. And then I took advantage of my position as guest of honor and immediately turned to my hostess.

"Carrie, how pretty that ring looks on your hand. It matches your dress so perfectly," I said. The words sounded superficial to my ears, but the astute Carrie quickly responded.

"Thank you, Eva. It's a yellow topaz—a good-bye present from Richard. He has taken another business trip to India. Isn't it beautiful? It was dear of him." With great delight, she held it up for all to see.

I did not venture to make further conversation, but simply smiled numbly and observed the women around me, wondering at their strategies and the fact that this fascinating female society existed just a hundred miles away from my own humble home!

Upon returning to Paine Hollow, I shared the details of the dinner conversation with Nettie, although I could not bring myself to talk with Mama about the preventive powders.

In her practical way, Nettie said, "Thank God Carrie had the friends and the finances to help Clara as she did. She must be credited with saving Clara's life."

We learned more about Clara's fate just before Christmas. In a letter received by Nettie, Clara wrote that she did not stop in Missouri for long, but traveled all the way to the north Pacific coast. And, within a week's time of arriving by railroad in Seattle, she married! In an uplifting missive, Clara reported that she had dozens of bachelors fawning over her at the laundry where she worked, and she quickly chose an established lumber merchant to end the competing attention, as the rivalries were becoming physical and she feared a gunfight.

Women are very scarce here and highly valued. I daresay that there are a hundred men to every female in town! I am happy with my new husband. He has built a house for me, and I truly have a new life, thanks to you ladies. But I do miss you all so. Would you please send me word of Little William? My life has changed immensely in two month's time, and I feel as though I live in another world, but I do think of you all the time, dear Nettie and Eva and Aunt Sarah.

Clara did not mention her father. Nettie has chosen not to inform Captain Jenkins of his daughter's new life; she says that Clara must do that herself. Captain Jenkins did not search hard for Clara after her disappearance, nor did he question any of the women in the neighborhood. He simply made the announcement in church that he was indeed sad because his little Clara had "run off." Noticeable tears rolled down the captain's cheeks when he stood and informed the congregation of Clara's sudden absence. They were taken for tears of grief by many. I hope they were also tears of remorse.

On Sunday mornings, when Reverend Moss asks if there are any prayer concerns, Captain Jenkins always makes the request that we pray for his "poor lost Clara." I believe he should ask that we pray for him as well, which I do. I also pray for myself, as I am fighting the continuous struggle to purge the wicked habit of judgment from my heart. The Lord will judge and treat the good Captain Jenkins accordingly; it is not my task to do so. If Captain Jenkins is truly repentant, he will have earned the Lord's forgiveness.

Little William is bereft, and my heart leaps out for him every time I see his sad little face. The boy has no idea where his big sister Clara has gone. He roams from house to house, hoping someone will play checkers with him until he goes home to his father's sparse cooking. Nettie takes pity on him and gives him a hearty tea time goody when he comes home from school, and I make sure he has something edible in his lunch pail as he leaves with Mr. Poole from my front yard every morning. Somehow, William will survive the winter. The world always seems a more hospitable place in the spring.

~

December 31, 1888

Reflecting back upon this past year of my marriage, it's clear that Henry and I have reached a deeper level of understanding with each other. I know as certainly as the tide comes and goes that there are times when Henry governs his temper, and there are times when Henry's temper governs him. Henry knows that I will yield to that tide.

I am married to two men—no, perhaps more than two. There is the master at sea—competent and authoritative on the water. And there is the land-bound Henry—industrious, but restless and unhappy with the local state of affairs, from politics to economics.

There is the reasonable and rational Henry, who sees things so clearly before others do, and there is the irrational, stubborn Henry, who is certain that once he has declared his mind on a subject, he cannot change his position, afraid he may look the fool by wavering. It is difficult, to state it in the most tactful way, to live with a man who is so intelligent, and yet so stubborn.

Perhaps it would be easier to live with an ignorant man than to live with a stubborn, intelligent one, but I shall never know. As I approach the third winter of my marriage, I know that I am living "for better or for worse." Henry and I share many areas of agreement, and mainly because of his stubbornness, just as many areas of disagreement.

We agree that it is cold outside, but disagree as the mercury drops on how much cold the cat can stand before she should be let into the house from the barn.

We agree that our accounts should be paid in "a timely fashion," but disagree upon what that turn of phrase actually means.

We agree that we should be prepared for storms, but disagree as to how much food and fuel to store in reserve.

We agree that Winslow feels poorly, but disagree as to whether we should call the doctor in.

When Henry is out to sea, I make decisions with ease. When he is in for the winter, I feel as though I have lost my mind, and there is no use in having an opinion. Sometimes I think I may as well take my brain out of my head and put it on the shelf until Henry sails out again. Henry continues to be an arduous husband, but I have resigned myself to the fact that he is not a man who readily listens to my suggestions.

~

Winslow and Henry have settled into the winter routine. Henry will chide his father for not seeing to tasks that Henry believes Winslow should complete. Winslow calmly ignores Henry and continues to read, settled into his chair next to the parlor stove, with purring Polly sitting safely on his lap. Newspapers pile up around Winslow's chair until I remove them to twist for fire starters. I must take care when I cull the newspaper pile, for Winslow has marked "keep" on the top of many articles. I have no idea why he is keeping these articles, unless it is to help him remember what he has just read.

A day may begin with a tender encounter in the early morning as Henry and I wake from our separate dreams. The Henry coming down the stairs will then bellow out that he cannot find his suspenders—did I remove them before I took his trousers to wash? The next Henry is burping in satisfaction as he pushes away from the breakfast table, full of fried eggs, oatmeal, and brown bread toast. Here he must stop to irritate his father.

"What are you doing today?" he demands to know. "I could use some help out in the woodlot. What do you mean, too cold? You're the one who taught me long ago that wood warms twice—once when you cut it and then again when you burn it in the stove. Keep busy and you'll be warm enough! Come on, old man, give us a hand!"

Winslow may or may not be roused to action, depending upon the barometer and the ache of his rheumatism. I know when Winslow is feeling his aches; the expression on his face shows it—a tense set to his jaw which has caused lines, like parenthesis, to form around his mouth. Henry fitfully locates his gloves, hat, muffler, woolen socks, and the proper boots for the task, and goes out to the barn to harness the horses before they have finished eating their morning oats.

Henry has taken to using our beautiful carriage horses for dragging timber from the wood lot. I worry that they do not get enough water all day, knowing how much water I carry to them when Henry is not home. It is hard for me to sit still when Henry takes charge of the pair. I know Henry is ignoring their needs, because he ignores his own needs and is outside from morning until dusk, cutting and dragging trees, and never returning to my kitchen for his noon meal.

Henry is lonely when he is in from the sea—lonely for that constant male companionship that is an arm's length away on every sailing vessel. Accustomed to expecting every order, every whim, every task attended to immediately by his crew members, it frustrates my husband immensely to have to do it all himself, but many days, do it himself he must. I understand his frustration, finding myself in the same situation so much of the time.

Lewis has come and worked along with Henry upon occasion, but after a day of it, Lewis does not come back to offer help again for a month. Henry simply cannot communicate without an ever present tone of authority. I wonder if Lewis is leaving to work in Boston to escape the prospect of being ordered about by Henry.

I strive not to jump and scurry to Henry's side when he has a bout of "captain-itis," as I have diagnosed the condition in my own mind. I constantly work to remain calm, look him in the eye, and ask him how I can help. Of late, this question may elicit a flood of mumbled insults and oaths conveying Henry's opinion that if I were the perfect housekeeper, then everything would be precisely in its place. I smile to myself that I would have to be a magician to achieve this level of order, taking into account the way that Henry strews his belongings about.

I stay inside most of the day. In spite of my flannel bloomers, when I go out to do the yard chores, the cold wind quickly reaches up my skirts. I sew and I write, and I wonder that this has become my life. When I complete the traveling dresses ordered by Carrie's friends, I look forward to piecing together a new quilt with jewel colors. I favor vibrant colors that brighten the dull winter days: emerald green, ruby red, sunflower yellow, royal blue, and deep purple.

My tired ankle warns me when to stop sewing and pick up my pen, for the hours with my foot on the treadle exact their toll. I have taken to wearing spectacles in the dim afternoon light. I suppose a bright lamp would be just as useful, but Henry says we must not use the kerosene too liberally. If those Bostonian ladies could see the way we scrimp! They thought it so romantic and adventurous that I am married to a sea captain.

A semblance of harmony exists because of my visitors. I frequently invite Mama and the other ladies of the hollow over for tea. Winslow puts down his newspapers and becomes very sociable, and Henry is pleasant and polite when there are other women folk in the house. Even my mother is unaware that there is another side to Henry. The ladies think him charming and even-tempered.

I am indeed fortunate that the Ladies Social Union is so active, and we continue to raise monies to support the seemingly tireless Susan B. Anthony, who will celebrate her sixty-ninth birthday this February. Whenever I feel discouraged, I think of how Miss Anthony has traveled the nation for so many years, lecturing and campaigning on behalf of the women's vote. I have nothing to complain about.

I look forward to our fund-raising activities at our own little de-commissioned Pond Hill School House—be it a drama, or a lecture and discussion, or an evening of singing, which Henry enjoys. Henry states that he is in favor of women winning the vote because, "That will be two votes from our household for my choice." Little does he know that I will vote my own mind when I finally have the right to a ballot. But it is good to have him in agreement and acting supportively with the ladies.

When I wash dishes, my view is of our precious little schoolhouse. The empty school yard is less troubling now that the building has become the favorite gathering point for the Ladies Social Union. With so many memories residing within those walls, we recently voted unanimously to raise yet more funds, this time for the purpose of purchasing the school building from the town and establishing a neighborhood library. As a body, we find it very exciting and adventurous that we ladies will purchase real estate in the name of the Ladies Social Union.

And now, 1888 is finished. I do hope that 1889 brings happiness and good fortune, and perhaps the good Lord will grace me with motherhood if I do not pray for it so intensely.

~

CHAPTER NINE
Storm of the Century

January, 1889

The New Year arrived in the middle of a frozen night as Henry and I lay sleeping, wrapped in two down quilts. The first dawn of 1889 was sparkling and bright—blindingly so. The snow and ice in the barnyard reflected the sun into my eyes so intensely that I wore my summer sunbonnet over my earmuffs to do my morning chores, causing Winslow to laugh. Henry smiled in spite of himself. He doesn't like to agree with Winslow.

In celebration of New Year's Day, I prepared a holiday breakfast of corn meal pancakes, applesauce, bacon and eggs. Mama and Papa and Lewis came to join us, and I set the dining room table for six.

As I brought the platter of pancakes to the table and took my place, Winslow said, "I'd like to say the blessing."

Lewis politely put down his fork. As we sat with folded hands, waiting expectantly, Winslow looked around the table at each one of us. "For this once," he said, "let's all join hands. The whole family is here, and this is very special to me."

Winslow can be such a dear. We joined hands, making a circle around the table. I held my brother's hand with my right and Henry's hand with my left. The contact with the two strong men flooded me with a loving warmth. Across the table from me, Mama smiled as she held Papa's and Winslow's hands. Winslow paused for some moments before speaking, causing us to savor the moment. My busy mind danced around the table, dissecting the order of the circle: Henry, Papa, Mama, Winslow, Lewis and myself. None of the younger generation held the hand of their own parent. Each man held the hand of one woman and one man. Each woman held the hands of two men and sat directly across from another woman. How had we arranged ourselves into this orderly pattern? I felt extremely grateful for the abundance of love reflecting back at me from the faces around the table.

Then Winslow spoke a brief but fitting blessing. "Dear Lord, thank you for your bounty of which we are about to partake. Please look down upon us with good health and good fortune, and help us to be more appreciative of the dear ones that you have placed in our lives. We pray for those who have gone on before us and trust that you are holding them in love, especially my dear wife, Arozana. Amen."

"Amen," we heartily repeated. The men dropped hands and pounced on the food as though they hadn't eaten for days. Papa spoke across the table to Winslow.

"This year can't be any worse than last year. And see how fortunate we've been. We're eating well and have sound roofs over our heads. Most of all, we've been able to stay here in our own homes and haven't been forced to move off as so many of our neighbors have." Papa addressed his comment as one head of the household to another, but Henry responded before Winslow had a chance.

"You're right, Captain Paine. But let's not forget that Lewis here is heading off to work in Boston for the winter. We'll miss you, brother. I almost think you might fancy a lassie up there, you're leaving us so willingly." Henry smiled slyly at Lewis.

"Henry!" I couldn't help myself. But Henry must have noticed something I hadn't, because Lewis blushed as easily as a girl.

"Well," Lewis stammered, "there is a miss from Nova Scotia who works in the bakery. Her name is Margaret McCloud. She's worked there for the past two years." Lewis looked over at Mama, as if for approval.

She raised her eyebrows. "Lewis, you didn't tell us."

"There's nothing to tell yet, Mother. I can't even say if she likes me. I told her last spring when I left that I'd be back this winter, but I don't know if she still works there."

"Nova Scotia—is she Catholic or Protestant?" Mama asked.

"Mother, I don't know. I haven't questioned her on religion, but I'll be sure to ask her for you if I get the chance."

"Oh, no, no. I was only curious." Mama waved away her question.

Papa assumed a serious expression as he looked at Lewis. My mind immediately jumped to the assumption that Papa was contemplating the extension of the family. Lewis is Papa's only son. Papa himself has many brothers and sisters, and most of those brothers and sisters already have grandchildren. But of all the little Paines in Paine Hollow, none of them are my father's grandchildren. I know he looks to Lewis to provide at least one son with the last name of Paine. But Papa didn't say anything to Lewis. Instead, he turned to my husband.

"Henry," Papa said, "I'm driving Lewis to the station tomorrow to give him a proper send off. I'll stop by and pick you up on the way by. We'll smoke a cigar with him on the platform. What do you say?"

"Of course, I'll be ready," Henry nodded.

"And you come along, Winslow, if you're up to it. It's below freezing outside right now, but maybe it will be a little warmer tomorrow."

"It's not the temperature, it's the dampness that bothers me," Winslow said. "A good, dry cold snap feels much better than the dampness. I'll be coming along to see Lewis off, especially if he's going off a-courting!"

Mama and I nodded knowingly at each other. The men had demonstrated something we'd agreed upon many times—the men of Paine Hollow are just as excited by gossip and imagined possibilities as the women are, if not more so.

"Aw, come on, you don't have to make so much of it," Lewis protested. "I don't know what will happen with Miss Margaret."

"We will pray for the best outcome, and of course we don't know what that might be," Mama said, always the diplomat. "Now let's enjoy Eva's cooking with a little more attention to it. Eva, I do love these lacy pancakes. How much cornmeal do you add to get this texture?"

"I sift an equal amount of cornmeal into the flour. And add a little more sugar to the batter than normal, that's the secret." I didn't say that Arozana had taught me.

"I'll have another serving," Lewis said. "You've outdone yourself, Eva. And some more coffee, too, please."

Lewis stood before I could and went to the kitchen to pour himself more coffee. While Lewis was out of the room, Mama turned to Papa. "Leave him be, Otis," she whispered.

Papa nodded solemnly. "As you wish, Sarah." This is Papa's standard response to all of Mama's requests.

Henry put his hand on my shoulder, and I knew he was up to some mischief.

"Perhaps a sister-in-law has been found for you, Eva," he said, theatrically somber.

"Henry, be good now." Mama reached over the table and fondly tweaked Henry's ear. Henry smiled at the attention.

~

The one man who Henry takes a bit of direction from, to my surprise, is my father. Whether it's for my sake, or for appearance's sake, Henry reacts to requests from Papa as soon as he receives them. Or perhaps he truly loves my father, which would be the best reason of all.

With Lewis gone to Boston for the winter, a change has come over Henry. Henry assists Papa with chores that require the joint effort of two men. And when Winslow is crippled with rheumatism and can't move from the warmth of the parlor stove, Papa is frequently the man who comes to help Henry. There has been a shift in the wind; Henry has assumed the helm from Winslow concerning the demands of this house and property, and he has also become a more attentive son-in-law.

Of course, I am happy that Henry has stepped in to fill the void left by Lewis, but it does pain me that Henry treats his own father, the dear Winslow, with an edge of contempt now that Winslow's health is obviously failing. It is certainly not through choice or fault that Winslow has grown older and lost his strength. My own father has been exceeding lucky in that regard, and is still as strong as most men twenty years his junior.

"I'm not so prosperous that I can pay a hired hand to lift heavy things for me, Eva, so I do it myself," Papa has explained to me. "But the work keeps me strong. When I stop working, I will lose my health, and so I won't stop working." Papa is an illustration of his own philosophy.

The shortest day of the winter has come and gone, but cold months stretch out ahead of us. Henry and I find ourselves retiring when Winslow does. I've made up the beds with flannel sheets, and I spend more time between the covers now that it gets dark at five o'clock in the afternoon. I think fondly of my pillow at that time. Retiring by eight o'clock saves on the lamp oil, and makes it all the easier to rise at four-thirty in the morning to stir the kitchen stove to life and begin the barnyard chores.

Since Mama and Papa had planned to be south for the winter, and I had tried to prepare myself for their absence, I am finding myself extremely appreciative of their presence now that their plans have changed.

Henry and Papa are cheerful together. And although I am sorry that Mama is not enjoying the milder Virginia climate, it would be strange in the hollow without her. Together we attend the Ladies Social Union events with Nettie and enjoy sleigh rides on sunny days.

The school children continue to provide me with entertainment as they wait for their morning ride to Wellfleet. They have built snow forts at my gate, and snowballs fly every afternoon upon their return from school. It never hurts to bake a dozen extra cookies, and they are accepted with much enthusiasm.

~

March 4, 1889

Last night I woke up from my sleep, crying and shaking. Henry was instantly awake and concerned. "What is it Eva? What, dearest?" he asked.

I couldn't see him in the black darkness, but I felt him leaning over me. With effort, I shook off my nightmare and tried to explain my terror. "I dreamed that we had a son, and he was beautiful and loving. And then he was lost. We couldn't find him anywhere, and I couldn't bear it." I was shaken. "I'm sorry to be so upset by a dream, Henry."

"I'm sorry, too. I know how much you want a child." He stroked my forehead. "I'm sorry you are so unhappy."

"Are you disappointed in me?" I asked.

"Disappointed in you?" He hugged me in the dark. "Not at all! Perhaps the fault is mine. How can I say that it is you? My parents only had one child, and that result remained the same in spite of years of trying for another. I heard the bed springs in their room creaking plenty as I grew up. This tendency may come down through my parents. How can I say, how can I blame you?"

"Oh, Henry. Thank you." I felt weight being lifted from me. "What should we do?" I whispered to him. "Should we adopt a child?"

"We should accept the Lord's will. It may take some time for you to become pregnant, as we have seen. I am not impatient." Henry drew the quilt up under my chin, tucking me in. "And if the Lord wants us to adopt a child, he will present us with one, I am sure. We would never refuse. Now try to go back to sleep, Eva. Morning comes soon enough."

Henry's perspective was sensible and concerned, which was a welcome surprise. Why have I waited so long to ask him his feelings on the subject? How stubborn was I to carry the burden alone? I have been singing today as I go about my chores. I am reminded that heartache can be relieved through earnest conversation.

~

March 12, 1889

We've had a fierce Nor-Easter that began yesterday and raged through the night. Highland Light reported winds at fifty miles per hour yesterday, according to the engineer when the train came through this afternoon. The roar of the ocean breakers can be clearly heard from our front yard, even though we are two miles from the back shore. Several days of threatening weather before the big blow gave cause for all merchant vessels to seek harbor, and no wrecks have been reported. But the roaring ocean is unsettling, and I hope it simmers down soon.

I have received more orders from Boston, all for my traveling dress design. Carrie's friends have more friends, and the ladies of Boston do travel in the winter. I've received orders for heavy dresses for steamer decks and lighter dresses for Egyptian pyramid tours. The joke in her social circle, so Carrie writes to me, is that a lady must eat a good dessert before she takes her measurements for Eva Smith—this to ensure the comfortable fit that is so desired.

I sew from the time my chores are done in the morning until it is tea time, unless Mama comes by to take me to a meeting or visit a sick neighbor. Bless her for harnessing Duke herself today, and driving over through the snow to fetch me.

"Eva, you've got to get your head away from that sewing machine," she scolded me as she came in with her hands on her hips, stamping the snow off her feet.

"Well, Mama, I just can't. Winslow's medicine is costly, and Henry's money has run out. And the property taxes are due. I really don't mind. The truth is, I like earning money."

"But not at the expense of your friendships and other social obligations. Now put on your coat and gloves, and come out with me." Mama was not to be put off.

"Yes, I'll come with you, Mama, but we have to stop by the station so I can mail these packages to Boston," I said. I picked up two bundles bearing Newbury Street addresses.

"Good, we can do that. Now where is your coat, Eva? Oh look, your coat needs mending! You must pay attention to your own garments—you know you are your own best walking advertisement."

"I thought you wanted me to work less, not more," I teased. I know she is proud of me and my skill as a dress maker. Mama has her own traveling dress that I made for her, but she has hung it in the back of her closet, saving it for her eventual winter in Virginia. Over my protests, she insists it is too special to wear.

"Oh, Eva, don't be so difficult," Mama laughed. She had succeeded in getting me out of the house. We both need female companionship and conveniently find it between us.

Henry, Winslow and Papa spend their day in Papa's workshop feeding the potbelly stove and trading yarns. Henry's purse seine net is ready for the fishing season, and he has bought an extra one in sad condition and is now repairing it with Papa and Winslow's joint supervision. The project gives them a reason to light the stove and smoke their pipes.

Papa is waiting for warmer weather to varnish his masts and booms again; he's had them off the *Nautilus* since November. The vessel rests safely in her cradle up above the creaking ice pack, waiting for the ice to melt so she can be let back out on the flood tide of spring.

Henry and I have a new stumbling block to surmount. Henry has taken to chewing tobacco and reeks of it when he comes back into the house at the end of the day. I will not allow a spittoon in the house, but he has one in the outhouse. The habits men learn from other men! I am sure that the expression on my face when he comes home tells him what my nose has detected, and he heads straight to the wash basin to scrub his face and mustache with soap. I keep hot coffee waiting on the stove, as to my mind, coffee on his breath smells a good deal better than tobacco.

I must be thankful that he hasn't started with alcohol, as some of the men have done to combat this dreary winter. Of course, they all protest that the consumption of alcohol is medicinal. But it seems as though more than the proper dose is consumed by a few. Mama and I observed a man sway and totter on the railroad platform as he waited for the mail arrival. Perhaps it is because Henry spends his days with his father and mine that he governs himself to the extent that I have never detected the sour scent of alcohol on his breath, and for that I am very thankful, indeed. I will settle for the tobacco if I must.

All in all, we are having a good winter, even though we've been attended by several storms as severe as this last one.

We've had no word from Lewis regarding the mysterious Miss Margaret. He sends us brief letters from Boston containing very little news other than that he is well, and his fellow boardinghouse residents are a cheerful lot. I am glad he is able to leave this dormant place in the winter. A young man like Lewis needs more of a range than this little frozen neighborhood can provide him.

In the meantime, my sewing brings me perfumed dollar bills through the mail from the good ladies of Boston. I must carry on!

~

March 26, 1889

Suddenly, Henry will be setting sail quite soon. I couldn't be more relieved. The tension has been electric these past ten days as he sought a master's position for the fishing season. However, the time has come when the only position he can find is to run a trading schooner for Joe Stubbs—the new *Mary Stubbs*, named after one of Joe's daughters.

This is not a sorry situation; the Stubbs Boat Yard is well regarded for launching sturdy vessels. But I do think of the situation offered to Henry by Captain Lorenzo Dow Baker. Had Henry accepted, he might well be an officer now on one of the Boston Fruit Company steamers.

But of course, Henry would never go to Captain Baker—not after turning down his kind offer several times. Aunt Elizabeth's husband, Captain Wiley, continues to be quite happily employed by Captain Baker's company, and is currently in Jamaica taking on a load of bananas. Boston's craze for the fruit has made a millionaire of Lorenzo Dow Baker. I daresay that the lowly banana supports the Methodist Church in Wellfleet, as Captain Baker is by far the most generous benefactor.

There will be no banana cargos for my dear husband. Henry is to sail to Norfolk, Virginia, with a load of ice, and bring back immature oysters for fattening on the Wellfleet flats. As he prepares to leave, his mood has been subdued one minute, maniacal the next. All winter he has fussed over his fishing nets, and yesterday he rolled them up and stowed them away in the barn loft.

I haven't dared to comment on the change of plans. Several pleasantries jump into my mind—*It's all for the best, dear. We knew the fishing would come to an end. How nice that you are running a newly launched schooner.* But none of these have I uttered, as Henry marches about with a frown on his face and his mouth turned downward.

Once again, the ritual—"Where is that new logbook, Eva? My wallet? Where's my new fountain pen? I just had it."

Once again, I am on the run like a little brown hen attending to her rooster. Here is his sea chest. I must fill it with clothes to keep him warm—the Atlantic is still so cold and gray. Wool socks, union suits, wool shirts, wool pants, wool coat. Nothing cotton, as it remains so damp once sprayed with sea water. An extra bottle of ink for his pen. A pocket compass so he can read it from his berth when not at the helm. Three more pairs of wool socks, as Henry Young, who is going along as first mate, may not be so fortunate as to have what he needs. Mr. Young's wife has taken ill with the spring croup that is going around, and she has been in bed for a month. I must go look in on her while the men are out.

It will be a crew of two, just my Henry and Mr. Young. Joseph Stubbs is of the opinion that two skilled seamen can sail a schooner, and he says he will pay for no more crew on this cargo voyage. Luckily, Henry doesn't mind cooking; he will be at the galley stove when Mr. Young takes the helm.

Papa has decided to make the same run with the *Nautilus*. Henry could navigate with charts through the waters off Virginia, but he has never done it before. Papa has sailed the route so many times that he can sail without charts, if need be. Lewis is returning home from Boston to sail the *Nautilus* with Papa.

Mama shared my anxiety that Henry would be sailing in an area out of his expertise, and it was she who prevailed upon Papa to make the run with Henry. I immediately felt so much better when I heard this would be the case and that Henry will have a guide, although Henry will never see it that way.

Much bantering has gone on between the men, which is good to hear. Papa strives to distract Henry from the loss of his heart's desire to go fishing. They were at it this morning in the driveway, carrying on in the loudest of voices, as if they were already at sea, yelling over the wind to each other.

"Henry, now we'll see how the *Mary Stubbs* sails, won't we?" Papa joked. "With the *Nautilus* sailing alongside, there will be a benchmark for you to measure yourself against."

"I'll give you a run for your money, Captain Paine," Henry answered the challenge. "I'll wager my right arm that I'll beat you down the coast."

"That's hardly a fair bet—I wouldn't want to collect on that one," my father roared back. "That would leave my daughter with a one-armed husband."

"There's no fear of that. But if you don't want to bet, so be it."

Men do have the most ridiculous conversations. But I wish Henry would show me a bit more appreciation, if not affection. Although I am trying to see things from Henry's point of view, I am still reverberating from his foul mood this morning.

~

As we woke up at dawn and were lying in bed for a few luxurious minutes of stolen time, I mentioned to Henry that Clay Thomas had stopped by at the end of the day yesterday. In Clay's opinion our windmill, which was torn from its tower during the recent Nor-Easter, is not repairable. Clay said he could order us a new one, and I told him to go ahead. Henry's reaction to my report was alarming. He shot out of bed and stood towering over me.

"Eva, that Thomas is full of bull," he shouted. "Of course the windmill can be fixed!"

I knew Henry was building up to a full-force tirade. My mind fought going blank. I recalled the many times Henry had insisted upon the newest, best, most efficient products, from his precious seine net, to the bathtub, to his new fountain pen.

"Yes, Henry." I looked up at him from the bed. "I just thought you'd rather have a new one than take a chance on a repair. An unbalanced windmill could wobble off its shaft and crash down again, possibly hurting someone this time."

Henry looked down at me with a furious expression. "It's quite clear, Eva, that I am the one who should be making the decisions about this property." As he shouted at me, he bobbed his head back and forth on his neck as if it were a bobber on a fishing line. "Now I'm going to have to cancel that order immediately and take the windmill down to the blacksmith before I go out. I don't know what you were thinking."

He opened our bedroom door and stomped out of the room in his long johns. Winslow cleared his throat from his bedroom. I know there are a dozen ways Henry and I could have discussed the matter in a civil manner and arrived at a mutual decision. But Henry chose to stand over the bed and shout down at me. More confusing to me, we had just shared a passionate interlude during the night, knowing that we wouldn't be with each other for at least a week.

On days such as these, I whole-heartedly agree with Nettie. Living with men is very difficult, indeed. Every one of them is of the opinion that women are inferior, and after the courtship is over, that sentiment shows itself in so many ways. If women didn't endure the task of birthing and raising sons, there would be no men. Perhaps we should all boycott motherhood for a decade and demonstrate that we can bring the human race to a halt. These men are here at our discretion!

Arozana coddled Henry, but even so, he respected his mother. I should have thought he would respect me enough to maintain a civil tongue and a reasonable temperament, like Papa does for Mama. But it isn't so. I am wishing it was.

Enough! I must get Henry organized for his voyage. But today I'd rather shovel horse manure than spend time with Henry. I am quite beside myself. This too, shall pass. Forgive me my temper, Lord. It is becoming as unreasonable as Henry's.

To be fair, I must acknowledge that Henry has his unspoken reasons for being upset. He has lost his beloved profession. He will not be following the fish again soon.

~

April 2, 1889

A day is a strange measurement of time. This afternoon is passing by in eerie stillness. I'm sitting here writing with Polly purring on my lap. Winslow is content reading his newspaper beside the parlor stove. If Henry walked in the door at this moment, he'd be pleased to find the house orderly and peaceful, with everything in its place.

This morning I completed the tasks of three women in a few hours of time—scrubbing and sweeping and dusting and baking. The air is cold and still, and the sun has failed in its attempt to burn through the gray fog. There are no shadows on the soggy ground, and sounds do not carry through this heavy weather. Henry and Papa cannot be making very good time out on the water with this hint of a breeze. A few low piles of snow remain in the woods, but they are quickly melting, lending their moisture to the damp atmosphere.

My daffodils are pushing up through the soil, and the forsythia bushes host tight little yellow buds. Spring is just ahead, and I welcome it wholeheartedly. I am done with winter. I look forward to long walks where I don't have to cringe against the chilly wind. A little more snow and a few more blows—and then it will be May. On the fourteenth of that month, Henry and I will mark the end of our third year as man and wife.

Perhaps now is the time for us to have a child. I do count on it. Once again, I hold the hope that I carry a life within me. As the time of the month for my menses approaches, I pray with all my heart and soul that it does not occur. Lord, forgive me for trying to direct your will, but I can't help myself. It is my strongest desire to have a child to love.

Nettie and I will go to the library soon, and then to the market.

Before he left, Henry stored the sleigh away and brought the buggy out for me. I must finish my tea and bring Winslow one more cookie, and then go out to harness the horses. They will enjoy the trot into town as much as Nettie and I will.

~

April 5, 1889

A dreadful blow has come up. The men are on their way home. Papa telegraphed Mama two days ago from Norfolk:

> *Dear Sarah,*
> *Ice sold, oysters loaded. Hot baths and roast beef enjoyed by all at The Red Lion. Leaving from Hampton Roads on April 4, by five AM.*
>
> *Fondly, Otis*

I pray that they are heading in to safe harbor for the night. If the winds are as fierce off the coast of Virginia as they are off Cape Cod, the *Nautilus* and the *Mary Stubbs* will be wanting a harbor. Winslow is anxious, and so I try not to be. I don't want to alarm him. Both Henry and Papa have sailed through dozens of storms. I rely on their experience and the Lord's guidance.

Winslow and I have secured everything we could in the yard, and shut the horses into the barn. The trees are blowing back and forth in the wind as if they were daffodils, and the daffodils themselves have been destroyed.

~

April 7, 1889

The extreme calm of the day belies the fact that the worst possible storm has happened. When the stationmaster received the marine report today via the telegraph line, he learned that the catastrophic storm has devastated the coast of Virginia, and dozens of vessels are unaccounted for. Mr. Newcomb immediately sent a boy over with a message to me, knowing that Henry, Papa and Lewis are sailing in that area. Mama and I anxiously await some direct word from our men. She was here all afternoon, but has gone home to feed her chickens.

In this late afternoon hour, the sun has broken through briefly but fiercely to warm the cold damp earth. Hope springs forth loudly as the newly emerged peep frogs in the pond sing their first intense song. I want good news.

Now that the winds have subsided, Winslow does not seem perturbed. "Henry has sailed through many a blow and your father twice as many. Settle down, Eva. The Lord will see them home," he said.

I'm holding on to his words. I cannot sit. I cannot write. I am pacing, and waiting for some news.

~

April 14, 1889

I am in Mama's front parlor. She has placed me on the settee in front of her coal stove and covered me with a shawl to keep me warm. I can think only about Henry rolling around in the frigid waves. Mama has been weeping, but she keeps very busy. I am unable to assist her in any useful manner—I find myself feeling light-headed and extremely forgetful. I cannot remember what I am supposed to be doing from one minute to the next.

After a dreadful week of waiting and praying, Papa and Lewis sailed in yesterday. Clive Townsend alerted Mama that the *Nautilus* had sailed past the point, and then he ran up to the Smith house to give me the news. Within minutes, Mama was at my door step with Duke and her buggy, and we made our journey to the old wharf.

Papa's haggard face frightened me as he threw the lines up to waiting well-wishers. The hull of the *Nautilus* was strangely stripped of her recent coat of paint, and bare boards showed through. Mama and I rushed onto the *Nautilus* as soon as she was secure. We knew it had been a terrible ordeal they had endured—according to the updated marine report, the Virginia coastline received the worst of the Atlantic storm, and more than forty vessels had been wrecked there.

Mama and Papa clung tightly to each other, and then Mama let go and ran to Lewis and embraced him, her hands barely reaching up around his neck. Papa took me into his arms, but he was as stiff as a wooden block. He pressed me against his chest until I struggled loose. I looked up at him, wanting to know.

"Henry?" I waited expectantly.

Papa was reluctant to reply, but I shook his shoulders, demanding.

"He's gone, Eva," Papa said, his voice choking.

I grabbed at the lapels of his coat. "Why didn't you wire me, Papa?" I cried. "Why didn't you?"

I don't remember falling, but I do remember Papa picking me up off the deck.

"I wanted to be here, Eva. I didn't want you reading it from a telegram." Papa held me up as my knees buckled again.

My mind went blank and the horizon tilted. A guttural voice from deep down inside me began to wail, "Oh, Henry. My Henry." I heard the strange rawness of the voice, but didn't recognize it as my own.

Papa asked the men gathering on the wharf to watch over the *Nautilus* while he saw me home. Lewis picked me up and carried me to the buggy. I can barely recall the drive. Mama sat holding me, Papa drove, and because there was no more room on the seat, Lewis stood on the side step. I remember my brother looking down at me from his strange position outside the buggy.

My cries drew people from every house along the way. "Oh, Henry. My Henry." The words became a chant that kept me conscious.

As we passed the train station and general store, my father shouted over at Mr. Newcomb, "Would you wire Wellfleet and get the doctor down here? Tell him Winslow Smith's house."

Mr. Newcomb waved acknowledgement and stepped into the telegraph office. We attracted the stares of the men who loitered regularly on the railroad platform. They fell in behind the buggy. The voice that continued to scream out was not my own; it came from some primitive place inside of me, and I had no control over it.

Winslow came out into the yard as the buggy rolled to a stop. Immediately, he knew his son was lost and clutched at his chest. The men who trailed behind us ran to Winslow and sat him down on the front step. Papa jumped off the buggy and joined them. A whiskey flask appeared from Papa's pocket, and Winslow took a hard pull from it.

I watched what people around me were doing as though I was separated from myself. Sounds continued to come from my mouth. I looked up into the dripping pine trees. The sky was cotton gray with no depth to it, and the air was cold and clammy. My hands were cold. Lewis got me out of the buggy and through the back door into the kitchen as the neighborhood women started to arrive. Mama held the door open for us, and then placed a kitchen chair next to the warm cook stove.

"Here, Lewis, she is shivering. Put her here," she ordered Lewis. Aunt Elizabeth's face appeared at the doorway. "Elizabeth, go out and see to Winslow, would you please?" Mama asked her, and immediately Aunt Elizabeth complied.

"Hot tea. Hot tea. I'm putting the kettle on now, Eva. Where are your salts?" My mother tried to get my attention. She stood over me, patting my cheeks quickly with her hands.

"Nooooo," was the long syllable I was now mouthing. "Noooo."

"Good Lord, who is having a baby?" Mrs. Townsend stepped into the kitchen. "I was on my way up to the store when I heard a woman giving birth—Oh, Eva!" She immediately realized her mistake. "I am so sorry. I didn't know. I am so *sorry*."

Little Rebecca was at her mother's side, wearing a dress and pinafore I had made for her. "Mama, what's wrong with Auntie Eva?" Rebecca asked.

"Hush, child," Mrs. Townsend said, hugging her daughter. "Her husband's been lost at sea, Rebecca. Be quiet, now."

Rebecca regarded me with large eyes.

"Nooooo," my wailing continued, while my mind studied the faces of the people I knew. Within minutes, ten women were in the kitchen, and their men could be heard coming into the front room with Winslow. Mama loaded wood into the stove to bring the kitchen temperature up, and women searched the pantry cupboards, taking note of what food would be necessary in the household during the grueling hours and days ahead. The murmur of low voices surrounded me.

Lewis went out to the barn to saddle Silkie. Soon I heard him gallop for town center to tell Mrs. Young in person that her husband had gone down on the *Mary Stubbs*. From the paddock, Sinbad shrieked his unwillingness to be left behind, filling the air with his wild protests. I could not remember a time that Sinbad and Silkie had ever been separated. My mind registered these details while my heart continued to pour out its angst. Aunt Elizabeth was back in the kitchen.

"For God's sakes," I heard her say, "She doesn't need tea, Sarah. She needs some laudanum. Or whiskey, rum, brandy. Where's the medicine cabinet?"

Aunt Elizabeth had entrusted Winslow to the men. But I wanted to see Winslow. It was the two of us who would feel Henry's loss the most. I tried to stand, and fell back into the chair.

"Where do you think you're going, Eva? Stay here." Mama put a cup of tea down in front of me, and pressed a vial of smelling salts to my nose. Then she took a cold wash cloth to my face.

"I need a handkerchief, Mama."

She handed me the lace trimmed hanky from her purse, and I blew my nose. I needed another hanky, so Aunt Elizabeth offered hers up. Finally I had a bit of a hold on myself. Then Nettie walked through the door, and upon seeing her, I couldn't prevent myself from wailing again.

Nettie bent over to hug me and then drew a chair over beside me. We sat there crying and blowing our noses together. Mrs. Townsend found my clean laundry basket and took out several of Winslow's clean red handkerchiefs. "Eva, keep these about you—I'm afraid you're going to need them."

Nettie was effusive in her sobs. I was relieved my rock of a friend could do nothing but exhibit this very tender side of her heart. I relied upon the stoicism of the older women in the room, but Nettie was my true friend. Had Nettie maintained her usual stiff upper lip, I would have been ashamed of my own outpourings. My thoughts returned to Henry's father.

"I want to see Winslow," I said. The women did nothing to help me get up. "How is he taking it?" I could not imagine Winslow's pain. I had no way to measure the agony of losing an only child—a full grown man at that.

"He's lying down. Your father is with him," Aunt Elizabeth said. She had found some rum on the pantry medicine shelf, and she heated it on the stove. She poured a few tablespoons into a glass, and added a heaping teaspoon of sugar. I took it and drank it and felt warmer.

"Now I'll drink the tea. I do want your tea, Mama, and pour some for Nettie, too. But please, I want to go in and see Winslow now. Please." I experienced the sensation of a reversed telescope as I thought of the great chunks of time I'd spent alone with Winslow, my dear father-in-law. The ladies relented and helped me into the front room.

Winslow lay on the sofa and Papa sat in a chair by his head. Other neighbors were there, sitting with the concerned loiterers who had followed us from the train station. Clive Townsend stood, hat in hand, having come in search of his wife who had taken far too long to walk to Ike's store. I sat down on the carpet next to Winslow and held his hand. His face was wet and crumpled. The ladies settled around me on the floor. Little William sat at Winslow's feet, and Captain Jenkins was there, too.

"I want to hear it all, Otis," Winslow said. "Tell me what happened."

Papa talked in low tones, and people became silent so he could be heard.

"Well my friend," Papa said, "You know that kind of weather that is all fickle—you've been out to sea as much as any of us have. The clouds started scudding overhead, but we didn't think anything of it at first. We felt pretty safe, running the *Nautilus* and the *Mary Stubbs* side by side. It seemed as though we would be getting a good following sea, and we'd get some speed up for the trip north.

"But without warning the wind shifted to the opposite direction, thunder and lightening moved in on us, and it rained in sheets. We reefed in the main sails. The rain turned to sleet, and then to snow. It was like that all afternoon, but we held pretty well to the compass." Papa stopped and cleared his throat.

Winslow's eyes were closed. "Go on," he said. Tears seeped out from under his closed eyelids and traveled across his cheeks as he lay on the sofa.

My own face was soaked. Papa looked at me, probably fearing I would start wailing again.

"I want to hear, too, Papa," I said. I struggled to keep my sobs under control.

He nodded and slowly continued. "It wasn't much worse than

a good snow squall, and we were still making progress, although it took some effort. Lewis had to take the hatchet to the lines and chop off the ice every half hour or so. We could see the *Mary Stubbs* clearly as she was not far off. Henry had taken on two lads in Norfolk as deck hands, and they were doing as we were, chopping ice. Lewis and I got the storm anchor ready, and Henry was over on the *Mary Stubbs* getting his out—we could see him and Young pulling it up out of the hold."

Everyone in the room was quiet.

"Then it got very dark, about six o'clock. A tremendous wind rose up and the swells were at least fifteen feet, so it was rough seas all along.

"That's when we lost track of the *Mary Stubbs*. One minute her deck lanterns were there, and the next they weren't. We thought maybe we'd passed her too quickly, so Lewis and I put out the storm anchor, hoping Henry's lights would come into view through the snow. The wind speed was so terrific that we had all we could do to keep the *Nautilus* from slamming ashore; it was blowing from the north east and driving us back towards land, storm anchor and all." Papa stopped.

Winslow emitted a long sigh. "Go on, Otis," he said, with a catch in his voice.

"I'm afraid there's not much more to tell. The wind kept up like that for hours, and Lewis and I took turns at the bilge pump all night to keep from swamping. Near dawn the wind finally subsided, but the ocean was wild.

"We turned and sailed south along the coast, keeping off shore away from the surf. As the light came up we could see the beach was lined with wrecks, and from Chincoteague to Cape Henry, all was devastation. We got back into Norfolk Harbor, and took stock of the *Nautilus*. Even though she'd lost most of her paint and looked pretty beat up, she was sound, so we sailed back out that afternoon. The seas had already gone down, and we searched for the *Mary Stubbs* in the area we'd last seen her, hoping she'd lost a mast and was limping along. But after two days it was evident she wasn't there. She wouldn't be further out to sea, as the winds had been blasting towards shore.

"So we knew Henry and his hands were gone, and probably knew it from the moment we couldn't see the *Mary Stubbs* anymore. I'm sorry I have to be the bearer of such bad news, Winslow." Papa folded his hands and lowered his face into his beard on his chest.

All was quiet as Papa waited for Winslow's response. Winslow opened his eyes and took a deep breath.

"I had a feeling that something had happened," he said. "When we got the marine forecast from Newcomb that the Virginia coast was getting the worst of it, I had the feeling that Henry was in trouble. I do thank you sincerely, Otis, for taking the time to look for my boy."

Another wave of emotion came up through my gut and overwhelmed my body. The remembrance of the last dreadful day I'd spent with Henry pushed into my mind. Our argument about the windmill would never be resolved through a passionate reunion. My limbs would never again be entwined with Henry's. I shook and trembled on the carpet.

Soothing hands reached out to me. I accepted the permission they granted to screech as loudly as the northeast wind while I vehemently wished I could leave myself and go find Henry. An unknown amount of dark time passed, and gradually I was brought back to the parlor by my family and neighbors as they lay their hands upon me. Then there was stillness, interrupted only by my involuntary gasps for air.

"There, there, Eva," Mama said. "You're going to get through it. That's my girl."

"Praise the Lord," Winslow said. "Praise the Lord with me, Eva."

"Thank you Lord," I said numbly, as I had done at so many funerals. "Thank you for taking Henry home to you. We will all be there together in Heaven someday soon. Thank you for your loving welcome and for the time you gave us with Henry. Amen."

I said the words for Henry's father and tried to mean them. The doctor came into the room with his black leather bag. Everyone, except Nettie, Mama and I, got up and left the room so Dr. Brown could listen to Winslow's heart. Winslow tried to push the stethoscope away, but Dr. Brown insisted.

After a few minutes of listening, Dr. Brown said, "Your ticker sounds good, sir, even though I know it doesn't feel good. No heavy lifting for awhile, and don't be afraid to drink a shot or two of whiskey— that'll do you good right now. I'm truly sorry for your loss, sir."

"I thank you, Doc, but what I need right now is some fresh air," Winslow said. He rose from the couch and went out through the front door to join the other men in the yard. Then it was my turn. My pulse was counted, my heart was listened to, and a little white opiate pill was administered.

"This will help you sleep, Eva." Dr. Brown smiled kindly at me. In a few minutes the pill took effect, relieving me of my heaving spasms, and thus relaxed, I took in some deep breaths.

"The one pill seems to be enough for you, Eva." He handed a packet to my mother. "Sarah, when she needs them, here's six more pills," he said. The doctor moved towards the kitchen to refresh himself after the five mile gallop from town.

Lewis was out in the drive, walking the horses back and forth to cool them off. A warm thankfulness came into my heart that my father and brother had survived the wild storm. It was only by the grace of God they were spared, I knew.

"Eva, I think you should come home with us tonight," Mama said.

"No, Mama. I want to stay here with Winslow." I couldn't bear the thought of leaving him alone. Mama looked dubious.

"I'll stay," Nettie said.

"But you have your boarders," Mama said.

"I'll go home and put out supper for them. And then I'll come back and stay with Eva and Winslow tonight."

"Oh, thank you, Nettie," I said. "You are so good to do that. Thank you so much." Through my exhaustion, I felt relief that I wouldn't have to leave the house tonight. "I am so tired. I need to lie down."

Everything went quiet. I couldn't hear—I was heading towards a drugged sleep. Somehow I was upstairs and lying on my bed, and Mama and Nettie were loosening my clothes. My dress was removed, and then my corset and undergarments. My nightgown was placed over my head and drawn down. I put my arms into the sleeves as guided, with my eyes closed.

"Don't worry, Aunt Sarah," Nettie said. "I'll sleep with Eva tonight. She'll be safe." I sat on the bed as Nettie and Mama took off my shoes and socks. I could hear my mother softly crying. "I'll bring supper for Winslow, too. Now don't worry," Nettie reassured her.

"Sarah," my father called from downstairs. "I've got to go back to the wharf and check on the boat before I go home. Why don't you stay until I get back, and then we'll ride home together?"

"Hush, Otis," Mama shushed him from the top of the stairs. "I'll be right down to talk to you."

As Mama tucked me under my quilt, I fell into a dream where I was a tiny girl again, and there was no one in the world that mattered except for me and my Mama and Papa, and they would always make everything right.

~

Lord, thank you for Nettie. She is my stalwart friend. She stayed all night, and did not sleep very much, I am afraid, as I cried in my sleep. The little pill perhaps did the job of putting me to sleep, but the resulting nightmares from which I could not wake were terrifying. With Nettie's help, I laid out all my clothing this morning, but I then misplaced my left stocking before I could dress myself.

Once in the kitchen, I forgot the ingredients that I'd put into the morning muffin mix and had to throw out the dough and start over again. Nettie made sure Winslow was fed and comfortable, and then she walked me here to Mama's house before going home to cook for her boarders.

Mama has placed me in this room reserved for company, in front of the parlor stove. I am so confused. A part of me still waits for Henry to sail in, as that part forgets we have been informed otherwise. And this knitting in the basket beside me—Mama says I've been working on these wool socks for Winslow, but I cannot remember that at all.

Papa and Lewis are out in the kitchen with Mama, and I can hear their voices. They do not think that I can, but although my mind is a muddle, my ears work as efficiently as ever. Papa is repeating for at least the third time, "I shouted over at him to reef in, but he wouldn't! He waved over at me, but did nothing to bring in sail, nothing!" Papa sounds agitated.

"Henry couldn't hear you, Father," Lewis says calmly. "You know the wind was blowing too loudly—it carried your voice away."

"I know Henry heard me. He saw all the signs of the storm coming up as well as we did, the damn fool! He should have reefed in when he saw us doing it. So hard headed, and now Young is gone with him, and the two lads. What a loss of life, and for no good reason at all."

"Otis, please. Shush! Eva will hear you," Mama protests. "I know you're upset, but go out into the yard. Don't talk about it in this house. Why don't you drive me up to the Smith's to get a trunk of Eva's clothes? She can't go back there. I might as well start moving her now."

Mama's attempt to quiet Papa falls short. Papa's voice rises again.

"He made my beautiful daughter a widow! My little Eva."

"Why, Otis, this isn't like you. There was nothing you could do, dear," Mama's voice is soothing. "The newspapers reported that the storm was a cyclone, and how could anyone have known it was coming? It was the Lord's will. We all die someday, Otis, and Henry's time has come. You can't continue to say that Henry was so willful as to cause his own death. Now, no more talk like this. It does no good at all."

"He may not have heard me, Sarah," Papa continues, "but he did not heed the storm. He didn't use the intelligence the good Lord gave him—he let his pride block his ears when I shouted over to him. I can't tell you how quickly he sailed that boat under! One moment he was there next to us, and the next, the bow of that boat dove straight down into a wave. The full spread of sails just pushed him under. He sailed down to the bottom, and was gone in the blink of an eye." Papa's voice rises to a crescendo. "He could be here with us right now if he'd used the intelligence God gave him and not been so bull headed!"

"Enough, Otis!" Mama says. "You don't want Eva to hear this, do you? Come now, we're going up to the Smith house. Think of poor Winslow. First he loses his wife, and now Henry, and Eva, too.

"But it would be improper for her to stay on with Henry gone. She is coming home to live with us. Now let's go! And not a word of this foolishness to Winslow. "

I can hear Mama brusquely putting things away in her kitchen.

"All right, Sarah. As you wish," my father says, but he is not contrite in his tone. My mother's footfalls approach the parlor door.

"Eva, your father and I are going up to see Winslow." Her voice is soft, as though she is speaking to a fragile invalid. "Lewis will be here in the kitchen. I see you found your pen and ink, and you have Winslow's socks to finish. Are you all right here in the parlor for a little while?"

"Yes, Mama." I close my eyes. She crosses the room and kisses my forehead and then turns to leave. "Check the chickens for me, please, Mama. And Silkie and Sinbad."

"Of course. You rest now, Eva." A waft of her lavender toilet water comes my way and she is gone. Soon the buggy rolls by the window with Papa driving and Mama beside him. I am alarmed, and yet too dizzy to be alarmed. Henry did not take in sail during a cyclone? Why would he be so foolish? Did he really hear my father, and then choose to ignore the warnings? It is unbearable to think Henry might have avoided death if he had taken precautions. It cannot be true. Papa is upset, that is all.

I have a slight tear in my skirt, as if I caught it on a nail. The air in the room is stuffy, and the gilt wallpaper fails in its purpose to proclaim stability and permanence. The carefully hung portraits of my grandparents, Nathan and Dorcas Paine, look down at me with dour faces. They both died when I was young, and they cannot help me. They had nine children, three of whom predeceased them. I begin to understand their somber expressions.

This carpet needs a good beating. I shall help Mama with that soon. It takes two to drag it out and hang it on the lines for a good smacking. My body feels so heavy. My head is filled with cotton. Didn't Henry care enough about me to be careful? Am I to live without him because of his willful carelessness? How foolish I have been. Henry was everything in the world to me. Was I not everything in the world to him? Wouldn't he err on the side of caution for my sake?

I shall never know. There is nothing to do but hope his body will be found, washed up upon the great outer beach. Until then, I don't think I can go on. I will not wholly believe that Henry is dead until I see his body. My heart spins fantastic scenarios of Henry swimming through the storm to safety.

~

May 12, 1889
A New Widow

I do so love the blue color of robin's eggs. The eggs are such sweet reminders that there are things bright and beautiful in this harsh world. Their color is just slightly greener than dear Henry's eyes. Henry had that color of eye which is rare for a man—the sky blue that is startling and youthful.

I keep watch over the robin's nest that nestles in the forsythia bush just outside my mother's kitchen door. I am living with Mama and Papa again, and Henry's father is all by himself at the Smith homestead. Papa says Winslow wants to be alone and refuses male companionship. I wonder if Winslow is eating. I must go dust the house and put some food by for him. His laundry—it will need tending to. Nettie and Mrs. Townsend have been taking turns cooking for Winslow, and minding the hens and the horses.

I will go visit Winslow soon. I will. Mama insists that I need this time, and much more time, to properly mourn as a widow. But I know Winslow misses me as I do him. As I miss all that I so recently reigned over—the kitchen, the bathtub and the barnyard of the Smith homestead—my home. Now I have lost it, along with my husband. The house is Winslow's; it never belonged to Henry, and therefore, it cannot be my home any longer.

I spend too much time up in this bedroom of my childhood. I lie on the bed and watch the dust sift down through the invading shafts of sunlight. When I stand to look out my window towards the sparkling bay, I can see down into the robin's nest. She sits faithfully on her eggs. I am so very envious of her coming motherhood.

Yesterday morning the blood on my sheets was as brilliant as a red cardinal's feather on snow. Henry is gone, and now the final hope of bearing a son or daughter has vanished. I have quite taken to hating the color red today—all the more reason for me to preoccupy myself with the color of these eggs in the yellow bush below me.

What a cruel trick my body has played on me—to withhold menstruation just long enough for me to believe that a pregnancy had finally occurred. But it is not to be. When I wept, I had to hear Mama tell me one more time, "It is the Lord's will." Why would the Lord want to be so hard on me? What have I done to deserve such deprivation?

I cannot erase my last terrible day with Henry from my mind—how senseless our argument was about the windmill, how dismaying my eagerness to see Henry off on his voyage. Was our heated disagreement a reason for the Lord to withhold my most urgent prayer request?

Mama has called up to me, telling me that she would like me to drive her to Wellfleet to visit the doctor at his office. She wants to buy some pills for Papa's cough, as Papa will never go get the pills for himself and won't hear of the doctor coming to the house for a mere cough. Duke has been quite lively lately, and Mama does not want to drive out alone with him. Doesn't she realize that my wedding anniversary is the day after tomorrow? I'm sure she does—she tries to distract me.

The blue eggs are visible now; the mother robin has flown off to find herself an earthworm. I have a terrible urge to reach down and pluck those eggs from the nest, and throw them against the side of the house. If I could reach them, I would do that. How wicked of me, but I am so angry. And so very sad. I do not know myself when I look into the mirror, and I cannot make my face smile. No, I will not drive in to town today. I don't want anyone to look at me. I am too wretched. I am grateful that I have the luxury of hiding myself away. I will tell Mama to take Nettie.

~

Chapter Ten
Cast Upon the Virginia Coast

May 22, 1889

We have received news—horrifying news. Just when I'd begun to reconcile myself to the fact that my Henry rests peacefully on the ocean floor, Winslow received a telegraph this morning summoning him to the town of Hallwood, Virginia, for the purposes of identifying Henry's body. Appearing in the *Boston Daily Globe* yesterday, but just received in South Wellfleet on today's morning train—this article:

> *IT'S HENRY SMITH'S BODY. May 21—Corpse Cast upon the Virginia Coast. Identity Established by the Name on a Photograph. Schooner Mary Stubbs Probably Sank With All on Board. The body reported cast ashore at Gargatha Inlet, Virginia, and afterward robbed of a considerable sum of money, was probably that of Captain Henry P. Smith of Wellfleet, who sailed from Hampton Roads, April 4, in command of the schooner Mary Stubbs, with a cargo of oysters bound for an Eastern port. The schooner was last seen off Chincoteague Bay just before the heavy gale of April 6, and no doubt foundered with all on board. Captain Smith was 30 years old, and supposed to have*

from $300 to $500 in his possession. The names on the photographs discovered on his person corresponded to those of his wife and wife's sister. Both pictures he carried in his pocketbook.

INQUEST TO BE HELD TODAY. Contradictory Tales Told by the People Who Found the Body. Hallwood, Virginia, May 21- The body of the unknown man found adrift in Gargatha Creek, making in from the Atlantic ocean, 80 miles above Cape Charles, and stripped of its valuables and turned adrift, was again found by the same parties, Turlington and Beloate, and was buried this morning early in Turlington's family graveyard. Turlington says now that his wife burned the two photographs of women, which were in the pocketbook of the corpse. Such contradictory information has thus far been obtained by your correspondent from the finders that very little confidence can now be placed in anything they say. An investigation will probably be held tomorrow upon the body, as which definite result may be obtained. The indignation of the entire community is aroused at the facts thus far developed in the case. The parties have hitherto occupied enviable social positions here. The parties agree that the name written on one of the photographs was Nettie S. Paine and that it was taken at Provincetown.

Thankfully, I'd already heard from Winslow that poor Henry has been buried in a Virginia graveyard under questionable circumstances. The newspapers should handle these matters with far more decorum. It is beyond shocking to read about a loved one in such sensational terms.

The effect on me is nauseating and visceral; I cannot help but imagine the thieves in the act of burying my husband's cold and decomposed corpse in a secret grave. I struggle with new horrific images of Henry. Human behavior is sometimes beyond deplorable. How could these men defile not only my Henry, but also the memory of their own ancestors by hiding a body in their own sacred final resting place?

Winslow did not ask me if I would like to accompany him south to Virginia. He assessed my emotions and chose to go alone. I feel badly about that, as the gentleman is not spry. But Papa reminds me that the spring weather is warmer in Virginia than it is here. Winslow will travel easily without the mourning Eva to watch over, and the constables will meet him at the Hallwood Station. Although the evidence appears to be irrefutable, I will not totally believe this gruesome development until Winslow informs me that it is so.

May 27, 1889

Today in the *Boston Daily Globe*:

> CENSURED BY THE JURY. *The Finders of the Body of Captain Smith Liable to Prosecution. HALLWOOD, Virginia, May 26- At the inquest held upon the body of the man found in Gargatha Creek, it was easily shown by Winslow Smith that the body was that of his son, Captain Henry P. Smith of Wellfleet, Mass. Captain Winslow Smith gave the body to Undertaker Littleton, who will prepare it for shipment to his home. All of the money found on the body was given to the coroner.*
>
> *The jury severely censured Turlington and Beloate, two of the finders of the body for their action in taking the money and turning the body adrift and commended the matter to the attention of the attorney for the commonwealth for action. The body was found again five days after and was brought here and buried. Great*

indignation is expressed by the people generally at the conduct of the men.

It is true, it is true, it is all true, and now I know it without question, as Winslow has wired to confirm it. I have not been able to stop crying. I thought I had done with that, but this confirmation has set me off terribly. I have quarantined myself in my bedroom.

Nettie brought me a new novel to distract my mind from the horrific images I am entertaining, but I cannot keep the characters straight. I have no idea what I am reading, and open the pages randomly to read a paragraph here, a paragraph there. Dear Nettie is well intentioned, but she has no idea of the total unruliness of my thoughts.

The street has quieted to a murmur. It is as if I am dying myself, the way that voices are lowered and serious expressions are worn by all who walk past our drive. I do have my faith in the Lord, but I wonder why he has deserted me, and given me this new burden to carry.

Mama is quite somber and has very little to say. I know she is as shocked as I am by the behavior of the incompetents who found Henry. It is of some consolation that the citizens of the village where Henry washed ashore are horrified by the chain of events, and their authorities have incarcerated the criminals.

The crime would never have been discovered had not the wife of one of the thieves confided to a friend that her husband had come upon a "gift from the sea,"—enough cash to buy a team of horses. The photographs of Nettie and I were there in Henry's wallet, although the thieves had taken care to destroy Henry's identification papers. The simple, silly woman showed the photographs to her friend, who noted our names written on the back: "Nettie S. Paine," and simply, "With love, Eva." I thank the Lord that the friend had a moral conscience and alerted the authorities.

I recall the happy day last summer when Nettie, Lewis, Henry and I went by train to Provincetown and posed for photographs. Had we not enjoyed that luxurious, frivolous day, then Henry might never have been identified.

It is irksome that the reporter for *The Boston Daily Globe* did not bother to verify the assumption that Nettie and I are sisters, but I understand the mistake. So many people have taken us as sisters; we have a strong family resemblance, even as distant cousins. I do think of Nettie as my sister, and so I should not be put out now that the world has read we are.

Papa spoke with the undertaker, Mr. Snow, this morning. I watched them through the parlor window as they talked in the front yard. They stood in the same spot where, just three years ago, Henry and I stood side-by-side to be married. I am relieved that I had no part of their conversation.

Henry is on the train even now, bound for home as cargo, his father riding in the coach car. How far have they traveled? Maryland, New York, Connecticut or Rhode Island? How long can it take to travel by railroad from the eastern Virginia shore to Wellfleet?

Henry lies in a coffin, his blue eyes shut. Or are they open? Is he clothed or is he not? I picture him in his wool captain's coat, although I know it was stolen. I overheard Papa say that the crabs probably got to Henry. I don't want to think about that. I will not look at Henry's body. I want to remember Henry as the strong man he was. For once, I am going to heed Papa's advice, and I will not look at Henry.

Henry is coming home, and he will be buried next to his mother. Papa has ordered a headstone. He says that Winslow will not be able to afford one, and that since this stone will also serve for me someday, Papa wants it to be a stone fit for a sea captain and his wife. But I have refused to allow my name to be engraved in the stone. A stone mason can attend to that upon my death. For now, I certainly do not wish to see my name chiseled under Henry's on his gravestone.

My Henry will soon be buried deep. Perhaps I would have preferred him to be forever lost at sea. But if that had been the case,

I would have had to wait for my widow's benefits—something else I overheard. My father mentioned it, I am sure, out at the kitchen table. Yes, Papa did say I would've had to wait some odd years for the Marine Benevolent Society to pay my widow's benefit had Henry's body not been found. How very inconsiderate of the shareholders to deliberately cause a widow to suffer not only emotionally, but financially as well.

But Henry has been found, and he is coming home by railroad. He would be angry if he knew; he hated the railroad so. The train will pass by our graveyard and then come in to the South Wellfleet station. Winslow will get off, and Mr. Snow will be there to receive Henry and transport him to the Smith homestead by hearse in the proper manner. I will go to the train to meet Winslow and my husband. But I will not look in the coffin. Papa says I must not.

After Winslow has had a day to rest, Henry shall have a proper funeral service. Reverend Moss will give the sermon. I don't know how I will get through the day, or the rest of my life. Forgive me Lord, but I have lost my way. I do not understand. Why has this tragic sequence of events happened to my Henry, and to me?

~

June 2, 1889

We have had so much rain. Henry now lies freshly buried under the wet sand of the graveyard, asleep in Jesus, his feet to the sunrise in the east. I have nightmares about Henry lying in that box, so cold and so deep. I fight bitterness and I endure endless, empty hours of longing.

But I have no right to pity myself. The Lord has provided an answer to my sad inner song of "Why, why, why?" A calamity that no one could have predicted has occurred this week, on the last day of May—the same day we buried Henry. Because of torrential rainstorms, a whole town in Pennsylvania has been swept away, ruined in a few minutes time. A broken dam more than a dozen miles upstream sent a sudden flood of woe down upon the unsuspecting citizens of Johnstown.

Two thousand people have lost their lives, and a thousand more their homes. The Johnstown Flood, as the press is calling it, will be in the minds of the nation for months to come. The great Clara Barton is already on the scene, setting up her Red Cross station. The cry for volunteers has gone up, as survivors must be found and attended to quickly, and there is a great call for the services of doctors and undertakers, and the donation of coffins. The catastrophe is so extreme that we cannot comprehend the magnitude of suffering.

The Ladies Social Union has taken up a collection of blankets, clothing and money. Anything will do—the survivors have lost everything. Nettie and I are labeling crates of donations and plan to send them off on tomorrow's train.

The Lord's answer to me—*I have not singled you out, Eva. There will be loss of life. There will be storms. There will be catastrophes. This is the way it is on Earth. Heaven is a better place.* Although Heaven awaits the faithful, the pain and suffering on Earth is so very difficult to accept.

～

Winslow has brought me the sewing machine as a gift. I am so grateful; I am able to sew again. How kind of my dear father-in-law. I must regain my interests, even if I am to live here at home. It is time for me to walk up to the Smith house to visit with Winslow. Mama says, "Eva, you are very kind to worry so much about Winslow."

But I truly love him. I married Henry, and I am Winslow's daughter-in-law. He has no one else. I will sew and continue to make money. I cannot ask Mama and Papa to help financially maintain Winslow, but I can help Winslow myself.

The widow Matilda Chase has been visiting Winslow lately, enjoying the cakes and pies that Nettie brings over for him. I believe

Matilda still has designs on Arozana's china, if not on Winslow himself, and if he does not feel human kindness coming from someone, he will cave in to Matilda's wiles. Ah, there I go again, being judgmental. Forgive me, Lord. Matilda must have some redeeming traits; she does, after all, consider herself to be a Christian.

~

July, 1889

For weeks after Henry's funeral, I couldn't bring myself to visit the Smith house, but eventually I summoned the courage to go. I can now pay Winslow a call like a proper daughter-in-law. I do bring something good to eat with me every time I walk or drive up the road with Duke. It is good discipline for the antsy Duke to be fastened to the hitching post at the Smith house. Winslow's two black beauties whinny to Duke—and he answers back—while I run into the house with my offerings. Perhaps a loaf of bread. Perhaps a cake. Something, every few days. I am concerned, as is every woman in the neighborhood, that Winslow is not eating properly. As a result, he has more food in his larder than anyone else does.

The first time I visited the Smith homestead was difficult, indeed. Winslow graciously let me wander by myself. He sat in his chair and read, indulging me my weeping. "It's alright, Eva," he said kindly every few minutes, without looking up from his newspaper.

Already, Nettie had rearranged the pantry, the kitchen shelves, and Winslow's closet. Walking though the house, I reacquainted myself with details that had been obscured by the dense fog of grief. I examined the wood grain on tabletops I had dusted. I admired the design of the parlor curtains—and these I had sewn myself. I climbed the stairs that I'd scrubbed and oiled, and I peeked in at the bathtub that had been installed for my benefit.

The bedroom I shared with Henry was neat and tidy—our wedding quilt was folded neatly at the foot of the bed, the feather comforter was smoothed, the pillows were plumped. Some of my belongings were still arranged on the bureau top. A stack of books, the largest on the bottom and the smallest on the top, sat arranged in perfect order. A brooch that Henry gave me brought bittersweet memories of the birthday I received it. My hand mirror rested face down. On impulse, I picked it up and looked into it.

The woman staring back at me had never been in this bedroom before. My face appeared hollow, my expression gaunt and hopeless. My hair was a mass of frizz tied up into a lopsided bun. I resolved to look into a mirror more often. It was not a pretty sight I presented to the world, and some premeditated practice of a smile was perhaps in order if I was to be out visiting. I packed my belongings into the carpetbag I'd brought with me for the odds and ends Mama had not already collected.

The bed called out for me to lie on it, which I did, with some trepidation. Once there, I wished myself dead along with Henry. To never feel his arms around me again, to never feel the stubble of his whiskers against my cheek, to never again feel his passion and his love for me—I didn't want to live. I said a prayer to the Lord, begging him to please take me, but he did not.

Reluctantly, I stood and rolled up the wedding quilt Arozana had made for us and laid it gently in the carpetbag. I looked about for Henry's personal belongings. He had taken the most important things with him, and they were lost at sea—his sextant, his spy-glass, his derby hat, his shaving box which contained his razor and shaving brush, his pocket knife, and his sea chest. Although my husband had been able to quickly create chaos from household order, he had not actually owned many things.

I opened the closet door. Mama and Nettie had already removed my dresses, but I wanted to touch Henry's clothing. The deep green vest he wore to church hung on a hook. I took it into my hands and felt the cloth. Here was the essence of my husband. Faint perspiration stains showed under the armholes, and I rubbed the vest on my face, drawing in the scent.

I closed my eyes and easily imagined him in the room with me. *Henry, my darling—I miss you more than words can say. You were everything to me. You took up so many of my thoughts and so much of my heart, and you always will.* I folded his vest and put it in my bag.

A pair of leather shoes that Henry had declared uncomfortable lay on the closet floor, along with the good leather boots that he would not bring out to sea. His two white shirts were freshly pressed, as I had left them, and the clean collars were stacked neatly on the shelf. His navy blue winter coat was there as well, made with a soft merlot wool that I had snuggled against many times as we rode to church in the sleigh. I couldn't find the suit he wore when we were married, but then I remembered. Of course, Winslow would have given that suit to Mr. Snow, the undertaker, and Henry wore it now.

I took the carpetbag in one hand and the wool coat in the other and looked back at the room from the doorway. I had become a woman here. It was a modest bedroom, with a slanted ceiling and a dormered window. I'd made the simple yellow curtains from grain bag prints, and the rag rug had been braided by Henry's mother. For the first time, I noticed the wallpaper was mismatched on two seams. I had never cared much about the décor of the room. The man with whom I'd shared the bed had been the main focus of my attention. I turned and went down the stairs.

Our framed marriage certificate hung in the front parlor. It was quite beautiful, featuring photographs of Henry and me, and also one of Reverend Moss as the officiating minister. The etching of a man and woman sailing together in a decorative boat was finely detailed and, although fanciful, strangely comforting.

"May I take this with me, Winslow?" I did want so much to have the record of my marriage, although I knew Winslow would miss it. He'd been watching me from his chair. A pained look crossed his face.

"Yes, Eva. It's yours."

"Thank you so much." I kissed the top of his head. "And this wool coat, would you like me to alter it for you? The sleeves would need to be shortened, and the shoulders taken in, but it will keep you very warm." I held up Henry's coat.

"No thank you, dear. I have a winter coat."

"Well, then, may I have it? I'd like to cut it down and make it into a coat for myself. I will think of Henry every time I wear it." I knew Winslow would not refuse.

"Yes, take it, Eva. Take whatever you would like." He looked very tired and sad as he said the words.

I felt immensely selfish as I kissed him good-bye and promised I'd be back soon. I have Mama and Papa to keep me company, and Winslow has no one now, except Polly, the cat. I'm glad that it's summertime, and the weather is comfortably warm right now. For Winslow to go through this grieving during the cold winter—I think it would kill him. He looks to me as though he has lost twenty pounds in these few months. He has given me his trousers to take in; they will not stay up without suspenders.

The summer and autumn will give Winslow time to regain his strength. Even so, arrangements will have to be made for the outside care of the animals and wood supply during the cold winter months. It is very unfortunate for Winslow that I am no longer living with him, but that is the way it has to be. My proper place is with Mama and Papa.

I am not to look at the Smith household financial ledger again. Mama made it clear that it would not be prudent to do so, since I will no longer be seeing to the accounts. Of course, I will not ask for a return of the money I earned and spent on the bathroom improvements, or the money I spent for coal through the lean winter months. I do not begrudge Winslow that.

Winslow has generously given me the sewing machine, and I can earn more money. But Winslow cannot. With pleasure, I will make certain the property taxes are paid so he can remain at the homestead. But Winslow will have to take in a boarder to help pay the other household expenses. My heart goes out to him. I will visit him often and pray for a worthy boarder to appear. And for myself, I pray that this iron anchor leaves my heart soon. Henry is gone, and there is nothing I can do to change that.

~

My dear friend Lily almost lost her father. Captain Wiley has survived a drastic event—Lorenzo Dow Baker's pride and joy, the *L.D. Baker,* caught fire and steamed ahead at full speed until she sunk in the Atlantic on July 15. Aunt Elizabeth was frantic when the vessel was overdue coming into Boston from Jamaica. Lily arrived with her children to wait with her mother. We all prepared to hear the worst news. The Boston Fruit company could offer no updates. How well I recalled that Henry had been offered a position on this vessel by the beneficent Captain Baker. It seemed that tragedy followed too closely upon tragedy, and that Henry would not have escaped unscathed in any case.

But miraculously, we received word that an unlikely rescue occurred. The captain of the *Franklin,* a seasoned New Bedford whaling vessel, had sighted the burning steamer on the night horizon. The *Franklin* sailed to the location of the wreck and picked up twenty-eight survivors as they clung to life rafts in rough water. It then took a week for the *Franklin* to sail her grateful passengers back into New Bedford.

According to all accounts, Captain Wiley did everything he could to save all aboard, but lost two of his crew members. The Widow Chase has stirred up a neighborhood controversy by declaring that if Captain Wiley was an honorable man, he would have "gone down with the ship" along with the two souls lost.

My poor uncle is feeling disgraced in spite of the fact that all six passengers were saved, including a woman, and only two crew members out of two dozen were drowned in the catastrophe. He is devastated, and says he will never get over it. Henry was right. Steam engines are not a perfect solution to the modern demand of adhering to a printed schedule.

Due to the constant boiling of blubber on board, a whaler is the most odiferous of all the sailing vessels on the sea, easily detected downwind for miles. How ironic that it was a stinking old whaler that came to the rescue of the Boston Fruit Company's modern flagship. I am greatly relieved, along with Lily and Aunt Elizabeth, that Captain Wiley is safely home, even though he is not a happy man right now.

~

August 3, 1889

Rather than stopping in on Winslow today, I decided to be brave and go on to the burial grounds to visit Henry and his mother. Their stones are side by side, to the north of the abandoned church. I've cried so much during my little turn about the cemetery, I'm afraid I look like I've been stung by a full hive of bees.

I've never been more attached to my sunbonnet. My protests of "old fashioned" have desisted. I do so appreciate the way I can hide inside it, and even pretend that I do not see other people.

After spending my hour with Henry and strolling around the cemetery to acknowledge all who recline there, I was in no condition to stop to see Winslow. I left some cookies in a brown paper package at the door, and know he will find and enjoy them.

~

Carrie Bolton has returned to Pleasant Point for the month of August. She is so refreshing, as are her boys, and visiting them gives me brief respites from my morose moods. Of course she read about

Henry's death in the horrid columns of the *Boston Daily Globe*. She sent a lovely condolence card, and she wrote me several empathetic letters, but it is so much more comforting to have her here in person.

Carrie is always eager to rush one's mind ahead, and she has done it again. When I sigh about not having had a child with Henry, she immediately offers me one of her boys, sometimes in their presence.

"Take me, Auntie Eva, take me," they beg. Richie and Tommy clearly delight in our little neighborhood. This summer, being another year older, they leave the cottage on their own and play barefooted on the sandy shore. Mrs. Coughlin is quite challenged trying to keep track of them—they have been punished several times for hiding from her and not answering her calls. Little William has attached himself to Richie and Tommy, and together they make an energetic threesome.

"Oh, come on, Auntie Eva. Do come out sailing with us," Richie frequently begs me. He has expectantly waited for his father to visit on the week ends, but that has not happened this summer. Therefore, I am constantly urged to do what Carrie won't. However, I do not have enough confidence in Richie's skill level as of yet. He learned to sail on the Charles River with a junior yacht club. But the Charles River flows in one direction and has no tides to consider.

"No, not until you have sailed a hundred times," I tell Richie. "And stick close to Captain Winslow over there, in the *Zephyr*. He will help you if you get into a fix." Winslow has ventured out in his catboat with his fishing pole and is looked up to by these visiting summer boys, who have followed Little William's lead. It does Winslow good to get out on the water.

～

From my widow's benefits, I've commissioned an artist to do a life-sized portrait of Henry in charcoal. I sent my favorite photograph of Henry to a studio in Boston. The result is a large framed version of the photograph that was taken that golden afternoon in Provincetown. The portrait is soft and inviting; Henry's eyes are expressive and warm. I find myself staring at it. Carrie Bolton recommended the artist as one who could accomplish my wish, after trying to dissuade me from it.

"You must come out of your shell eventually, Eva. Hanging a large portrait of Henry will only discourage potential suitors."

"No one will see the portrait, because I've hung it in my bedroom. However, I would view the discouragement of suitors as a positive outcome, rather than negative. I cannot imagine being married again."

"You're not serious, Eva," Carrie protested. "You're so pretty and talented. Why do you say that?"

"Because I don't want to experience such intense emotions again," I said. "I don't think I could bear it. Henry was my one true love, and I am finished with marriage. If I find love once more, then I may well have to go through the pain of losing it."

"In time, you'll change your mind. You'll see." Carrie spoke with certainty.

"No, I won't. I loved Henry, and I don't think I could ever love anyone the same way. I am content to say that I will not marry again." I thought I was finished, but then I blurted out, "And you, of all people, Carrie, should be the last one to try to talk me into the supposed bliss of courtship and marriage." I was as surprised as Carrie by my outburst.

～

My role as the mistress of a home is over. Mama is the queen of her house, and I am the daughter. It has been difficult to make the change, although I do respect Mama's wishes. She will allow me to tend the hens, and I may take care of Duke when Papa is out to sea. I have been demoted to a barnyard hand. I will have to unobtrusively relieve Mama of some of her tasks, now that I know how to perform them.

The day will come when I start the laundry without asking Mama if I should; the day will come when I cook a meal for Mama and Papa and surprise them when they return from an errand. But for now, Mama is adamant. I am to do very little but recover from my husband's death.

This morning after breakfast, Mama shooed me out of her kitchen. I walked directly to Carrie's cottage. I found Carrie on the porch writing out her marketing list. Finding her at that simple act brought me to tears. I have not written a marketing list since leaving the Smith house.

"I feel so very useless and unimportant. I am not to make any decisions, and it is difficult after making so many for so long," I said.

"Eva, why don't you consider coming to stay with me in Boston this fall? I think a month in the city would do you good." Carrie looked at me with concern.

"That's very generous of you, but it's too much for me to accept!"

"Oh, come on, Eva," she chided me. "You can sew. I will buy a sewing machine for the guest room. Will that make you happy? You can make me a dress if you insist on doing something for me in return. But I just want you to come as a friend. You are such a good friend!" She was quite persuasive in her sincerity. A surge of warmth came over me, and I hastily made up my mind.

"I *will* come and see you, Carrie. I'm not sure if I can be there for a full month, but I will stay for two weeks." I thought of Nettie and how she would miss me while I'm gone. She has given me so much of her time in the past several very difficult months. As a child, I never wanted for a sister with dear Nettie just across the road, and now that I am home again, our bond is closer than ever.

"Two weeks is a good start," Carrie grinned. "I will buy whatever model of sewing machine you desire—you just let me know. It does get quiet while the boys are at school, you know. I could use some company in that big house. I wander around all day there by myself. Richard comes home for dinner a few times a month to see the boys, but otherwise, he is totally consumed by his business and his latest mistress. Not that I'm complaining. It's convenient for me, except for the loneliness."

I thought it sad that despite our obvious marital differences, Carrie and I both endured loneliness.

"But surely you have lots of friends?"

"No one as sincere as you are, Eva. You couldn't tell a falsehood if you tried, even if it was the polite thing to do. I like knowing who I am dealing with, and not having to guess what the hidden agenda might be. You have no idea how the ladies in my circle calculate. It is, unfortunately, something I have to steel myself for."

"Enough, Carrie. Let's go for a walk down to the shore. I see Winslow coming in with his catboat."

"Winslow, Winslow. Yes, I will go see Winslow with you again. Will he let us use the team and buggy this week to drive into town for a little shopping?" Carrie is always thinking about the days ahead while I work at getting through a day. She tries not to be exasperated with my frequent need to visit with Winslow.

"Yes, Carrie, I know he'll be happy to let us take the buggy. Winslow would accommodate me in any way. We must ask Nettie to come with us when we go. I am not feeling up to driving, and you don't know how to. Nettie will be delighted to go into Wellfleet with us. She loves to drive."

I'm sure I was transparent in my desire to bring my two friends together. When we are a trio, I feel my most comfortable. I find that I can bow out of the conversation for brief periods and let them entertain each other. It is wonderful that I have two dear friends, and I hope that they will be good friends to each other.

~

The summer days pass by pleasantly enough. Papa and Lewis are out to sea with the *Nautilus*, and it is a petticoat government here at home. Mama enjoys my presence immensely. I'm aware I'm not the happy daughter my mother said good-bye to three years ago, but Mama remains the loving, patient parent. She frequently invites Carrie and Nettie to stop over in the late afternoon for a cup of tea, a blueberry scone, and a good chat.

Mama has said to me several times, "I never imagined that my daughter would be a widow before I was." I know that it is difficult for her to see me so sad and crumpled. I have practiced smiling in the mirror for her benefit, since she is the one who sees me the most frequently, and I don't want to be such a dark rain cloud all the time. Strangely, these little acting sessions in front of the looking glass do make me feel better.

It is the nights that consume me. I long for my Henry, even though during the summers of our marriage he was rarely home for more than two days before he was out to sea again for fourteen. The persistent longing is in possession of me, as firmly as Henry was.

After reading deep into the night until I can no longer do so, I blow out the lamp and fall into a troubled sleep. Then my confusion begins. Henry stands over my bed and glowers at me, as if he wants me to save him. But it is too late. In my dream, I remember that he is dead and buried. I wake with a start. Then, by the moonlight, I look at the portrait of Henry smiling from the wall over my bed. I am reassured he is not angry. I fall asleep again.

I know that Henry is gone, and yet he is still with me. I cannot exist for an hour without comparing my thoughts to what Henry would have thought. It is unnerving.

I find myself recalling little incidents in our life together—they randomly enter my mind, unbidden, and I re-live them as an observer rather than a participant: the sunny winter afternoon we joined the children skating on the pond and had such fun; the disappointment he showed when I served him lumpy gravy; the affectionate way he brushed his horses; the argument he had with his father over heating the front parlor in the winter.

I smile at the good times we had and try not to dwell on the unpleasant memories, which are painfully bitter. I tell myself that the longing I now feel is no more unpleasant than the hurt I felt when Henry shouted at me, inflicting sharp wounds that lingered in my heart too many days after the event, even though my intention was to forgive.

I now realize that there are five women in Paine Hollow who have been widowed. Our eyes meet with recognition, and several have offered me reassurance that the longing will fade.

"There is good reason, Eva, for the old rule that a widow should wear black for a year," Mrs. Townsend told me. She was married and widowed as a young woman before marrying Clive. "It takes at minimum a full turn of the calendar year to fully recover, and the advances of other men should be discouraged for at least that long. But soon, you will go for an hour, and then a day, without thinking of Henry. And the time will come when you know, even in your sleep, that Henry is gone."

I do hope that Mrs. Townsend is correct. I want my old self back again. I did not realize that I had lost myself until Henry was lost. I have resolved never to allow another man to possess me as completely as Henry did. If this is the result of a marriage—that "two shall become as one" so completely that a woman can no longer think her own clear thoughts—then I shall be a widow forevermore.

Some may think this is selfish of me, but I am certain there are ways I can be of help in this world without giving myself away to a man again. Henry was more than enough of a husband for me, God rest his soul.

~

September 16, 1889

To our astonishment, Papa and Lewis arrived home on this morning's train. Mr. Newcomb sent the service wagon to deliver the men and their luggage to the house.

"My word, this is a surprise," Mama cried as she ran to the wagon from the kitchen, her apron strings flying out behind her. "What is it, Otis? What has happened?"

I rushed out behind her, expecting to hear that the *Nautilus* was in dry dock somewhere after a mishap, undergoing a necessary repair.

"Now don't go getting upset, Sarah, everything is fine!" Papa jumped off the wagon, as fit as ever, and Lewis stepped down on the other side.

"Oh, Lewis, tell me," Mama said. "I must know, and your father is so frustrating!"

"Just a minute, Sarah." Papa searched for his wallet. "Let me tip the driver here. You'll hear all about it soon enough." Papa was sober and calm. Lewis came around the wagon and kissed Mama's cheek.

"Father should tell you, not me," Lewis said quietly to Mama. "Don't worry; there is no cause for alarm." He turned to give me a hug. Papa heaved his sea trunk up onto his shoulders and turned toward the house.

"Come along, Sarah and Eva," he said as he went up the front steps. The kitchen door was too narrow for the large trunk. Papa took his time in spite of Mama's fretting, and after he had washed his face at the kitchen sink, he sat down in his chair and faced us.

"Sit down, all of you. You, too, Lewis. Stay with me, son." Papa looked up at me. "Eva?" He motioned me towards the chair he wanted me to take. Mama sat next to him.

"Sarah, please don't be upset," he said. "What I am about to tell you is for the best."

"I'm not upset. What is it? What?" Mama wrung her apron on her lap.

"I've sold the *Nautilus*." Papa held up his hand to signal that he wanted to say more before we spoke. "A fellow down in Norfolk made me a very good offer, and I decided to take it. I'm sorry, but it is for the best." Papa tried to sound cheerful, but failed. His voice caught as he went on. "I'm getting on in age, and Lewis won't always be available to come out with me. And after Henry, well, I wouldn't want you to have to go through what Eva is going through, Sarah. My heart's just not in it anymore."

I didn't trust what I was hearing. Mama sighed loudly and looked down at her hands. There was a moment of silence around the table as we waited for Mama's reaction.

"Oh, Otis," Mama said. "I'm so relieved. I have always worried about you. I never know if you're going to come home when you sail out."

She started to cry. Papa reached over to take her hand, and Lewis and I got up together and left them alone in the house. We walked toward Duke's pasture, and he trotted a circle for us.

"He's been trying to sell the *Nautilus* all summer, Eva," Lewis said. "And I certainly couldn't afford to buy her. He said he wouldn't want me to, anyway. He wants me to take the permanent position up at the bakery in Boston."

"No! I don't believe it. This is all so sudden, Lewis."

"Not really. You've been unaware, understandably so, that our father has his own nightmares about Henry going down." Lewis looked at me nervously and quickly added, "And he knows that I'm sweet on Margaret up there, and that she's sweet on me."

"Is that so? You haven't said a word about her since January."

"We like each other and have an easy time of it together. She's a nice girl. Hard working. She sends most of her earnings back home to her parents in Nova Scotia. I know Margaret and I could make a life of it together. We write to each other. She's been waiting for me since April to come back up to Boston again."

"But you'd live in Boston? Oh, Lewis. I can't bear the thought. You belong here in Paine Hollow. You're Papa's only son!"

"He says different. He says go and make the money while I can and marry the girl who waits so patiently. He wants me to be safe. It's hard to think I won't be out on the water, but with money the way it is, I'd be mad to turn down the bakery position. I'll be leaving in a week." Lewis looked past the pasture out towards the bay, squinting his eyes against the sun.

"I'll miss you," I said. I wondered if he knew that. "But I wish you the best, Lewis, I truly do. I hope all goes well with Margaret. You'll come home to be married?"

"I don't know. It depends on whether Margaret's parents can come down from Nova Scotia, and if so, Boston would be the better location for the ceremony. But that's still a ways off in the future. Margaret and I are in no rush. We want to save up enough money so when we leave our boarding houses, we can afford a decent flat."

"That's sensible of you. But what about Papa? I find it hard to believe that he will never sail out on the *Nautilus* again. And I can't imagine him staying home all the time. It's not like him."

We looked towards the house.

"He'll keep busy enough, and sail some with Winslow. But he says he's all done with the ocean and her storms. He doesn't want you and Mama left alone, should something happen."

We were both quiet. Lewis bent down and picked up some pebbles and then pitched them one by one at a fencepost. He was handsome with his tanned face and strong arms.

"Margaret McCloud is a fortunate girl," I told him. "I can't wait to meet this mysterious lady. You'll have to introduce us when I go up to Boston this fall to visit Carrie. You're going to give me a sister-in-law!" I paused, recalling how I had given Lewis a brother-in-law— just three years and some months ago.

"There's something I must ask you," I said. I put my hand on his arm to stop him from pitching a stone. Lewis looked at me expectantly. "And please do me the favor of telling me the truth. I overheard Papa the day after you two came home with the news that Henry had gone down. Papa was very angry. He said that Henry had been 'bull headed' when the cyclone blew up and had willfully ignored Papa's warnings to take in sail. Tell me, is that true?"

My brother slowly shook his head, as though he didn't want to think about it.

"I have to know, Lewis," I said urgently. "You're moving to Boston. You must tell me now! Papa never will." I steeled myself, knowing that if Lewis saw tears I'd have no hope for an answer.

Lewis again looked out towards the bay. It was dead calm, with not a ripple showing on the water. I didn't say a word more and resolved not to until he spoke.

"Eva, you have no idea how loudly the wind was screaming through the lines," Lewis said, his voice flat. "It came up suddenly, with a roar. I couldn't hear Father shouting, and I was standing right next to him on deck. I couldn't even hear myself shouting. There is no question in my mind—Henry could not hear Father shouting over to him." Lewis removed his gaze from the bay and looked at me. I was extremely grateful for his answer, but I had one more question for him.

"But why didn't Henry take his mainsail down when you did?" I asked the question as though boring a drill into Lewis. He was my witness; he was the only person I could count on for a fair answer. Lewis winced, but didn't turn away. He looked me straight in the eyes as he spoke.

"I really don't know, Eva. I've thought about that so many times. Maybe Henry's mistake was to think Father was being overly cautious. But Father had thirty years out on the Atlantic over Henry, and he knew by that strange roar of the wind that it was going to get much worse before it got any better. But no one knew it was a cyclone bearing down upon us, or none of us would have been out there."

"Then why was Papa so angry with Henry?"

"It was the shock of losing him, I'm sure. And Father couldn't bear to see you suffer like that. But we all know it was no fault of Henry's that he foundered in the biggest storm of the century. Father would never repeat now what he said then—it was a very emotional time and he never meant for you to overhear him. He was blowing off steam, and Mama and I knew it."

"Thank you, Lewis," I said, hugging him. "I needed to hear that. It means the world to me." My brother's muscular shoulders were so broad that I could barely get my arms around him. He squeezed me back and then let me go. I took in a deep breath of the salty air.

"You must be hungry," I said. "Mama was going to make a beef stew for dinner—I think I'll go in and see to that for her. And corn meal muffins—I'll bake you some to take the edge off until the stew is ready. It's good to have you home, Lewis. It really is."

I bit my lip, knowing that the next time he departs, my life will change again. Perhaps soon I will have a sister-in-law, and then someday, if it's not too much to hope for, a little niece or nephew. I so much appreciate the fact that the Lord has spared Lewis and Papa. When Lewis presents Margaret to the family, I will be the very best sister-in-law and auntie anyone could ask for.

∿

Afterward

April 6, 1938

Several years after Henry's death, I fell into an annual habit of looking through albums of fading photographs and reading my old journals during the first week of April. Today I remarked that I was doing so to Nettie on our way home from our Wednesday afternoon prayer meeting.

"Reading my own handwriting brings it all back so clearly," I said before I could stop myself. "I had such hope for us, but I wanted more than Henry could ever give me in the way of intimacy." Nettie and I have known each other for so long that we think aloud in front of each other, sometimes with disastrous results.

"What do you mean, *intimacy*, Eva?" Nettie asked. "Are you trying to tell me that you and Henry never had relations?" Nettie held the Ford's steering wheel with both hands and peered straight down the road through her thick glasses.

"No, Nettie, that's not what I'm saying at all. I mean the intimacy of thought, of understanding. I mean intimacy in the broadest sense. My hope that Henry and I would understand one another—it was so naïve," I said.

Nettie reached across the seat and squeezed my hand. "Eva, you were young. All young people are naïve! Don't torture yourself. At our age, we've got to enjoy every day we have left, silly goose." She made a correction as the Ford drifted off the asphalt onto the gravel shoulder.

"Whatever made you bring the subject of Henry up right now, for goodness sakes? The minister's talk this afternoon? His theme of a woman's place being at home, rather than out working?" Nettie chuckled. "It's apparent the good reverend has no idea what women do, especially women like us who have no husbands. We are always working, even when we are at home. Especially when we are at home."

"No, it wasn't the sermon, Nettie, it's today's date," I said. "Henry's been gone forty-nine years today." I turned my face away from Nettie and looked out the window as we drove back to South Wellfleet.

"Almost a half century, where has the time gone?" Nettie accelerated on a straight section of the road. "Don't go all sentimental on me now, Eva. Henry's been dead far more years than he was with us."

"Nettie, slow down! I want to get home in one piece!" I gripped the armrest on my door.

"I just wanted to bring you back into the present." She laughed and took her foot off the accelerator pedal. "There's no telling if your life would have been better had it been spent with Henry. No telling at all."

I rolled my eyes. Nettie can be so full of opinion about matters she knows nothing of.

"Just because you never married gives you no cause to judge *my* marriage!" I said.

"Don't be so sensitive, Eva. I'm not judging, I'm just saying. Henry's been gone for forty-nine years, God rest his soul, and you've had decades of peace and quiet. How many women can say that besides an old maid like me?"

"Whatever do you mean?"

"It sounds like you know what I mean. It's no secret that when a sea captain comes in from the water he gets restless without his crew to boss around, and soon he's bossing his wife and children around, and his neighbors too, if he can get away with it. My own nephew is no different than the old timers were in that regard, even though he's got a new diesel engine and those expensive power winches on his boat. His poor wife, I wonder how she puts up with him when he's home!"

"Nettie, really—you are impossible." I crossed my arms against my chest, signaling my indignation.

"Yes, impossible, but there's the chance I might also be right." Nettie grinned and brought the Ford to a halt in my driveway. "Coming over for supper this evening? Young Veenie Pierce brought me some oysters, and I'm making a stew."

"No, thank you, not oysters. Not tonight. I appreciate it, but some other time." I leaned over and kissed my friend on the cheek and got out of the car. Nettie rolled down her window and leaned out.

"Stay away from those dusty journals, Eva," she yelled at me. "Read a *National Geographic* or something. It will do you good to get a broader perspective on the world."

I climbed my front steps, opened the door, and turned to wave at Nettie. Then I stepped into my house, closing the door firmly behind me. Nettie might think it foolish, but I find a great measure of contentment in reading about the days of my marriage.

~

Nettie and I talk about the difference an automobile has made in our lives. I don't have one because there is no good reason why we should both own one. We go most places together, so I helped Nettie buy her Ford and she drives me.

We can travel to the center of Wellfleet as quickly as I can walk from my house down to the shore. Paine Hollow Road is quieter now. People ride by my yard closed into their cars. I miss the sound of voices announcing the approach of a buggy—the chatter of children, the loud conversations between folks on the buggy seats and folks on their front lawns. Children no longer follow horses, laughing and shouting, but rather are shouted at to get out of the road when a car approaches.

Pavement is compatible with the rubber tires on which we now roll, but the soft sandy roads were so much more embracing if a child at play fell down. When Paine Hollow Road was paved a few years ago, I was actually sad as the sandy ruts were leveled forever and sealed below the black oily mixture.

The world has changed. My time as a sea captain's wife is long in the past. When I was still a young widow, I carried Henry's portrait from my bedroom to the parlor whenever I expected a male caller, and his presence kept other men from asking for my hand, just as Carrie predicted. Henry's observing portrait was the most effective deterrent that I could politely employ, and Nettie lent her full approval.

The raging blaze my heart once held for Henry has long since subsided to a comfortable glow, but it has never died. We will be reunited someday, and I could never see the sense of marrying again. One husband was more than sufficient for me. The smiling young man in the portrait brings me a peaceful happiness that is quite enough. The fact that Henry and I never had children still causes me sadness, but I have been able to give that love to other children.

Papa enjoyed his retirement for fourteen years, and then in 1903 his heart gave out as he and Mama and I wintered in Norfolk, Virginia. Mama and I never went to Virginia again after that, even though we enjoyed the climate. Mama couldn't bring herself to travel without Papa.

Winslow passed away thirteen years after Papa did—a surprise, because I'd mistakenly thought Winslow possessed a weaker constitution than my father. A summer resident soon bought the Smith homestead from the estate, and the new owners have no idea that I once slept in their house as a young bride.

Mama, bless her heart, kept me good company until just six

years ago. And then one day, she simply decided not to get out of bed. I telephoned her favorite doctor and he came to the house, but he could find nothing wrong with her. We had recently invited the whole neighborhood to celebrate her ninety-eighth birthday, and she'd been quite happily engaged with well-wishers for a full afternoon. I thought she might be suffering a bit of exhaustion as a result.

"Is there anything hurting you, Mrs. Paine?" Dr. Bell asked as he examined her.

"No, nothing hurts. It's time for me to die, that's all," Mama told him.

After a moment's pause, Dr. Bell said, "Well, Mrs. Paine, you are certainly old enough to hold that opinion, but the final decision will be the Lord's.

"I know that," Mama said. She then closed her eyes and refused all food and water. Lewis came and sat by her bed all day, holding her hand. I sat with her through the night. Neighbors came by to pay their respects, but she wouldn't speak or open her eyes to look at them. She passed away peacefully in two day's time. After all the years Mama and I spent in this house together, I feel that she is still with me now.

Lewis married Margaret, of course. They lived in Boston with their precious only child, Abbott Otis Paine, who was born three years after Henry died. Abbott was a beautiful, happy child with red hair and freckles. He delighted in coming and staying with me and Mama and Papa through the summers of his boyhood, and as a young man gave me my first ride in an automobile.

We all held our breath when he went off to fight in France during the Great War. Thank the Lord, he returned home to us in good health. A pretty summer resident from Worcester wrote to Abbott all through the war. Immediately upon his return, he married Ethel on the bluff over the sparkling bay, and they roared off to Niagara

Falls in a Stutz Bearcat motorcar. Abbott and Ethel have two sons—Jay and Bobbie. Jay is eighteen years old now, and Bobbie is eleven.

Bobbie is very special to me. He lived with me for two years as a little child when Ethel became bedridden with a strange illness. Now that Ethel has fully recovered, I immensely enjoy visiting the family in Cambridge, where Abbott teaches at the Rindge Technical School. They spend summer vacations here in Paine Hollow. If it wasn't for Lewis and Margaret having a son, who in turn gave me two great-nephews, I would not be blessed with the youthful male exuberance visited upon me every summer in this otherwise quiet house.

Lewis and Margaret now reside in their own little house just down the road, which Lewis built after he retired from the Boston bakery. Lewis owns half of this house, because we inherited it together from Mama, but when Lewis retired, Margaret wouldn't hear of living here with me. Margaret was as startled as I was, upon the reading of the will, that Mama left half of the house to me—a woman—rather than totally to Lewis. Mama always was forward thinking in her quiet way, and not one to be bound by tradition. Lewis had no trouble with the split inheritance—in fact, judging by his calm acceptance, I believe Mama consulted him before she wrote her will.

It is just as well that Lewis and Margaret did not move in with me. I do love Margaret dearly, but her Scottish sense of humor is just a bit too dry for me. This house will belong to their son some day; there is no question about that. If not for my brother's generosity, Mama and I would never have had a telephone or electricity installed.

Papa conceded to indoor plumbing before he died, but he never could see the need for electricity or "that time waster," the telephone. Lewis made sure Mama and I were comfortable as we aged, and so I must be thankful that Margaret has been in agreement with his generosity. I've been able to pay for the maintenance and taxes on the house; Lewis manages the improvements. He is and always has been a dear, concerned brother.

We ladies have been voting for eighteen years now. Nettie, Carrie, Lily, and I still get together to discuss the candidates with our neighbors, and the Ladies Social Union has evolved into the South Wellfleet Associates. Our husbands and brothers and fathers could no longer stand to be left out of our lively political discussions, and so we all discuss together, and the Pond Hill School has become the South Wellfleet Neighborhood Hall.

My dear childhood friend Lily has come back to live in Paine Hollow—she and Charles retired to a sweet house they erected next to Aunt Elizabeth's house. And so, once again, Nettie and Lily and I are together in our seventies as we were in our girlhoods. Carrie drops in on us from Boston whenever she wants a salt water swim and a walk on the beach. She is a generous grandmother to her brood of twelve grandchildren. Both Richie and Tommy married healthy girls from Cape Cod.

~

The days when Wellfleet was homeport to hundreds of sailing vessels are long over; only we elder citizens know what it was like then. Along with the rest of the country, Wellfleet has been through an industrial revolution, a world war, and a devastating financial depression. No longer does a daily line of sails pass by the ocean shore. Fishing boats and freighters alike are diesel or steam powered. Sailboats are now sailed for pleasure, rather than commerce.

Route Six is the favored route of transportation through town. Unfortunately, the railroad passenger cars have been retired, and only freight cars pass through on the tracks, pulled by diesel engines. Horses, like sailboats, have become a luxury, no longer a necessity. The use of telephones has replaced back fence gossip sessions. We instantly hear international news over the radio waves, although we are still very fond of newspapers for the local happenings. And washing machines have changed our lives forever, thank the Lord.

In spite of all the change in the world, Paine Hollow is a side road that time has forgotten. The Greek revival style farmhouses appear smaller then they did in the past, until it is time to paint them. Pitch pine trees and scrub oaks have grown up like weeds in the pastures, obscuring the view of the bay. But it is peaceful here, and I am satisfied. There is no better place for me. I sit and sew in the little room where I was born, and hope that someday I will die here, rather than in some distant hospital bed.

Dear Henry is less than three miles away, waiting for me in the cemetery along with our parents and our ancestors. I hope he doesn't mind that his bride will finally lie down beside him as an old lady. But I'm in no hurry. Bobby will soon arrive from Cambridge to visit his Great Auntie Eva for the summer, and I've promised to let him take me sailing in the catboat *Zephyr* with his Grandpa Lewis. Henry, my love, you will have to wait for me a little longer.

~

Dear Reader,

This book is a work of fiction, but it is steeped in the tea of truth. The Paine, Smith, and Cole family characters are all based on real people. Naturally, supporting characters were invented in order to personify the issues of the time period. Main characters that are totally fictitious: Annabelle Holbrook Crandle and her husband, Carrie Bolton and her friends and family, Captain Jenkins and his two children, and the dislikable Widow Matilda Chase.

Many of the supporting characters are actual people. Captain Lorenzo Dow Baker was indeed one of the primary benefactors of Wellfleet during the nineteenth century. Nettie Paine was Eva's distant cousin and best friend. Arthur Newcomb was the South Wellfleet stationmaster and post master for many years.

For more information on the historical details of Eva and Henry's relationship, including photographs, please visit their website at www.EvaandHenry.com .

Thank you for reading the book. I appreciate your comments, questions and feedback. Book club visits are sometimes possible, and I hope to meet you.

Sincerely, Irene M. Paine

Contact me at IreneMPaine@EvaandHenry.com

～

Made in the USA
Lexington, KY
17 March 2017